BADASS
Hell Yeah!

BY

SABLE HUNTER

BADASS

This is a work of fiction. Names, characters, places and incidents are either the product of the author's imagination or used fictitiously, and any resemblance to actual persons, living or dead, business establishments, events or locales is entirely coincidental.
Copyright © 2012 Sable Hunter
All rights reserved.
http://www.sablehunter.com

ALL RIGHTS RESERVED. This book contains material protected under International and Federal Copyright Laws and Treaties. Any unauthorized reprint or use of this material is prohibited. No part of this book may be reproduced or transmitted in any form or by any means, electronic or mechanical, including photocopying, recording, or by any information storage and retrieval system without express written permission from the author / publisher.

Isaac McCoy is every woman's dream. He's a cowboy, one of the Texas McCoy's of Tebow Ranch - tall, dark, handsome and sexy as hell. To add to the mystery, he's a biker - clad in black leather, riding a big Harley - he makes the girls swoon. To put it simply, Isaac is the black sheep of the family. And what his family doesn't know is that he's also a Dom. Always a little different from his brothers -Isaac has been into fast cars, fast women - and the kinkier side of sex. Until Avery. That's right's the Texas Badass has fallen for the angel of Kerrville County - the Baptist Preacher's daughter - Miss Prim and Proper. And that will never do. As much as he wants her, Isaac pushes her away - sometimes you have to be cruel to be kind. Avery has been in love with Isaac for years and she's ready to make her move. But Isaac makes it clear that they come from different worlds, there's no way she can fit in to his life. She's not the kind of woman he needs. So, Avery decides to take matters into her own hands. What she intends to do is take lessons in how to be a bad girl. Avery is determined to learn what it takes to please Isaac in every way. She's seriously after her Badass - and soon, he's not going to know what hit him.

Six brothers. One Dynasty—
TEBOW RANCH.
Meet the McCoy brothers—Texas men who love as hard as they play.
Texas Cowboys – nothing hotter.
HELL YEAH!

Note from the Author:

This is the fifth book in the McCoy group. As my readers well know, the events in all the Hell Yeah! take place in a relatively short amount of time. Therefore there are overlapping events at the beginning of each book. I write the books to either be read in order or as standalone books. Please be aware that there are scenes, which if you have read the others - to you will be flashback scenes. This is to tie the loose ends together and allow someone who picks up just one book to have some idea of the events that bring the family to this particular point in time. There is a full story here – well over 80000 words and new details have been woven in that only Isaac or Avery will know.

Happy reading – Sable.

If you love this book, please consider leaving a review. Thank You!

BADASS

Prologue - Chapter One

"I can do this." Avery coached herself as she stood at the door of Hardbodies. "It's a simple plan. I'll just walk in, sit down and tell him how I feel."

Before she could open the door, it swung open, hard, almost knocking her down.

"Damn, I gotta take a piss!" An inebriated cowboy came staggering out, swaying with every step. If a bleached blonde with way too much make-up hadn't been holding him up, he would have fallen right at Avery's feet. "Hey, why don't you get out of the way, Miss Priss? What are you doing here? You look like you belong in a nunnery!"

A wave of bad breath hit Avery in the face and she held her hand over her nose to avoid the smell, stepping aside to give the couple a wide berth. "Excuse me, Sir." Avery didn't argue with him or take offense. That was just her way. Ridicule wasn't new to her. Avery knew she was different, a little square. It was how she'd been raised. Her dad was a Baptist pastor and Avery had been expected to attend some kind of church service three times a week since she could remember.

"Sorry," his companion muttered, directing the short apology at Avery. The poor woman was struggling to support her companion's substantial weight. They disappeared into the shadows, and Avery let out the air she'd been holding in her lungs. Smoothing her palms down her skirt, she wondered if she was dressed properly. Perhaps she should've changed clothes before coming to talk to Isaac. Looking down, she sighed. Her outfit was nice, but conservative. She didn't really own anything which could be termed stylish.

"Here goes nothing." She smiled at her own trepidation. Her hand shook as she pushed open the heavy door. Suddenly it whooshed out of her hand, and a large body blocked her view of the drinking establishment.

"Miss Avery, what are you doing here?"

Good Gracious! Avery looked up and up and then she laughed. "Terence Lee, how are you? I haven't seen you since you came to church with your Granny on Grandparents Day."

The big, brawny man looked sheepish. "Sorry, Avery. I know I need to be in church, I've just been busy."

She placed a hand on his arm. "Stop. I'm not the right-wing religion police. You're my friend. I was just making conversation." Sometimes it was frustrating. No one saw her as a woman. Instead, men saw her as an extension of her father or the church. Most were afraid to speak to her, much less ask her out. Little did they know that Avery Rose Sinclair was not the prude they all assumed her to be. "Is Isaac here?"

"Yea, he's tending bar." Censure was on Terence's face. Apparently, he didn't approve of her interest in his boss. "He's not going to like that you've come here, Miss Avery. This bar is no place for a lady like you." Every time Avery tried to step around him, he shifted his big body to bar her way.

Enough! Placing her hands on her hips, Avery glared at her childhood friend. "Move, Terence. I'm a grown woman and I'll go where I please." What was the big deal? Wrinkling her nose, she pursed her lips and fumed. Was he trying to protect her or Isaac? Finally, the mountain of a man stepped back and Avery got her first real look at Isaac's place of business. It was packed. People were dancing and playing pool. There was laughter and the clinking of glasses. But all of it faded from view as her gaze settled on the object of her desire. Isaac McCoy. Avery Rose almost purred. She had been in love with him forever, and tonight she was going to make her move. Despite years of sending him every signal she could think of, he had never been anything but polite until last week.

Several times, she had caught Isaac looking at her with heat in his eyes, but that could've been wishful thinking on her part. But after what happened on the street in front of the drug store, everything had changed. That day, she'd walked out of the store, not paying a bit of attention, and bumped right into him. Isaac held her for a few moments, and then uttered words which would forever be inscribed on her heart. He'd said, "God, you're beautiful. I would give anything in the world if you were mine." Then, he kissed her once, hard. But it had been over too fast. She hadn't even had time to enjoy it. When he lifted his lips from hers, he'd looked funny, blinked and stepped back, as if he just realized what he'd done. Before she could catch her breath to ask him what he meant, he was gone. All she'd been left with was an incredible memory which had fueled many nights of hot fantasies and one hell of a romance novel. Now, she was here to find out if he felt the same way she did.

God, he was handsome. She began a slow, steady path toward Isaac, almost like she was stalking him. Avery was a wildcat sneaking upon her prey. She smiled at the thought. Her, a wildcat? Yeah, she could be, if given half a chance.

Isaac was her hero. Their paths had crossed many times over the years. He and his family were Hill Country legends. Everyone in the county knew the sound of his Harley, and when he rode his motorcycle down the streets in that tight leather jacket, every woman stopped in her tracks to watch him go by.

Oh, she knew the rumors. She was well aware of his less-than-stellar reputation. According to popular belief, Isaac spent most of his time in bar-fights, brawls, drag races and rowdy parties. But, rumors could be wrong. Avery knew for a fact that there was more to Isaac than most people realized, even his family. They didn't know *her* Isaac.

Because of her affiliation with the county benevolence board, they had worked together behind the scenes. Avery was privy to the fact that Isaac supported a couple of charities single-handedly and was very generous with several others. He wasn't aware how much she knew about his business. Confidentiality was important to the board, but she saw a side of Isaac few others knew existed. To her, he was everything she wanted in a man—gentle, kind and undeniably sexy.

As she walked, she rehearsed what she would say. Maybe, 'Hi, Isaac. Could I have a martini?' No, not a martini. Avery would order a beer. Good Lord, she wouldn't be able to handle a beer. 'Might I have a Shirley Temple, please?' Yea, she could drink a Shirley Temple. He had his back to her, which showcased those yard wide shoulders. Lord, what she wouldn't give to hold him close. There was no man on the face of the earth that looked like him. Avery stared so hard, she was afraid he might burst into flames. Only last night, she had lain in bed and imagined him on top of her, pumping inside of her, her hands kneading those magnificent muscles. Whew! Avery fanned herself. If the congregation only knew! Avery Rose Sinclair had secrets. And one of them was standing before her. She had lots of fantasies that featured the sexiest bad boy in Texas. And tonight, she was going to ensure her fantasies came true.

* * *

Isaac had been aware she was in the room the moment she walked through the door. Every nerve ending in his body reacted to her nearness. Avery was all he'd ever wanted in a woman and the very thing he could never have. Bottom line, he didn't want to want her, but he did. She was pure and innocent, untouched and sweet, while he was a biker boy with a bad attitude and a taste for the kinkier side of sex.

Lord, she was beautiful. A lady—that was what she was, a lady. He watched her, first in the mirror, then turning he pretended to wipe down the bar. But he saw every step she made. Tensing his muscles, he controlled his baser impulses. She would never know. He would make sure of it. To look at him, he appeared nonchalant, self-assured. Cool, calm and collected. When in reality, all he wanted to do was vault over the bar, grab her and ride off into the sunset with her on his Harley.

He didn't say a word to her. She came forward hesitantly, slipping up to sit on a barstool. "Hi, Isaac. It's good to see you." Her little smile was sweet and tentative, and Isaac's mind fought a battle with his heart. "Could I have a diet coke, please?"

Lord, he didn't even know if he had a diet coke. "Sure." At least spending the time to look for one kept his eyes, hands, and lips off of her. "Found one." Taking the time to pour it, he managed to get himself under control and debated what to say to her. Looking up, he almost lost his resolve, but he needed to do what was best for both of them. "Avery Rose, you need to leave. This bar is no place for you." Isaac set the glass of soda in front of the sexiest woman in Texas. "Drink this, and then you're out of here. I'll walk you to your car myself."

"I'd rather stay, if that would be all right with you," she said politely. Isaac's hand lay on the bar six agonizing inches from Avery's. She closed the gap slowly and covered his hand with hers, letting her thumb caress his fingers. This was bold for her. Avery could hardly believe she had the courage to make the first move.

Isaac jerked his hand away as if it had been burned. "All right, that's it. I don't get paid extra to baby-sit." Walking around the bar, he took Avery by her arm. She didn't resist, but let him lead her to the tavern door. Terence Lee gave her a sympathetic look and opened it wide enough to let both her and his boss exit the building.

Avery looked like she was about to cry. "Isaac, please don't make me leave. I won't cause any trouble. I'll be quiet."

Stopping at the door of her beige minivan, Isaac looked down at her conservative little skirt and demure matching blouse. Actually, she was so beautiful it hurt his eyes to look at her. He wanted to kiss her trembling, plump lips until they were fiery red from passion. "Don't you have an event to host, or a benefit to plan?"

Or anything else to keep her out of his sight. She had no idea how tempting she was.

"I've spent my life doing those things. Now, I want to be with you." Taking him totally by surprise, Avery closed the short distance between them and gave him a sweet kiss. Rising up on tiptoe, she fitted her mouth to his, letting the tip of her tongue dance over his lower lip. Hell! Isaac wanted to crush her to him more than he wanted to live another day. His arms rose and fell, rose and fell, his hands clenching into fists as he fought to keep himself from devouring her where she stood. Damn! He had to get control. Avery was not for him.

Jerking back, Isaac pulled away from her. "This is not going to happen, Avery." Isaac was about to do something he swore he would never do. He was going to hurt a sweet and innocent little thing. It was Isaac who picked up the kittens and puppies that people threw away on the side of the road. It was Isaac who climbed trees and put little birds back in their nests and fed baby squirrels with bottles when hunters killed their mamas and left them to starve. But sometimes you had to hurt somebody in order to be good to them. "Go home, Avery. I don't want you."

Avery looked stunned by his admission. "You don't want me?"

Frustrated, Isaac pushed his hand through his hair. "No, I'm sorry. I don't know where you got the idea, but you've misunderstood. I don't want you."

"But what about the other day, when you kissed me and said…" Avery's voice was small. "…when you said that you wished…" Her face fell and she stammered, unable to go on.

13

"I was just being nice." Isaac was lying like a dog. Preparing for the killing blow, Isaac braced himself. It was going to hurt him a hell of a lot more than it would her. "You aren't my type, Avery. In fact, I don't think you're anybody's type." At her wounded expression, he knew he was almost there. He pulled back the knife and waited to execute the final thrust. "I like my dates to excite me. Face it, Baby. You're just not woman enough to turn me on. Go home."

Isaac watched her little body reel backward as if he had physically hit her. "I'm sorry, Isaac. I won't bother you again." She fumbled with her keys and unlocked the van door. "Forgive me, I didn't know. I didn't understand."

Isaac forced himself to stand there and watch her drive away. He felt like something unbearably precious had slipped through his fingers and shattered on the ground.

* * *

Several days later, Avery came to a conclusion. She had cried herself to sleep for the last time. The way she saw it, she had a choice. She could either give up on Isaac McCoy forever, or she could attempt to transform herself into a woman he could be attracted to. Since she was already head over heels in love with him, it seemed that changing her looks and personality would be easier than giving up on her dream.

Just as there were things about him that most people didn't know, Avery had secrets, too. Some of her secrets would shock her folks and the church. One of them was the way she made her living. Avery was a writer. She wrote romance novels. Oh, they weren't too risqué, after all, she was inexperienced. But she did have a good imagination, one that was fueled by dreams of Isaac. She had been saving her money, too. And Avery was ready to declare her independence. Tricia, her best friend, had always dreamed of opening a florist shop. Now, Avery was financially able to go into business with her. In fact, by the time she got back, things would be in full swing. Tricia had already rented the building, stocked the store and had already started filling orders. All she had to do was dive right in and start helping. That way, she could stay in Kerrville near Isaac and still be active in the community. Her writing would have to remain a secret, but that was okay.

Yes, there were a lot of changes she wanted to make in her life. A born organizer, Avery knew how to set priorities, and Isaac was her first priority. Knowing she had to take serious steps to gain the knowledge she needed, Avery decided to go to an expert. No one would ever have to know. Discretion would be necessary. But like the TV commercial said, what happens in Vegas, stays in Vegas.

So, she made a phone call. After two rings, there was an answer: "Operator. May I assist you?"

She took a deep breath and plunged in. "Yes, Ma'am, I'm looking for a number in Nevada for the Shady Lady Ranch."

There was a pause and then the grandmotherly sounding operator had to put her two cents in. "Honey, you have a sweet little voice. I can tell you're a nice girl. Do you realize you are enquiring about the number for a house of ill repute?"

Avery cleared her throat, stuck her chest out and stood up for herself. "Yes, Ma'am, I am. I need that number, if you don't mind. I'm tired of being the good girl. I want to learn how to be bad."

Chapter Two

"I don't think one can learn how to give a proper blow job by practicing on a dildo." Destiny leaned on the table, resting her chin in her hand, while chewing gum with gusto, and popping one bubble after another. "Whatcha got against using a real dick, one that's hooked to a real guy?"

Avery stopped licking the thick pink shaft. She wrinkled her nose. The sex toy didn't taste that great and it made her tongue dry. "Because the only penis I want to kiss is attached to the man I love. I'm just here to learn how to please him." She turned the large dildo around in her hand and looked at it from all angles. "This is really big. Do real ones come in this size?"

"You *are* innocent, aren't you? I thought Margo was kidding." Destiny straddled a dining table chair and leaned forward, arms draping over the high back. "I don't understand what you're doing here. You let them parade you out at line-up, but Derek is always there to claim you. And we all know he just walks you to the back, kisses you on the forehead and goes back to bartending."

Laying the fake male member down, Avery settled back in her chair and looked at the girl in front of her. Destiny was Avery's age, maybe even a bit younger. But she was eons older in sexual experience. Yet, Avery felt protective of her. Did that make sense? It was probably her latent missionary instincts. "I came to Shady Lady to learn how to pleasure a man. Where I'm from…my face, my name, and my family…they are all synonymous with being strait-laced and having high moral values. I couldn't talk to my mother about sex, or to my best friend—nobody. So, I called here on a lark and my request intrigued Madam Margo so much, she invited me out for a few weeks."

"What does cinnanamous mean?"

Avery wanted to laugh so bad her sides hurt. "Synonymous is a word that means…never mind. All I'm saying is that where I'm from, nobody sees me as a sexual being or as a woman anyone would want to have sex with." She remembered what the drunken cowboy had said the night Isaac had broken her heart. "I might as well be a nun."

"Why didn't you just let your boyfriend teach you about sex?"

Destiny's naive expression and logical answer hurt Avery's heart. "Learning from Isaac would have been my first choice. Unfortunately, he isn't my boyfriend, and he has no desire to be, either. At one time, I thought Isaac liked me. I used to catch him staring at me, and once he said I was beautiful. But now I'm convinced he was only curious about me, because I'm so different than he is. That's what I want to change. I want to become a woman he could be attracted to."

Unbidden, Destiny's hand went to the top of Avery's bent head and she stroked her hair like she was comforting a frightened kitten. "You are a beautiful, desirable woman and I'll teach you how to make him glad he's a man. All I need to know is what he's like and what turns him on. By the time I'm through with you…you, Avery Sinclair, will be Isaac's dream girl."

* * *

Isaac was working double time; his more obvious goal was visible, out in the open and public. He was working on Hardbodies, renovating the bar into his vision of a seductive, exciting place for the locals to hang out on a Saturday night. All in all, he was pleased with what he'd done. You could get a cold mug of beer, or a glass of wine and listen to some decent live music. Austin was close enough that he had no trouble attracting quality bands. By his design, Hardbodies was a cross between a western/cowboy saloon and a biker haven. Both species were catered to and welcome in his establishment, mainly because he was a cross between the two himself.

Isaac McCoy was one of *THE* McCoy's of Tebow Ranch. He and his brothers had broken horses, raised cattle, rode in the rodeo, played football, done everything a Texas good ole' boy was supposed to do, and they had done it well. Tebow wasn't as big as the infamous King Ranch, but it epitomized what a Texas ranch should be like. More than a showplace, it was their home. For the past few years, he hadn't spent as much time there as he should have. It wasn't his family's fault. The walls just seemed to want to close around him.

Aron had done his best to keep them all together after their parents died, but Isaac and Joseph had found their solace in a different manner than the others. Jacob had made family a priority, making sure that nobody's birthday went unnoticed and no holiday went uncelebrated. Noah had become Mr. Conservative. He was way too serious and Isaac worried that his inflexibility would one day do him in. Joseph had become an extreme athlete, one of the best that Texas had ever produced, while he had become the wild child, the black sheep, the troublemaker of the family. At least that's what he let the others believe.

Oh, he ran in a rough crowd, sometimes, but Isaac had stood up for more underdogs than he could count. He had made it his business to see that outlaw biker gangs kept their distance and there was no violence or drugs in his territory. When he had been approached by Shorty to buy the bar, Isaac had jumped at the chance. Being the owner of the local watering hole would put him right in the middle of the action so he could make sure that all was as it should be. His family had been surprised and pleased that he'd taken on the responsibility of owning a business. They knew of some of his community involvement, but not all of it. And that was the way he wanted it.

Isaac had his good qualities, even he could admit that. On the other hand, he couldn't deny he had a dark side. Not even his brothers knew the whole truth. Isaac McCoy had a penchant for black leather, fast bikes, and faster women. And he had a secret. A big secret.

As Isaac stood at the door of his basement playroom, he smiled. Now, he wouldn't have to drive into Austin or Houston or Dallas to satisfy his sexual appetites. Isaac McCoy was a Dom. In some circles, he was developing quite a reputation. Several times submissives seeking to be trained had approached him. Even a few Dom-wannabes had asked for direction and advice. In the Texas BDSM world, he was known as Badass, and it was a title he had earned. Isaac was a badass. He liked his sex rough and hot, but most importantly he had to be in control. And that fact was why he couldn't have the one woman he wanted more than anything.

Shutting the door to his secret hide-a-way, he headed up front to the bar. It was too early for customers. Doris was restocking the liquor and cutting up garnishes. Meanwhile, he was doing his dead level best to forget the devastated look on Avery's face when he told her she wasn't woman enough for him. What a huge effing lie that had been! He wanted Avery Rose Sinclair, but he was afraid he would end up crushing her like a rose trampled on the ground. So, he was just going to have to forget her and move on. Letting her go would be the greatest gift he could give her.

First, though, he was going to have to find out what happened to her. After that fiasco in the bar, she had up and left, just disappeared. Her parents had moved out of town about six months earlier, when her dad had left his pastorate in Kerrville and accepted a church in the valley. Isaac had always suspected that Avery stayed in town to be near him. And now, she was gone because of him.

He had driven by her little house three times over the past couple of days. It looked deserted. Even though Isaac knew it was going to be a disaster, he'd looked up her dad's new church on the Internet and called the parsonage number to see if she might be visiting them. He needed to know that Avery was okay. At least her mother had answered his question before she discovered who she was talking to. He learned that Avery wasn't with her parents. And her mom hated his guts. No news there.

Isaac didn't share the same community social standing his brothers enjoyed. To the less pious members of the Kerrville community, he was their example of an upstanding citizen. He wasn't a front man like his brothers. Isaac did his good deeds behind the scenes. Most people didn't know how hard he worked for different organizations and the time and money he devoted to charitable events.

Avery knew.

Countless times they'd worked together, and if she needed something done, she'd always known Isaac was one of the few people she could count on.

Over the years, he'd watched her grow up and change from a pretty girl to a devastatingly beautiful woman with a natural grace and the sweetest spirit known to man. He smiled, remembering her quirky sense of humor. Avery always had a kind word for everybody, and one thing which amused Isaac was the way she loved to play pranks on people. Half the time they backfired on her, and she never had a problem laughing at herself. Avery was a wonderful person and truly a joy to be around.

Walking out the back door of Hardbodies, Isaac opened the tailgate of his truck and began unloading cases of tequila and rum onto a dolly. He racked his brain trying to figure out where she could have gone, ashamed to admit he didn't know who her friends were, or even what she did for a living. In his efforts to keep her at arm's length, he had failed to hold up his end of the friendship bargain. She always attempted to make conversation with him, asking him polite questions and showing interest in his life, but he hadn't returned the favor. So, where was she? Slamming the tailgate, Isaac let loose a blue streak of remorse. If something happened to Avery, he'd never forgive himself.

* * *

"That's right. Now, suck the head like you're eating a big ole' juicy plum." Three of Nevada's finest ladies of the evening leaned over Avery as she yummed down on a pink plastic Jackrabbit. She closed her eyes, trying to imagine she was kneeling in front of Isaac giving him pleasure. "Now, pump it as you suck it," Roxy instructed, moving her own fist up and down in the air. Avery tried to follow the instructions. After all, this was important to her. But she got the giggles.

"Watch your teeth. Don't bite the boy," Claret fussed, taking her job seriously. That thought sobered Avery up. She didn't want to do Isaac's private parts any damage. Extricating the faux penis from her mouth, she wiped her lips with a paper towel and announced, "Let's do something else. My mouth is tired." Hopefully, kissing Isaac's penis would be more exciting than this process seemed to be.

"How 'bout if we work on your wardrobe, Avery?" Claret got a sneaky expression on her face. She was having a good time playing erotic mentor. Just last week, she'd taught Avery how to walk, how to slowly strut and sway her hips, every move a flaunting of her sexuality. After putting on music, the girls had taught her how to use those moves in a pole dance or a lap dance. Several of them had worked with her on routines, going over and over the moves until she memorized them.

Every night after they finished Avery would retire to her room, and she would stand in front of the mirror to practice being sexy. She would put one hand on her hip, one leg in front of the other and thrust her breasts out. Much to her surprise, she seemed to be catching on, and Avery was her own worst critic.

It amazed her how free and easy she felt with these women. Here, she had truly been able to let down her hair. Avery swore she'd never laughed so much. She even confessed to them about her writing. In the quiet hours of the night, Avery had penned her first erotic story and sent it off to her publisher before she could change her mind. It had been called, "Cowboy Heat", and of course, Isaac had been the hero. All of the girls downloaded the free eBook reader app and bought her stories. A few even asked for her autograph. She had to admit she sort of enjoyed the attention. It had been difficult never sharing such an important part of her life with anyone. One night they sat up until the wee hours of the morning talking and laughing. She told them the plots of several more novels she had in the works and showed them how to find her website and her blog. Tricia was a good friend, but these were things she'd never felt able to share with anyone, before now.

"I ordered some biker clothes for you," Claret announced, proudly. "They're guaranteed to bring your Hell's Angel to his knees."

"All right, I'm game." She stood up and wrapped the dildo in a paper towel, so she could remember to clean it properly when she got back to her room. It had been a new one, of course. They'd allowed her to take it out of the plastic sealed container. The ladies were all very nice to her. She wasn't a germaphobe, but she was cautious. Despite knowing the sheets were carefully laundered, Avery slept in the childhood sleeping bag she'd brought from home. That sleeping bag had seen some action, lately. Even now, just thinking about Isaac made her nipples puff up and beg for attention.

Last night, Avery had touched herself. After her bath, she'd lain on her pink kitty sleeping bag and rubbed her breasts. It felt so good. She didn't make herself come, but she certainly gave kitty something to think about. Avery was determined Isaac would give her that all-important first orgasm. Perhaps she was being sentimental, but it seemed necessary to her to save all of those momentous experiences to share with him.

"Can I come too?" Sissy was the newest girl. In many ways, she was as unskilled as Avery.

"Sure. The more the merrier." Destiny sashayed down the hall, turning sideways as she met Madam Margo. "Hey, Boss Lady. How's it shaking?"

Margo held up a hand and stopped all four of them in their tracks. "We've got trouble, especially for you, Avery." She looked so serious, Avery got nervous. She couldn't imagine what the problem was.

"What's the matter? Did I do something wrong?" She was grateful for all of the girls' help and had no idea how anything she could have done would bother anybody.

"You didn't do anything, dear. But your being here isn't exactly a secret anymore." Margo held out a copy of the Las Vegas Sun. Avery took it from her hands, and right there in living color was a picture of the whole line-up of Shady Ladies, including herself. And the headline underneath the photo said "Modern Day Mary Magdalene - Preacher's Daughter Turns Tricks."

Avery gasped. "Holy Mother of God. Who could have done this? I thought I was incognito."

"I was afraid of this. Sonya's John said you looked familiar and he asked a lot of questions about you. He crept around after his session, like he was hiding from someone. I bet if you had seen him, you would have recognized his face. It's obvious he knows who you are."

Avery put a hand to her forehead. "Oh, what did Sonya tell him? Heavens! I'm so far from home. Surely, this photograph won't be picked up in Texas." Good Lord, she could just hear her daddy now. He would have a conniption fit, even though she hadn't done anything wrong—technically. She was just planning on practicing fornication with Isaac McCoy at the first opportunity, that's all.

"Let's hope not, Honey." But even Avery could tell she looked doubtful.

"I just hope he didn't make a YouTube video," Sissy said gravely, as she twisted her platinum ponytail around her fingers.

Avery leaned back against the wall and sighed. "This is just my luck. I get branded a good-time girl and I've never even been around the block. I'm probably the first virgin fallen woman in history."

* * *

"I can't believe you're gonna try and pull that old trick on Skye." Noah shook his head at Isaac's tomfoolery.

"Loosen up, Little Brother. She's a city-girl. It'll be fun." It was deer season and the McCoy brothers had taken time out during the past week for a hunting trip. Archery-only season began in early October and the tradition merited a festival-like atmosphere. The brothers hunted from horseback and harvested enough deer meat to keep the kitchen in sausage and venison for the next twelve months. This year their foreman, Lance, had invited his sister down from Oklahoma City for a few weeks. "Watch this. I pulled it on Jessie when she first got here and I thought she was going to deliver that baby right then and there."

"Yeah, and Jacob almost de-balled you for doing it, too." Noah watched as Isaac took a pair of buckeyes from his pocket and tossed them in the air. "Skye sure is a beautiful woman. Are you interested in her?"

Isaac stopped for a moment and looked at his brother. "She's beautiful, but I'm not interested. So if you are, go for it, Man. What about Harper?" Isaac knew Noah had set his heart on Harper years ago. But something had happened, something Noah refused to talk about. Isaac knew what it was, and he hoped to high heaven that knowledge didn't blow up in his face.

A funny look passed over Noah's countenance. "Harper and I just aren't meant to be." That was the truth if Isaac ever heard it, Harper was nothing but trouble.

"You'll find someone else, Noah. Someone who'll make you smile. I have no doubt about that."

Noah wasn't arguing with him. "Skye is something else, Isaac. Hell, she's just about damn perfect. I don't know if it's her Cherokee blood or what, but she makes my heart beat like a war drum."

"So, Paleface, is it okay if I tease your little Indian princess?" He was enjoying this, probably too much, but that was one of the perks of being the big brother.

"I'll be watching you," Noah joked with his brother, but Isaac could tell he was halfway serious. Figures. He was damn sure gonna quit drinking the water at Tebow. There were weddings and babies popping up all over the place. He'd be richer if he'd bought stock in garter belts and diapers.

Isaac held the door for Noah, and they walked in right as Aron threw a full beer can at Jacob. It whizzed right by Isaac and he caught it, neatly. "Thanks, I needed that. What are ya'll throwing cold ones around for?"

The eldest McCoy sat in his big leather chair, feet propped up on the ottoman. His boots were dusty and his black Stetson was pushed back on his head. "Because we're hot, tired and dusty, Hotrod. Hand your brother that beer, he's spent the day trying to convince Mrs. Trahan that Red Warrior wasn't trying to run her down and gore her to death."

Isaac handed the can of Shiner beer to Jacob, who was sitting on the couch opposite the big screen TV, watching a reality show featuring shooting competitions. "Thanks, Bud. You ever seen this show? These guys have all kinds of target practice, wild stuff. I think we ought to have war-games like that at our next party. What do you think?"

"Well, since the next two parties we have are Joseph's engagement party this weekend and your and Aron's weddings the next, I don't think that idea will fly very high with the womenfolk," Noah answered with his usual logical thought process.

"He's right." Aron took a swig of beer. "I can't see the girls going for target practice at their love fests. We'll have our gun shooting competition for Isaac's birthday at Halloween. That'll reward us for all the tedious romantic celebrations we've got to get through this month."

Isaac could see over Aron's shoulder and what he saw made him want to snort. Aron hadn't meant anything anti-wedding by his comment. After all, he was desperately in love with Libby. But at the moment, Libby was right behind him, and she didn't look happy.

Isaac started to stop him from putting his foot any deeper in his mouth, but it was just too much fun.

Aron started talking again, and he just made it worse. "I mean, how much lovey-dovey stuff are we supposed to endure before we get to do some manly shit? Life at Tebow has become like one of them chick flicks on the Lifetime Movie network. All we need is to hook you two up with a woman each, get Nathan a little girlfriend, bring Kane and Lilibet into the fold, and we could be the cast of that stupid 'Seven Brides for Seven Brothers' movie from the fifties. Next thing you know, all us men will be lined up like chorus girls singing them corny songs like 'Goin Courtin' or 'Lonesome Polecat'."

At Libby's face, the brothers who could see her drew back as far as they could. She was about to let it fly. "I don't think you need to worry about 'going courtin', Mr. Aron McCoy. But 'lonesome polecat' will definitely describe your sleeping arrangements for the foreseeable future." Libby was beautiful, pregnant and not amused. The expression on Aron's face when he realized she had overheard his joking diatribe was priceless. Isaac had never seen his brother crawfish so fast before.

He got up quickly and even though he was a foot taller and over a hundred pounds heavier than his fiancé, she clearly had the upper hand. Isaac could tell she wasn't really mad, peeved maybe. But, she wanted Aron to think she was mad. In fact, when Aron looked around for moral support from his brothers, Libby gave them all a soft wink to diffuse the situation. It wasn't often they got the best of Aron, and when they did, the family needed to take advantage. "Now Libilicious, you know

I want to marry you more than anything else in the world." He was reaching for her, but she kept backing up, staying just out of reach.

"That's not what I just heard, Aron." She pooched her little mouth out sexily, and Isaac realized that he and the others were getting a first-hand look at feminine wiles in action. "You dread our wedding, don't you?"

"No, no—hell no!" Aron was stalking her, slowly. "You know that making you mine is my highest priority."

"Are you sure? I mean, we could postpone it, and the ceremony won't even go to waste. Jacob can't wait to marry Jessie." Libby looked over at Jacob for confirmation. "Isn't that right, Jacob?"

Jacob jumped right in. "Sure can't. The sooner I get my ring on her finger, the better. I intend to tie the knot before little Bowie Travis makes his appearance."

Libby moved around Aron to talk to Jacob. "All we would have to do is cancel one of the cakes and order a few less flowers. The guest list wouldn't even have to be changed. We'll call the Reverend—" She didn't get to finish the sentence before Aron had swept her off her feet and up into his arms in the traditional 'over the threshold' position.

"Now wait a gosh-darn minute, both of you." He stared at his brothers like it was all their fault, and then he looked back at the woman in his arms. "It doesn't matter how frou-frou the ceremony or how many monkey-suits I have to wear, I wouldn't trade marrying you for a deed to the whole damn universe." He kissed her hard in front of God and everybody and marched out of the room with his treasure.

The other three sat there and then looked at one another. Jacob laughed first. "Maybe the ole' polecat won't be as lonesome as we first feared."

"No, I think he made amends for his macho carryings-on." Isaac couldn't help but be jealous of what Aron and Libby shared. He needed his brand of sex, if only it wasn't keeping him from having the woman of his heart, that reality was eating him alive. He would change if he could, but he didn't know if it was possible. Frankly, he was sick and tired of trying to be something other than what he was.

"Where's Skye?" Noah asked out of the blue.

"She's upstairs with Jessie. They'll be down in a minute. Jessie's showing her the nursery you put together for her." Isaac watched Noah's face and knew he was remembering the trouble he'd caused Jessie and Jacob. His interference had almost cost Jessie her life and the nursery had been his way to try and make amends.

"What was Aron talking about when he said Ms. Trahan was afraid of the Warrior?" Isaac knew the big bull was as gentle as a lamb.

Jacob sat up, drained his beer bottle and smiled. "It was funny. Now, ya'll know that bull. We've hand-fed and brushed him since he was knee-high to a grasshopper."

"He loves to be brushed with a curry comb. We've spoiled that old monster, but he sure does sire damn fine calves. As far as Beefmaster bulls go, he's top-notch," Noah commented, but Isaac was amused to see that he kept one eye on the staircase. The boy was besotted!

"I love to watch him when he sees Jessie or Libby come to the gate with some nuggets in their hands. He runs at them like a freight train. When we have company, they can't be still when he comes a runnin'. They dance in their shoes, thinking that big ole' bull is gonna run 'em down. But he always skids to a stop, nose to nose, with those sweet little girls. Why, I'd trust him to let Jessie ride on his back, if she had a mind to." Jacob took the remote and turned the sound down on the TV.

"So, where does Ms. Trahan come into play?" Isaac knew Jacob could spend hours telling a story if you didn't aim him in the right direction.

"She came to buy a few straws of War's semen and she wanted to take a look at him. So I took her over to his pasture, and told her to walk down to the pond where he was standing underneath one of the big oaks. He looked like a king surveying his domain. She was impressed, but decided to get up close and personal with him."

Isaac started laughing. He could see where this was going. "What did he do, decide to come and meet her and give her a proper escort?"

"Yeah, I guess she was expecting him to just stand there like some statue, but he's polite, he didn't want to make her walk all that way by herself. Besides, she might be packing a few nuggets for all he knew. He was willing to give her a chance."

"Lord, what happened next? Are we in jeopardy of a lawsuit?"

Isaac slapped Noah on the back of the head. "Down Donald Trump, this is just a funny story. Nobody's suing anybody."

Jacob snorted. "Actually, we're lucky Ms. Trahan didn't have a heart attack. She loves to play the rancher's wife, but she don't know a hill-a-beans about animals. Anyway, when she saw Red Warrior begin to mosey toward her, she got nervous and turned to come back to the gate. She picked up her pace a little and so did War. After all, he thought they might be playing a game."

"I just love the way you read this bull's mind. But, then again, you are the Bull Whisperer of central Texas. When do you think Skye and Jessie are gonna come down? Do you think I ought to go up and check on them?"

"Why don't you do that, Romeo?" Isaac watched Noah struggle with staying or going. He decided to stay. "Do you want to play the 'ball' game with Skye?" He held the buckeyes out to tempt him.

"Hell no," Noah groused. "I can't lie with a straight face like you can."

"Can I get back to my story?" Jacob had been patiently waiting, and when they settled down he resumed. "Anyway, when little Ms. Trahan realized that War was moving toward her, she panicked and started to run. Well, War figured if she was running, maybe something was after them both, so he might oughta run too. So the faster she ran, the faster the bull ran and when I heard her screaming, she was tearing across the pasture waving her arms in the air, saying 'Save me! Save me!'" Jacob was waving his arms, mimicking Ms. Trahan, and Noah and Isaac were cracking up.

"What happened next, or should I guess?" Isaac could just see War running with that big dick of his swaying in the breeze.

"I wish I'd had a camera, it would have won us a million dollars on one of them funny video shows. War never caught up with her, plus he kept looking back over his shoulder to see what booger-man was after him. And

33

by the time Ms. Trahan had reached the safety of the gate, and Lord, in heaven, don't repeat this at the bar. But she had tinkled on herself. I looked down and there were drops of pee falling in the dirt and running down her leg." They were all laughing, Jacob hardest of all. "And do you know what War did? He let it fly, too. I guess you could say they scared the piss out of each other."

"What did you do?" Isaac couldn't begin to imagine. Jacob had more couth than he did.

"What do you think I did? I pretended not to see a thing." There was movement on the stairs, so Jacob finished up his tale. "I finally got her to pet him and see that he's just a big old baby and she bought twenty thousand dollars' worth of his little swimmers."

"Here they come," Noah announced, his mind clearly not on War's pee party.

Jessie came first and Jacob lit up like a Christmas tree. Isaac felt a tug at his heart. Seeing his brothers so happy meant a lot. Jessie was gorgeous and her tummy was as round as a basketball. His older brother pulled her down onto his lap and started rubbing the place where their baby rested. The little boy wouldn't be Jacob's biological child, but neither he nor any of the family cared one iota. She had come to Jacob pregnant, thinking that the surrogate baby she carried was his. A mix-up at the sperm bank had been the best thing that ever happened to Jacob. But the baby would be a McCoy, a well-loved McCoy, through and through.

Then Isaac saw Skye, and he saw Noah watching Skye, and it was a sight to behold. She was slender and elegant, with long dark hair and the biggest doe eyes he'd ever seen. He didn't really blame his brother, after all Skye was a beautiful woman. It was a good thing he didn't have feelings for her or a new family feud might be in the offing. All right, show-time. "Skye, you sure did get a good deer yesterday. That buck dressed out at a hundred and a quarter. I saved the antlers for you, and I saved something else, if you want them." He held his hand out, palm up, with those two round buckeyes lying in the center.

She looked at him suspiciously, her bright black eyes shining with banked amusement. Perhaps, Miss Skye wasn't a typical city girl. She held out her hand. "May I hold them?" He gave them to her and she rolled them between thumb and forefingers. "These are very nice, but they don't belong to my deer. I dressed him myself and put the aforementioned delicacy in the stew I'm preparing for your supper. These balls are a little small for my deer. Have you felt between your legs to see if you're missing anything?"

Well, hell. Noah and Jacob literally bellowed their laughter and Isaac bowed his head, hiding his own smirk. Skye was nobody's fool. Jessie jumped up and took Skye by the hand and they began planning dessert for the evening meal. All of a sudden, Isaac didn't feel that hungry for stew.

"I'm in love," Noah whispered under his breath. "Yep, I'm in love." Isaac was glad, because the farther Noah stayed away from Harper, the better they all would be.

* * *

"I almost don't recognize myself." Avery turned sideways and stared at her reflection. Decked out in black leather, she didn't look like herself at all. Her hair was fluffier and her make-up was subtle, but somehow it made every feature look sexier. She leaned closer and looked at her eyes. They were a blue-violet with a gold starburst, but the eye shadow and mascara she had applied with Destiny's help made them look huge. She liked it, Avery decided. And her mouth was pink and glossed, making it, she had been assured, very kissable. Touching her face, she traced her cheekbones. "Do you think Isaac will like the new me?"

"He'd have to be dead to resist you now, Sugar." Margo stepped back and surveyed her handiwork. "Don't forget everything I've taught you. You now have skills that will make any man your slave." She reached behind her and picked up Avery's small pink Hello Kitty suitcase. "I've stocked this with a bunch of goodies and a list of reminders of the new weapons you have in your repertoire. Remember, you can now do a mean lap dance, you know how to work a stripper pole, you are proficient in oral sex and seductive moves, and you know more sexual positions than the writers of the Kama Sutra."

"That sounds good, Madame, Dear." Avery laughed. "But alas, all of that talent has been acquired without the benefit of a living, breathing male partner. Lord only knows if I'll be able to practice what you preach." At Madame Margo's amused, but pointed look, she promised. "Yes Ma'am, I will give it my best shot." That went without saying. It was why she'd come. The last couple of weeks had been spent acquiring knowledge of erotic techniques, most of which she hadn't even known existed. Now, all she had to do was go home and try them out on Isaac McCoy, if he would let her. At least she had lots of new stuff to write about. Her publisher had called and demanded more erotic stories. It looked like her writing career had taken an unexpected turn. They were asking her to accept interviews, but Avery couldn't afford to allow this new information to get back to her dad and his church. They would faint dead away.

Having already said her good-byes to the girls, she hugged the older woman who had broken all the rules and taken in a total stranger. For all Margo could have known, she might have come to cause the house a peck of trouble. Instead, she had obtained an insight into a world she had only heard of in the vaguest of terms. Wrapping her arms around the older matron, Avery placed a kiss on her rouged cheek. "I want to thank you, for everything. You've tried to teach me a lot of stuff, and I know I failed miserably in most of it. But one thing you have accomplished is an increase in my self-confidence. I'm going back to Kerrville a new woman." The bravado was a front, but she thought she could at least get her foot in the door at Hardbodies. And once she was in, she would have an opportunity to get Isaac's attention.

"You have my number, Sweetie. Call me if you need anything. And don't you forget, that man is gonna be lucky to get you." Margo walked her to the door, and watched as Avery strapped her bags to the back of the Harley Sportster. It had taken two days of intense work by the bartenders and some of the regular johns to get her to the point where she felt at ease riding the motorcycle. Trading in her minivan had not been a hardship. The conservative vehicle just didn't go with her new personality or even with her chosen career. It was time for the world to get a glimpse of the real Avery.

Climbing on the bike, she slipped on the helmet and turned the key. A roar greeted her ears and made her blood rush. The moment had arrived to set her plan in motion. Avery Rose Sinclair was going home, and it was time to show Isaac that the good girl had learned some new tricks.

Chapter Three

Isaac ran a hand over the sub's smooth tanned ass. She shivered in anticipation. "Please, Master. I need more."

A pleading, submissive tone used to be all it took to make him rock hard. Lately, it wasn't working, and Isaac was doing everything he could to regain the pleasure he used to get from sex. Dammit! He was a Dom! Taking his enjoyment from a submissive woman was one of the greatest thrills of his life. While he could still instruct and guide, he hadn't been able to bring himself to have sex during a scene. Each time he began, all he could see was... No! He refused to even think her name, not now. She didn't belong here, not even her name or a thought of her belonged in this setting. Focusing on the woman before him, he spoke, "Trust me, Madelyn. I'll give you what you need." He held his hand out to Levi who placed a leather quirt in his palm. "Are your nipples hard?"

"Yes, Sir." The woman who was strapped to the waist high bondage table spread her legs as far as she could, seeming to offer Isaac access to her very soul. "They need to be sucked."

"All in good time," he assured her. "Right now, I'm about to turn this perfect rump a nice shade of pink." He tapped the quirt on her rear, just to see how she'd react. When she lifted it slightly, as if seeking the sting, he knew it would bring her pleasure. One of the prime duties of a Dom was to give a sub exactly what she needed. But instead of the quirt, he first used his hand, slapping her bottom lightly. She yelped in shock. Liking the response, he massaged her cheeks, trailed down the tender inner flesh of her thighs, coming close…so close to her tender sex. Isaac felt his cock stir, but his heart wasn't in it. The rampaging excitement which used to accompany a BDSM session like this was missing.

"Oh, please. Oh, yes," she whispered. He knew what to do. In fact, Isaac could do this in his sleep. Pleasuring a woman was a gift. All of his adult life, he had known his sexual needs were different from his brothers'. Domination was as much a part of his soul as Tebow was. And if he couldn't function in this manner any longer, he was lost. His fingers pressed deeper, sliding through her slit, grazing her clit in circular patterns until he could feel it respond. Madelyn tried to move her butt to push back against his hand. Even though the straps held her in place, he felt her muscles strain. Isaac was pleased, and slapped her rump again. Maybe, just maybe. "This is my body to use," he said and thrust two fingers into her so hard and fast, he felt her go onto tiptoe, her vagina grasping in shock. "Sub, you have presented your ass to me for my pleasure. Your orgasms belong to me. You will come when I command you to and not before."

A red blush flared up the beautiful woman's body as his finger moved inside her. But Isaac knew she would need more stimulation than that. He pulled his hand from her vagina and slapped her again on the one firm cheek. She whimpered, and he knew she was desperate with want. This was the part Isaac always loved the most. He got off watching a woman in the throes of lust. There was nothing more arousing than bringing a woman to the point of begging for his touch.

Stepping in front of her, he admired the twin plump mounds that hung down like rich, ripe fruit. "You have such pretty breasts. Look at those succulent nipples…they are raspberry red and so very plump, Little Sub." He gently squeezed her breasts, and his thumb brushed over the tips, making her moan. Taking the quirt, he traced around her breasts lightly, brushing over her swollen, sensitive nipples, sliding the implement of pleasure over her shoulder and down her back, teasing her with what was to come. With a sharp flick, he slapped her round ass with the leather quirt, pausing to gauge her reaction. As he expected, she gasped, arched her back and pushed her rump toward him, a look of pleased surprise all over her face. Today was her first experience with the bite of a whip. As always with subs, she had agreed to it, but imagining it and experiencing it were two different things.

Isaac slowly increased the intensity and frequency of the whipping, and Madelyn moaned. Waiting for his own lust to build, he lashed slightly harder and quicker, pleased to see beautiful pink streaks appear, as if in watercolor on her smooth, white flesh. With each slap her cream flowed more freely, until it was making a milky trail down her thigh. His little sub mewled, closing her eyes. Isaac knew how it worked. Her mind transformed the energy from each bite of the quirt, making her hungry for more and more. Upping the ante, he smacked the insides of her tender thighs with the small whip, making her legs quiver. The intensity rising, she groaned as he whipped the soft skin, each blow sending jolts of pleasure surging through her body. Damn! She was like a Roman candle about to shoot off and he felt—nothing. Disgust at himself almost overwhelmed Isaac. What kind of a damn Dom was he?

Useless, he was flippin' useless and it was his own friggin' fault. The whole family teased him about his tender heart. If he gave free rein to his soft side, he would have every stray in the county at Tebow ranch. And now, he had gone and fallen in love, but not with a woman who could tolerate or enjoy his lifestyle. Hell no, he had to go and fall head over spurs for a sweet, pure angel of a virgin who would be horrified to know Isaac McCoy got off on bondage, domination, whips and chains—the whole leather and lust scene.

Refusing to give up without a fight, he fondled the sub's perfect rump and lightly whipped the backs of her thighs. She sighed heavily and cried out, "Harder! Oh, please, Master, I need you to whip me harder!" She was groaning, moving her hips back and forth. "Ohhhhh, I'm going to explode! I can't stop it!"

"Stop! You will not finish until I allow it. You must wait for my signal." Isaac's voice was gruff and he quickly stepped away from her. She let out a harsh sob, needing more, needing to orgasm. And Isaac was furious with himself. He stood there, unable to continue. Nothing had changed; he simply couldn't do it anymore. Motioning for Levi to take over, he almost apologized to the sub. It wasn't her fault. Tears slipped down her flushed cheeks and her breath flowed rapidly between her parted lips. He admired her strength as she pulled herself together to await the new Master's desire. Levi glanced at Isaac, not in censure, but in understanding. They had spent hours together as Isaac tried to work through his problems. So Levi had been on alert, waiting to see how Isaac would do.

As Isaac stepped away, Levi knelt before the sub, running his hand up and down the inside of her thighs. Madelyn's reaction was to automatically tilt her ass toward him. He snapped the whip once, hard against her mound. Madelyn cried out, begging for more. Taking the handle, Levi played with her, teasing her opening, pushing at the tender hole and dragging the cream up and down her slit. Obviously, he had no qualms about pleasing the little sub. As Isaac watched, Levi knelt behind her and licked her pink, swollen folds. With a groan of lust, he sucked and nibbled on her throbbing clitoris. She groaned in gratitude, pressing against his mouth. "Now come for me, Baby!" Madelyn shuddered in release as a Master gave her permission to take her pleasure.

Unable to watch anymore, Isaac left them alone. Levi was a fine Dom and he had excelled under Isaac's tutelage. Flinging a towel over his shoulder, he looked at his hood and cape hanging on a hook. How many times had he worn them in scenes? Too many to count. The hood was custom made with the Tebow brand in the center of the forehead. Funny, now he didn't want to wear it at all. Feeling disgusted with himself, he retreated up the stairs. Crowbar was polishing the railing. Isaac nodded to him. Levi's simple friend had proven to be invaluable to them. Completely trustworthy, he worked nights for them, doing what needed to be done and helping Terence Lee with crowd control. "How you doing, Crowbar?" he acknowledged him as he headed to his apartment behind the bar.

Only lately had Isaac begun spending nights at Hardbodies. Tebow's main house was becoming a bit crowded. After Joseph and Cady got together, there was just a little too much happiness in his own home for him to be comfortable all the time. Isaac realized his attitude was selfish, but bottom-line, he was flat-out jealous. And the worst part was, there wasn't a damn thing he could do about it, but to just wait until he worked Avery out of his system.

Little by little, he had created a haven for himself in the space behind the bar. It was connected by a breezeway, and if you didn't know what was coming, you were totally taken by surprise. Isaac's sanctuary fit him to a tee. Like the main house at the ranch, there was a lot of wood and ceramic tile. A small kitchen and den were the first rooms you came to, but behind them he had a huge bedroom and a bath fit for a potentate. In the corner was a hot tub, and the guys who installed the shower had called it a carwash.

Stripping as he walked, he got tickled at his own pitiful self. Wasn't this just his damn luck? As he shucked his leather jeans, his cock sprang free. Great…now, he was hard. Looking down at his contrary dick, he had to admit the truth. It wasn't the naked, horny sub that made him as stiff as a steel beam. It was thinking of that sweet, soft witch of a woman who haunted his every thought.

Damn! Just picturing Avery had his mind going places which ought to be against the law. How many times had he imagined her naked? Her skin would be smooth and soft, and that hair! God, he'd spent hours just fantasizing about her hair! It was long, dark and hung in the sweetest, fattest, little ringlets, and God as his witness, it bounced as she walked. He would give almost everything he had to watch it bounce while she rode him. "Sweet Jesus, I'm losing my mind," he lamented as he tugged at his rod with long smooth strokes. Hell, he should just take a cold shower, but he was too weak. What he needed was relief, even if it was by his own hand.

Hanging the towel he had brought from the playroom over the rack, Isaac turned on the water and adjusted the spray. What he wouldn't give to see Avery standing here waiting for him to hand wash every inch of her curvy, luscious body. She might dress conservatively, but nothing could hide those magnificent breasts. Stepping onto the dark marble, he let the warm water run over his skin. Getting clean wasn't his highest priority, Isaac needed release. He was tired of trying to go to sleep with a hard-on. Right now, there was no ignoring his desperation. Leaning back against the shower wall, he began to fist his manhood. "Oh, yeah," he breathed harshly. "God, Love, I need you so bad. My Avery, so sweet, so lush, you are so hot." Spreading his legs in a wide stance, Isaac began to jerk himself off. God, it felt good. "Avery, I want you so much." Throwing his head back, he massaged his length, rubbing it up and down with just the right grip. Lord, what he'd give to be pushing inside Avery right now, his kingdom for her heat. God, yeah. She would be exquisitely tight, because Isaac knew without a doubt that Avery was saving herself, just for him.

God, his pleasure came boiling up fast and furious from his tight, hard balls. Throwing his head back, he let out a bellow. "Avery!" Jets of his seed shot out from his manhood, spraying the wall of the shower with white ribbons, each a testimony to how much he wanted the one woman he could never have.

Laying his head on his arm, he rested his entire body against the cool surface. God, what was he going to do? He was caught between a damn rock and a crappin' hard place. He couldn't be satisfied with a life of vanilla sex and the one woman he would die to possess would never understand or accept his lifestyle in a million years.

After washing and drying off, he redressed for work in his signature black jeans, black shirt and a leather vest. This was Thursday, not his busiest night of the week. But there was a biker-rally in town, so his bar would be ground zero for those who needed to unwind, cool-off and get drunk, or were just looking for some tush.

There might be some tension from the cowboy regulars, but Isaac was ready for anything. He knew how to handle both kinds. In fact, he was no stranger to trouble. He and his family had had their share of ups and downs over the years. And most of it had been his fault. He was man enough to admit the truth. During high school and all through college he had drunk too much, partied too hard and made some questionable decisions. The man who had been sheriff before Kane had gotten him out of more scrapes than he could count. Drag racing, fistfights, you name it and he'd tried it. The only things he'd stayed clear of were drugs and stealing. A man had to have some principles. Padding around the apartment in his socks, he gathered his wallet and keys, and was just about to pull on his boots when his cell phone rang. When Isaac saw the name of the caller, a glimmer of hope flashed in his mind. Maybe Vance could tell him something he wanted to hear. "Talk to me, Brody."

"Good evening to you, too."

"Is it good? Did you find her?"

"Well, we're not sure. We think we saw her."

"How in the hell could you not know? I gave you a picture."

Vance chuckled. "If it was her, she didn't exactly look like the picture. She was, uh, dressed sorta differently."

"Look, I know she dresses in those little twin sets, matching sweaters and skirts. Avery is a throwback to the fifties. But she's a sweet girl." Why did he feel like he had to defend how she dressed? There wasn't anything wrong with the way Avery looked.

"We're going to do a little bit more checking and make sure before we give you a definite answer."

Still listening, he locked up his apartment, walked to the bar and went right to work. Vance was still trying to explain where a woman resembling Avery had been seen and by whom. Yet, they couldn't be certain the report was a hundred percent correct. "What are you telling me, Vance? Either you know where she is or you don't?"

Listening to his friend talk, Isaac could admit that the last few months had been wild and he was more than ready for things to go right for a change. Damn! "That doesn't give me a lot of comfort, Brody. I don't care how good Heath is supposed to be. Avery is still missing." Proving he could do three things at once, Isaac poured a shot of whisky, motioned Terence Lee to oust a drunk, trouble-making customer, and listened as Vance detailed the dead-ends his comrade had come up against as he had hunted for one small, innocent woman. The funny part was that Avery was evading a tracker who had been on the seal team that took down Bin Laden.

"Give me one more day and I promise I'll have an answer for you, or you can tie me to that funny little table you have in the basement." The line went silent. Vance Brody had hung up.

"Hell!" How did Brody know about his playroom? Damn, he might as well put a billboard up on I35. He could see it now: 'Isaac McCoy - Find your pleasure in leather…at Hardbodies.' Actually, it didn't sound half-bad.

* * *

Avery couldn't bring herself to park in Hardbodies' main parking lot. She wanted to give herself the few moments of calm a short walk would offer. Instead, she guided her bike to the street behind the club and pulled into an alley between the lumberyard and the feed store. Both establishments were closed for the night and she wouldn't be in the way of any traffic. Kerrville hadn't changed since she left and neither had she, not really. Oh, she was more aware of the physical aspects of sexuality, but she was still innocent. Avery was afraid her circumstances were like a fighter pilot who had only trained in a simulator. When thrust into battle, they discovered reality was a thousand times more intimidating than the safety of the control booth.

Removing her helmet, she locked it in place and climbed off. Glancing down, she made sure there were no runs in her stockings. A tiny smile played across her lips. If her dad could see her now, he would throw the book at her, the Good Book, that is. As she made her way across the lot, she wondered if Isaac would recognize her. When she'd studied her reflection in the mirror, Avery had practiced a sultry look, only to burst out laughing at the image in front of her eyes. She supposed she looked sexy, at least she hoped so. Her hair was longer, now hanging a couple of inches above her hip. It still had a mind of its own, long dark ringlets that always put her in mind of a Mother Goose character. Mary who had the little lamb would have hair like hers or Miss Muffet who sat on a tuffet or whatever. How she wished she had sleek blonde hair like some of the girls back at the ranch. Men preferred blondes. At least that was what she'd always heard. A wolf whistle cut through the air and Avery jumped, looking around to see who was attracting the male attention. There was no other female in sight, and the whistler lifted a can of beer in her direction. "You are one hot babe, Honey. Are you looking for a good time?"

He was talking to her!?! "Thank you, very much." She gave him a sweet smile. "I appreciate the compliment, but I'm on my way in to see an old friend." Her Pollyanna answer put a quizzical look on the bearded man's face. Shoot! She had to get her act together or this was going to be a colossal failure. Slowing her walk, she put a swing in her step, making her hips sway seductively like she had been taught. Flipping a strand of hair over her shoulder, she tilted her head upward and tried to manifest a dangerous air of mystery. Fighting back a giggle, she figured she would be okay until she opened her mouth.

"Sorry, Miss. My mistake," her admirer said with a confused backward glance over his shoulder. 'Great', she thought. 'If you can't convince a stranger you're a bad girl, how will you ever hope to fool Isaac?'

* * *

"It's about time you got here," Isaac growled as he noticed his younger brother Noah coming across the bar. He set a Coors in front of him. "Say something funny, I need to laugh." That absurd thought alone made him smile. Asking Noah to crack a joke was like asking a lion to roll over and play dead. It just wasn't his nature.

"Uh-uh..." Noah thought quickly. "Virginity is like a soap bubble, one prick and it's gone." Noah looked so pleased with himself, he smiled. Isaac appreciated the effort, but the topic of the joke was too close to his problem. Avery was the virgin, he was the prick and their future happiness was as fragile and elusive as an iridescent sphere of airy hope.

"Nice try." The band had been cranking out one hip grinding dance number after another, but as they stopped for a break, an odd hush settled over the room. A lone voice sounded through the silence. "Holy Shit! Hot Damn! Who's the babe?" Another male spoke in a hushed, reverent tone. "Get a load of that piece of effing perfection."

Noah turned around on the bar stool, looking to see who everyone was gawking at. "Christ! Who in blazes is that?"

Isaac looked. 'Sweet Lord!' A heart-shaped butt encased in black leather short-shorts filled his vision. Knee-high leather boots with a five-inch heel, a short little crop vest and one sweet strip of naked skin. "Mmmmmm…" He couldn't help but groan. Now, that was one hot little body! Where had she been all of his life? His manhood, unexpectedly, perked up and saluted. Long dark hair hung in ringlets to the middle of her back. Ringlets? He stared. Hell, those ringlets looked familiar. "No, surely not. No wonder Brody was questioning his intel." Isaac gritted his teeth and watched as the woman was surrounded...no, engulfed by men, and not once did she turn around. But, he did see her ease back from the men as if she thought they were too close for comfort. That one little nervous gesture had him moving out from behind the bar.

A gruff, bearded biker stood up at the same time. "Man, I gotta go get me some of that, put the five F's to work. You know what I mean?" He held up his rough hand, fingers splayed, and enough dirt under his nails to plant a garden. Elbowing Isaac, he sought another male's approval. "You know what I mean, the Five F's: Find, Flirt, Finger, Fu…"

"Shut up!" He didn't give the moron more than a second glance. A man like him would touch her over Isaac's dead body, not before. It wasn't Avery, it couldn't be, but his body was reacting to the possibility. And then she turned, and by God, his throat went dry, his heart jumped and his dick almost filled to bursting. Avery…it *was* Avery. The leather cropped vest was all she had on and it was cut low enough so all of her generous breast flesh was mounded up like luscious dollops of coffee ice cream. Isaac wanted to lick those beauties to see how sweet they must actually be. He couldn't help it. His feet started to move; there was no way in hell he could stay away from her.

* * *

Was it working? Was he watching? He dang well better be watching, that was all she could say. Avery Rose was scared to death. How much longer could she stand to be ogled by these questionable, smelly men?

But showing weakness or distaste for these people would be unacceptable. Isaac wasn't attracted to good girls, so she never wanted to be described that way again. Okay, yes, her new demeanor was a front, a false front. She could admit the truth. Avery was still as untouched now as she had been before, but she intended for that to change, hopefully tonight. She could do this. Her knowledge of the erotic and risqué was vast. Hands on? Not so much. Still, she looked the part and that was a start.

"Avery?" She jumped. Hell, her feet cleared the floor. She would know that voice anywhere. "Avery? What in God's name do you think you're doing? And what in the hell do you have on?"

He took her by the arm as if to pull her away from the crowd, when a barrel-chested gorilla protested. "Hey wait a minute! Leave the little lady alone. We were just about to get better acquainted."

"She comes with me, now!" Isaac ground the words out, as if they left a bad taste in his mouth.

Uh-oh, this couldn't be good. He didn't seem to be very happy to see her. His grip on her arm tightened. Isaac wasn't hurting her, but he had taken complete control. Avery was getting a distinct sense of déjà vu. This was going to be an exact replay of their last meeting. He was about to show her the door. "Isaac, you have no right. This is a public place and I'm over twenty-one. And I wasn't causing any problems, not till you walked up, anyway." She faced him with what she thought was a determined look on her face.

With a not-so-gentle tug, Isaac pulled her against his hot, hard body. He buried his face in her hair, and whispered right in her ear. "I have every right, as you well know."

Avery looked up at him, to see what he meant. Was he claiming ownership of her? God, please, yes. His next words dashed that hope. "I own this bar, my word is law."

Fine. He may not want her here, but that gave him no right to manhandle her. "Let me go, Isaac. I'm perfectly capable of walking out of here by myself."

About that time, ape-man decided to intervene on her behalf. "The little lady said 'no', Barkeep." He made the mistake of grabbing Isaac by the shoulder. "She wants to stay here with me. Don't you Sweetheart?"

Frankly, both men were getting on her nerves. This had been a mistake. Isaac was never going to admit he wanted her. Stopping in her tracks, she tried to extricate herself from the iron grip of the man she loved with all of her heart. "Why should I go any place with you, Isaac? I wasn't bothering you. I just came in for a drink like all the rest of your customers."

"Yea, she just came in for a drink." Avery's self-appointed hero stepped up right in Isaac's face. Big mistake, but one he might have gotten away with. His next move, however, became his downfall. Before she could react, the bearded wonder had the audacity to reach out and cup her bottom and, as the old saying goes, that was all she wrote. Isaac lost it and knocked the big ape sprawling, and then all hell broke loose. Cowboys, good ole' boys, bikers—it became a blur. Avery realized she was witnessing, no, correct that, Avery realized she had *caused* a knockdown, drag-out bar fight. She didn't know whether to be flattered or insulted.

The brawl kept growing. Chairs flew, tables crashed, and the sound of breaking glass filled the air.

One biker piled up on top of another, they ganged up on cowboys and vice-versa. She put her hand over her mouth and managed to avoid flying fists. Isaac looked up once and cursed. He grabbed her hand and managed to head Avery toward safety, motioning for Crowbar to come get her. She went, reluctantly, dodging a half full bottle of whiskey that was tossed across the room. "Avery, I'm Crowbar, it's nice to meet you. I'll take you to Mr. Noah." He gave her a friendly smile.

"Thank you, Crowbar. It's nice to make your acquaintance." Avery didn't know this big, gentle man, but Noah she would recognize. He was the only blond McCoy. She always thought he looked like a young Brad Pitt. His shoulder length hair and chiseled features made him look like an avenging angel. When they reached the bar proper, Noah intercepted. "It's good to see you again, Noah," she spoke politely, realizing she was trying to maintain Southern gentility during the midst of drunken mayhem.

"Hey, Avery, you sure know how to liven up a party. Let's get you somewhere safe." He steered her toward the back door.

A loud crash and a grunt. "Noah, I think Isaac needs you more. Most likely, I can find my own way out, thank you. I've been shown the door before." She smiled at him sadly. "Tell Isaac that I apologize and will be glad to reimburse him for all the damages."

Noah looked at her quizzically, but he didn't argue. Thankfully, he went over to assist his brother who didn't seem to have the upper hand at the moment. Avery gave him one last wistful glance and left.

* * *

Wham! Ummph! A chair came crashing down on his head. Hell! A voice at his shoulder sounded entirely too amused. "Need some help, McCoy?" Isaac glanced over and saw Kane, sheriff of Kerrville County. He was looking way happier than the circumstances warranted.

"Nope, I started it." There wasn't any use lying about it.

"Do you need help finishing it?" Kane dodged a blow, but Isaac caught it, unfortunately.

"Yeah, probably."

Weaving through the mass of bodies, Isaac tried to figure out exactly who was on his side. There was no use hitting somebody who didn't warrant it.

"I thought you weren't gonna do stuff like this anymore. After all, you're trashing your own bar." Kane noted dryly as he apprehended a couple of noxious no-counts.

Isaac wasn't arguing the facts, it was a puzzle, but there was only one answer that made sense. "Avery's back."

Kane nodded solemnly as he cuffed one spitting, snarling biker's hands behind his back. "Ah, well that explains it." He pushed his fresh arrest toward Terence Lee to deposit outside, and hauled another one up short. "Where is she?"

Isaac turned too soon, and a strange cowpoke landed square on his back. He swatted him off like an unwanted insect. "She's right over there." He pointed, then cursed. "Damn!" She was gone. "Well, hell."

* * *

Avery didn't look back, but held herself tightly, fighting off the chill of the late evening. Sheesh! She didn't have on near enough clothes. Still, she hurried, stepping carefully over the rocks. Turning an ankle in these high heel boots was the last thing she needed. All she could think of was getting away from Isaac. He wasn't going to get the chance to lecture her in the parking lot this time.

Running away from him wasn't exactly how she hoped the evening would end, but perhaps it was for the best. She needed to get back to the motel and come up with a strategy. Avery made her way across the street to where she'd parked her bike. Tonight wasn't the best night for him to see what she was riding, either. She grabbed a pair of blue jeans out of the knapsack on the back and slipped them on over the skintight shorts. Her outfit was supposed to be seductive, hopefully, but it wasn't worth a burn from the muffler. Straddling the Harley, Avery fired the engine up and pulled out into the street. Even before returning to Kerrville, she had decided against staying in her own home. The eyes of her neighbors were way too sharp, and several of them had her mom and dad's phone number. So she booked a room at the Long Stay suites, instead.

A smile played on her lips. If nothing else, riding this motorcycle was a lot of fun. When she had been planning this whole 'mission impossible', Avery had imagined riding behind Isaac, holding onto his strong chest or riding alongside him as they traveled across country. Silly dreams, she admitted to herself. Isaac would probably never see her as anything other than the church mouse she was. Cutting her eyes down at her chest, she almost laughed out loud. God, she was silly. What had she been thinking? Goose bumps covered her arms and shoulders, making her anxious to get out of the daring clothes and into something more comfortable.

Only Tricia knew where she was, and she wasn't telling. Her friend was bugging her about taking on more responsibility and now she was ready to do it. Her dad and mom had been informed she was okay, she'd made certain of that. She wasn't in the mood to listen to more arguments about moving to their home in the valley. Avery had apologized for not contacting them. But if they'd known she'd been staying at a Nevada brothel getting educated in the finer sexual arts, they would have moved heaven and earth to come after her. Apparently, Isaac would have also. It had come to her attention he had hired private detectives to find her. They hadn't even come close, however. The Shady Lady Ranch would have been the last place anyone would have thought to look for Avery Sinclair.

The motel parking lot was deserted, thank goodness. Easing in between two pickup trucks, she parked and got off. This time she took her helmet in with her. Avery hated to think about people stealing from her, but she knew it could happen. As she walked to her door, she pondered why Isaac had been looking for her in the first place. It seemed farfetched to think he might have been helping her dad, but she couldn't come up with any other possible conclusion. It certainly wasn't because he wanted to find her for himself. What would he want her for? As much as it hurt her to admit the truth, Isaac had been right. The old Avery was as far from his type of woman as a female could get. Whether or not he'd give the new Avery a chance, well, that was debatable, but she wasn't giving up without a fight.

The sounds of car horns and a child's laughter wafted on the night air. As she stepped up on the concrete sidewalk, Avery looked up at the night sky. It was clear and there were a million stars scattered over the black velvet expanse. For just a moment, she let herself stand there and wish on those stars. She prayed Isaac could see her for the woman she was deep inside. "Let him love me, please." Sending the wish up into the heavens, she let it go and pushed the key card into the lock, hearing the beep as the door opened into her lonely room. Lonely, was right. At twenty-three years old, Avery had only been on a couple of dates in her life, and they had been structured, chaperoned church events. And she had shared a kiss with a man exactly twice, the first time when Isaac kissed her in front of the drug store and the second time when she had kissed him the day he had told her to leave. Those meager exchanges were the sum total of her pitiful sexual experience.

Pushing aside those thoughts, Avery decided to have a positive outlook. She had changed, at least as much as she could. Isaac would have to take her the rest of the way, if he cared enough to try. So far, that alternative didn't seem to hold much promise. He didn't seem to be very glad to see her, nor did he give any indication he was any more attracted to this Avery than he had been to the old standard model. Nevertheless she was determined to give it her best, and if she failed, she wouldn't have any regrets.

Who was she kidding?

She was desperately in love with Isaac McCoy and if she didn't win his love, she would regret it every day for the rest of her life.

Dang! It was cold in here! She scurried into the bathroom and turned on the bright overhead lights, seeking to generate a bit of warmth. Undressing, she turned the water on as hot as she could stand it and took a quick shower. With hurried, economical movements, Avery dried off and rummaged in her suitcase for something to wear. "No, nothing sexy tonight. There's no one here but me and I'm freezing." She talked herself into wearing the least attractive garment she owned. "I love you, granny gown." She held it over her head and shimmed it down and then laughed out loud. Glancing in the mirror, she realized that nothing showed but her head, the ends of her fingers and the tips of her toes. The offensive sleepwear was made of flannel and the color was baby blue with pink flowers, perfectly disgusting. And it felt wonderful.

Avery wrapped her arms tightly around herself and spun in a circle, and was a little surprised when she became a tad dizzy. Of course! No food in eight hours would make you dizzy. Her stomach growled in agreement. "Pizza sounds good," she murmured as she flipped through the phone book. After she had placed an order, Avery turned on the TV and curled up on the bed to wait. Tonight wasn't the time to cry over the ill luck she had experienced at Hardbodies. As Scarlet O'Hara would say, 'I'll worry about that tomorrow'. At least Isaac knew she was back in town.

* * *

He couldn't find her anywhere. Isaac was pissed. It was after midnight and he was hungry, horny and hotheaded. For two hours, he'd driven all over Kerrville hunting that beige little minivan Avery drove. The first place he'd looked was her house, but it was as deserted as it had been the last time he checked it. Next, he went to every motel and hotel he could think of, but her vehicle was nowhere in sight. Isaac had always been able to recognize it because of the little crocheted cross that hung from her rear view mirror. That and the license plate, which said it all. It was accidental, and he was sure she never realized it, but it read 2GO-OD4U. Its cryptic message always spoke volumes to him.

Pulling into Hardbodies, he cut the engine and just sat there on his Harley, defeated. The only other thing he could think to do was call every motel in a twenty-mile radius. As he stared at the door of his club watching people come and go, he noticed Terence coming toward him. "Hey, Boss. I know where Avery is."

"Where? And how did you know that's what I was doing?" Isaac wasn't looking a gift horse in the mouth, but he was curious.

"I didn't figure you wanted to misplace her again, not after all the trouble you've gone through trying to find her." His bouncer had been paying more attention than Isaac realized. "Avery's my friend, Isaac. When she left, I followed her, just to make sure she was safe. She took off from here riding a little Harley roadster and she's got a room over at the Long Stay Motel just off Main."

A Harley? No way! Damn! "Thanks, I owe you one." Isaac started up his bike and took off, relieved to have some idea where to find her. As he drove, he rehearsed a speech. He practiced it until the moment he slid into the parking spot. But nothing he could think of sounded right. It didn't matter. He still had every intention of confronting her. The fact that he just wanted to see her wasn't a factor. Yeah, right. Hell! Rapping on the door, he waited.

"That was quick," she greeted him with a smile, but it only lasted a second. "Isaac! I thought you were my thin crust pepperoni. What are you doing here?"

She didn't sound glad to see him. Still, he felt his heart being squeezed as if it were caught in a vise. There was no doubt about it. Avery was the sweetest, sexiest woman in the whole world. Standing ramrod straight before him, arms crossed over her mouth-watering chest, she was wearing some kind of flannel gown that covered every inch of her body. Isaac thought she looked absolutely adorable. "Now, this is how I expected you to look." The sexy, seductive siren he had seen at the club might be unfamiliar to him, but this kitten he recognized. Isaac stared at her. Yes, this was his woman and every molecule in his soul was chanting, 'Mine, Mine, Mine.'

"How did you find me?" Avery ignored his comment about her gown. Drats, she was so mad she was sputtering. Why did he have to show up when she had on the drabbest, unsexiest nightclothes in existence? Why, oh why hadn't she kept her biker clothes on for just a few more minutes? "And why did you come looking for me? I thought the only thing you wanted from me was to get out of your sight." He was here, right in front of her. She wanted to grab him and pull him in, but she didn't think she could stand to be rejected twice in one night. So, she decided to play it tough.

"Step in, Sweet-Doll. The whole world doesn't need to hear our business." He walked toward her as she backed away from him. "We've got some talking to do." About that time, the pizza guy came and Isaac infuriated her further by paying for it and setting it to one side without a word to her, one way or the other.

"I can't think of a thing in the world we have to say to one another. I believe you've said it all." She dug in her purse for money and held it out to him. He ignored the gesture, so she flung the bills toward the bed. He could tell she was torn. Her eyes flashed between warm and wary like a Walk/Don't Walk sign.

With a predatory gleam in his eye, Isaac stalked her deeper into the motel room. "You've been out of town for a while. Where have you been, exactly?" He wasn't making polite conversation. He really wanted to know.

"I'm surprised you noticed." She waved a small hand in the air, dismissively. "But, you wouldn't believe me if I told you."

He pushed on. "What were you doing at the bar tonight, Avery? I told you before. Hardbodies is no place for a girl like you. What if I hadn't been there? Do you have any idea what could have happened to you? You could have been gang raped!" He watched her little face flush with emotion, as she was getting angrier by the minute. She'd never know how much he wanted her. God, what he wouldn't give to scoop her up and kiss that mad right out of her. And he could do it too. There wasn't a doubt about it.

"That wouldn't have happened. Terence Lee was there, and that nice guy called Crowbar. Besides, I wouldn't have stayed if you hadn't been there. I was only there to see you, as you well know."

This time it was his turn to ignore what she said. "And what kind of clothes were you NOT wearing?" He was egging her on and for some reason, loving every second of their sparring.

"Clothes? You want to discuss my wardrobe?" Avery spit out the words, totally furious. He'd driven all this way just to fuss at her some more, just because she had dared enter his precious sanctum.

"I almost didn't recognize you in that odd get-up you had on tonight."

"You didn't approve of what I had on? Why not? I dressed the way you like your women to dress." Maybe she had looked silly to him. A shaft of pain cut through her. She had never thought of that before.

"Leather and chains are not for you, baby." He picked up a bit of the granny gown, rubbing the material between his fingers. "This is more your style."

Avery looked affronted, majorly affronted. "This? You like me in this?"

Almost laughing, he answered, "Yea, it's kinda cute." Kinda? Sexy as all get-out was more like it.

"You think this is me?" A look of determination came over her features. "You've certainly never seen the real me." And before he could blink, she picked up the hem of her garment and skimmed it over her head, leaving her standing there totally, completely, gloriously naked. "Now, what do you have to say to that?"

The breath was literally torn from Isaac's body. "Hell, I say Sweet Merciful Heavens." He stared at the most gorgeous little shape designed by a gracious God. No fantasy image he'd ever conjured of her came close to the perfection which stood before him. Isaac didn't know where to look first, so he began a thorough item-by-item inventory. Creamy magnolia hued skin, so soft looking he knew velvet would feel like burlap in comparison, an hourglass figure that made him want to spend endless minutes memorizing every square inch of her delectable body. And those breasts! His hands rose, itching to cup the round high full globes that were tipped by pink puffy nipples. God, they looked like cupcakes iced with fluffy strawberry cream. Isaac licked his lips. "Damn. I know it's not right, but I'm weak. I can't resist you."

Her anger dissipated when she recognized hunger on his face. Miracle of miracles, Isaac wanted her. "Who wants to be resisted?" she whispered. When he reached out and cupped the back of her head, pulling her close, she didn't wait. Avery took what she wanted, and she wanted Isaac. With a tiny whimper, she gripped his hair, closed the distance between them and placed her mouth on his.

It was no tentative kiss. She pushed her tongue in and tasted…sucked. Avery bit at his mouth, hiking up his level of excitement by showing him the depth of her need. Isaac got rock hard and his heart was thudding with a jackhammer beat. Damn! Holding nothing back, she kissed him wildly, framing his face and devouring his lips with deep, drugging kisses. Damn! Isaac was sure his package would bust out of his jeans. Fisting her hair, he pulled her back an inch so he could take a breath. "Sweet Baby, you are so hot! I can't believe we're doing this."

"I beg you, don't stop," she whispered, burying her head against his throat. "I want you, so much. Please, don't stop. I need you to kiss me over and over again." Isaac couldn't stand it another moment. He took over, his dominant nature coming to full force. Yet, Avery met his every demand with unwavering joy.

"I am so damn hard." He licked a path from her lips to her throat. Those succulent globes were mashed up against his chest. He couldn't wait to get those hard little nipples in his mouth. "I need more, and I need it my way," he growled.

"Yes, I want what you want, anyway you want it," she agreed, straining to get as close to him as humanly possible.

Isaac knew she had no idea what she was saying, but he was too weak to be strong. "Put your hands behind your back, Avery," he directed. When she looked at him questioningly with those big purple eyes, he repeated his command, softer this time. "Hands behind your back, Honey. Now." She did as he instructed and he rubbed his hands down the softness of her upper arms and across to cup those luscious mounds. Avery trembled beneath his caress. Isaac's callused thumbs stroked her nipples. "Lord, you're pretty. I love to see you like this, so beautiful. I've never touched softer skin." Leaning over, he nuzzled the upper swell of her breasts, pressing open mouthed kisses all over the creamy flesh. With a grunt of impatience, Isaac curled his tongue around a swollen areola. Avery leaned back, pushing her breasts closer to his face. "Oh, you like that, don't you?" He laved and kissed and lapped his way all around the eager little nipple, but never closed his mouth around it to suck like he was dying to.

He cut his eyes up at Avery when she made a frustrated little grunting noise. She was holding on, trying not to beg, those pearly white teeth biting down on that suckable bottom lip. Why was he waiting? He wanted it as bad as she did. Isaac got down to business and suckled her nipples. Long Hard Pulls. Swirling his Tongue. Deep Thorough Sucks.

"Oh My Lord, I love this, Isaac…" she whispered. He left one nipple and captured the jealous twin, slowly, no rush, reveling in her unique flavor and the heavenly way she felt in his mouth. Avery gasped when he pushed the soft globes together so he could worship both nipples at the same time.

"You know what I plan to do, Girl?" Isaac was past thinking. He was as turned on as he could ever remember being, and he was saying what he felt, no holding back. "I'm gonna suck these nipples while I'm deep inside you. I want you to ride me, dangle these beauties in my face and let me smother myself in your softness. I want to feel these fat, hard nipples drag across my thighs as you take me in your mouth. You want to do that for me, don't you?"

"Please, yes." She arched her hips, pressing her heat hard against his thigh. His erection was huge and she couldn't wait to feel him pumping inside of her. Avery's body knew what it wanted and needed, even though she wasn't experienced and she didn't know how to ask for it.

Isaac sucked his way up her neck, smooching on the silky expanse, scraping his teeth, marking her with little nips and tastes. His hands couldn't be still. He had to touch her. Running his palms down her body, he circled around and cupped that incredible heart-shaped rear, lifting her, grinding her naked sex up against his denim clad crotch. When she would have reached up to grab him to balance herself, he stopped her. "Keep your hands behind your back," he reminded her. Walking, he sat down on the bed and arranged her across his thighs so he could delve his fingers into her cream. Avery's whole body went completely still. "Shhhh, it's okay. I'm not going to hurt you." He knew that wasn't her concern. She was just innocent. His innocent baby. "I have to touch you. I can't help myself."

Avery let her head fall back and she lifted her hips slightly, canting them, offering everything she had. When his fingers finally dipped into her wet, bare slit, her eyes widened and she bucked just a little under his hand. "Easy, love, this is gonna feel so good." Isaac swirled his fingers in the lush softness of her vagina. She was slick and hot, and when he looked into her face, he saw all the trust in the world. It humbled him. Pressing a kiss into her deep cleavage, he gentled her with reassuring words. "You like what I'm doing to you, baby?" Avery bit down on her lip with force and nodded. Isaac pushed his middle finger into her and she almost came out of her skin. "You're so wet and swollen." He wiggled his finger inside of her. Avery's entire body shuddered. "You want me, don't you?" Avery mutely nodded her head. "Do you like being under my control?"

"Oh, yeah," she moaned. He couldn't help but smile. Who knew his good little girl would be so responsive? Her breath hitched as he pumped his finger in and out, rubbing her slit, luxuriously spreading her cream before he added a second finger.

"Do you like this as much as I do?"

"Yes, Isaac…but I …" Her body gave its own answer. Isaac watched a rose red flush of excitement wash over her breasts and up her neck. What a treasure she was!

"Yes, but what?" Whatever she asked for was hers. No question about it. "Tell me, Honey."

"It feels really good. But, I…don't know." He held her gaze, willing her to ask him for what she wanted. "It makes me want…more!"

"More?" He pushed his fingers up inside of her, hunting that magic spot that would turn her world upside down. At the same time, he took his thumb and found her sensitive button and began to strum it. "Is this want you wanted?"

"Yea, yea. " She gasped. "I think that's it." Her expression was one of wonder. Isaac had never enjoyed turning on a woman this much before. To up the ante, he bent his head and closed his lips around her nipple and began to draw on it with strong pulls. All the while he stimulated her with his finger, moving in and out, massaging her clit, watching her flare like fireworks. Isaac's manhood was so engorged, it was pushing against his zipper like an inflating airbag. If it had been any other woman, he would have thrown her down and buried himself to the hilt. But this was the one woman he cared about most, and watching her climax was going to be the single most erotic experience of his life. Her whole little body started to shake. Sweet little moans escaped her lips. Determined to push her over the edge, he bit softly at her nipple as he kneaded her vulva with his hand. Avery lost it. "God! Isaac!" Throwing her arms around his neck, she pushed her nipple further into his mouth as she squeezed her legs together trying to trap his hand right where she wanted it. Watching her fly apart was the hottest thing he'd ever seen and chastising her for moving her hands never even crossed his mind. All of his fantasies had been right on the money. Touching Avery was freakin' unbelievable.

"Thank you, Isaac."

She laid her head on his shoulder so sweetly he couldn't resist kissing her, long, slow, and deep. "May I please you?"

He only delayed a moment. Tomorrow might hold a world of regret, but having Avery in his arms, safe and sound, was too miraculous to resist. "Get on your knees and undo my pants."

The commanding tone wasn't lost on Avery. She didn't understand it, but she complied immediately. This was the moment she had been waiting an eternity for. Going to her knees, she tried to hide the fact that her hands were trembling as she unbuckled his belt. Concentrating, she began tugging at the fastening of his jeans. She was too nervous and after failing twice, she rested her head on his knee, too shaken and embarrassed to face him. He would never believe she had any experience or could be what he wanted, if she couldn't even unbutton his jeans! "I'm not very good at this," she admitted, shamefully.

Any other time, Isaac would have used the admission against her, but at this moment denying her was impossible. He had to feel her lips on him. His body, heart and soul weren't giving him a choice. Stroking her cheek, he cajoled. "You're perfect."

Glancing at him, she wanted to pinch herself. Was she really here, kneeling at Isaac's feet? Heavens, he was beautiful. The trademark McCoy good looks were magnified in this brother. He was a deadly combination of ruggedness and masculinity. Yet, he possessed a sweet spirit that few men had. Oh, he did everything he knew to hide it, especially from her. But she had watched him with children and animals, how he dealt with his brothers and how he always went out of his way to help people. The Biker bad-boy was an angel who'd been rescued from the fall, and in her book, he could do no wrong. His face was chiseled with high cheekbones, an angular jaw and eyes so blue she felt like she was gazing at sapphires. And those lips had taken her to the gates of heaven. God, she wanted him so much. What could she say to make him want her back? "Isaac, will you kiss me?"

Without hesitation, he pressed a kiss to the corner of her mouth, sliding his lips across hers. Shivers of delight moved over her body. "Your lips are like candy. But what I want to do now is look at you while you love on me.

Avery felt her skin go hot.

"Damn, you're sexy when you go all pink and flushed." He stole another quick kiss, laughing as she rose up, following him, wanting more. "Uh-uh. I need something else, Love. You've taken me too far. I have to feel your lips on me or I'll go crazy."

Determined to please him, she reached for the button, but this time he helped her, pulling the tab of the zipper down until the firmness of his erection was right in front of her. All she could see was the shape of it, thick and long behind the white of his underwear and a drop of wetness drew her hand. She laid her palm on top of it, molding it, amazed that she could feel his heat. "Oh, Isaac, I want you so much." At her admission, Isaac groaned audibly.

They both worked to tug on his pants legs until the jeans were far enough down so Avery could make herself at home. Isaac couldn't take his eyes off her jiggling breasts. They moved like a dream and she was excited. There was no missing that fact. Her nipples were hard and swollen, and if he weren't in such need, he would have pulled her up and sucked some more. God, he never knew he had a breast fetish. But, he guessed he did. Or an Avery fetish might be more like it.

While he was contemplating his needs and desires, Avery surprised him and began unbuttoning his shirt. When he covered her hands with his, she begged. "Please? I just want to look at you." The desire in her eyes was his undoing. Isaac almost popped off a couple of the tiny black buttons, helping her. Libby was gonna fuss at him if she had to sew them back on. When it was all undone, he whipped it around and tossed it and the vest to the floor. Avery stared and licked her lips. "Isaac. Oh, Isaac." She pressed both palms on his pecs and began to rub. "As it says in the Psalms, you are magnificently and wonderfully made. I could just eat you up." Without waiting for an invitation, she mimicked his earlier action and rubbed her mouth across one copper colored nipple before circling it with her tongue.

"Enough!" He framed her face and stopped her erotic play before he embarrassed himself by shooting his wad in his shorts. "I need your attention to be focused a little lower down."

"On your penis?" Her delicate way of speaking made him smile.

"Say it, Avery. Any woman who is about to give a man a blowjob ought to be able to call a spade a spade." She looked at him skeptically, but the pulse point at her neck was visible and fluttering like a butterfly behind silk.

She gulped, but gave it a shot. "Your...cock." As soon as the words left her lips, she smiled in triumph and Isaac's heart did a swan dive. Damn, if he didn't toughen up toward this little darlin', she was gonna completely ruin his Badass Dom reputation. "Free me," he directed gruffly. Turning her attention to his rapidly expanding manhood, she set out to divest him of his briefs. The look of concentration on her face was priceless. At the corner of her mouth, a little pink tongue emerged. And when she unveiled him and gasped at what she'd uncovered, he thought she was the cutest, sweetest thing he had ever seen. "Goodness!"

Isaac forced himself to be still and just enjoy. Avery held out her hand, fingers almost touching his member, as if she expected it to jump up and grab her. And he was so hard, he just might. She let out a harsh breath and ran a finger from base to head, tracing the ridges and veins. "You're beautiful," she breathed. With tender care she circled the swollen plum head and gasped when it jumped in her hand. She measured it, holding it up to his belly and against her palm. Isaac didn't know how much more he could stand. "Avery if you don't get down to business, I'm gonna expire from sheer exasperation."

She locked eyes with Isaac as she carefully wrapped her hand around his rod and squeezed. "You are so hard and hot," she moaned as she whispered the words. Moving her fist up and down, she watched his face as he closed his eyes and let his head fall back. "Does that feel good?" she asked, needing to know she was doing it right.

"Hell, yes," he hissed. "But I need your mouth. I need you to suck me." Honesty, he believed in honesty. She pumped him twice more, her hips working back and forth in an agitated motion. "What's wrong?" He knew, but he wanted her to tell him.

"I feel needy, like I did when you were touching me a bit ago."

Her confession mesmerized him. "Don't worry, I'll give you what you need," he promised. When she reached between his legs and found his balls, his breath hissed from between clenched teeth. Yes, he'd give her what she needed, but not right yet. "God Almighty!" She was killing him.

"They're so hard and big." She rolled his testicles between her fingers and his hips lifted, begging for more. "Avery…." he warned.

"Don't worry." She smiled at him and wiggled as if hunting a comfortable spot. "I can do this. I've been practicing."

Practicing? What the hell? Isaac started to think what that might mean, but when she covered the head with her warm, wet, velvety mouth, his mind went absolutely blank. And when she began to suck, while stroking him with that magic little hand of hers… "Holy hell!"

Avery stopped what she was doing, "Isaac? Did I do it wrong?" She looked at him with fear in her eyes. Had she displeased him?

"Hell, no, it's too good. More!" he demanded. With a renewed sense of confidence she continued to love him. Taking him deep like she had been taught, she swirled her tongue, licked and sucked, pumping him with her fist with one hand and caressing his sac with the other. The girls at the brothel had promised her she could please Isaac this way. So Avery put her whole heart into it and every time he grunted or moaned or ran an approving hand down the side of her head, she wanted to beam. But her mouth was too busy for smiling. Other parts of her were getting downright perky; her nipples were peaking, her clitoris was throbbing and she was feeling wet and wiggly. If this operation didn't require two hands, she would touch herself to find some relief.

Isaac's whole body shook. Jesus! She was killing him! And, by God, she was beautiful. He couldn't take his eyes off of her. Never in his life had he expected to see the erotic scene before him, his Avery Rose on her knees, at his feet with a look of absolute wonder on her face. Her lips were stretched around his thickness and she was making the sweetest most contented little sucking noises. There was no way in hell he could last. "You're so good, angel." His words were barely coherent, coming out more as growls, but she seemed to understand. Her big eyes found his and Isaac recorded the image forever. Was there ever a more beautiful sight than your woman looking up at you, beseechingly, while she gifted you with ecstasy? "Take me to heaven, Avery." A tiny nod. She understood. She closed her eyes, bobbed her mouth and sucked harder. Circling her fingers loosely at the root, she pumped him in rapid, short strokes.

"Hell, yeah! I'm fixing to come. Let me." He tried to pull himself out of her mouth, but she pushed back on his hand. "Damn!" He hadn't expected that. Hell, he hadn't expected any of this. Twisting those fat ringlets around his hand, he anchored her to him, so she wasn't going anywhere. With a rough groan, he closed his eyes, lost in perfect bliss. Almost. Almost. "God!" Jets of his hot essence boiled up from his balls and erupted into her sweet mouth. He could feel her swallowing around him, and Lord help him, she swallowed every drop. He never would've dreamed of this happening in a million years. Her small hands were caressing his thighs. She was petting him, touching him like he was something special.

Special? Him? Heck, yea he was something else all right. This was Avery. What had just happened? Had he lost his mind? She was holding his rod and licking it from base to tip like an all-day sucker. And he wanted more, he wanted it all. Isaac wanted to dominate her until she begged him to take her, over and over again. Impossible! "Stop!" Isaac got up so fast he knocked her sprawling. "Damn…" He started to help her up, but she scrambled away from him with a confused look on her face.

"What's the matter?" she asked him. Her heart was in her eyes and he felt like a heel. "Did I do it wrong?"

"This was a mistake, Avery. I never should have come here. We never should have done this." He redressed quickly. It hurt his heart to see her rise from the floor and cross her arms over her breasts. A few moments ago she had been completely at ease with her nudity, and now she seemed ashamed. "Look, this isn't you, it's me."

At the age-old cop-out, she choked out a half-laugh, half-sob. "Isaac, I thought we…" Her voice trailed off as he turned to walk away. "Wait!" She followed him, padding across the motel room floor in her bare feet. "What did I do?"

Isaac stopped. They stood frozen, him a few feet in front of her with his back to her. He didn't turn around. "This shouldn't have happened. We're too different. Our worlds are too far apart."

"It doesn't feel like they're far apart. I think our worlds collided quite nicely a few moments ago, Isaac." She didn't intend to plead, but she couldn't help it. "I've changed. For you." She walked up right behind him and touched his arm. "Please."

Damn! "This is for your own good. I'm not the man for you." Resolutely, he continued to the door. "You'll see that I'm right. You'll meet a nice guy, someone who can be what you need." Avery didn't move.

"You're wrong, Isaac. I'm not as innocent as you think I am." He opened the door and she wanted to pull him back, beg him to stay. But she didn't. "I could be the kind of woman you wanted, if you'd just give me the chance."

With a heavy sigh, Isaac leaned his head on the doorjamb as if he were regretting ever coming to her at all. She thought she would die.

"Listen, you're a sweet girl. And I wish things were different, but you need a suit and tie, a banker, an insurance salesman, you need respectability." Casting one last look over his shoulder, Isaac summed up the problem as he saw it. "You need to go home to your parents. You don't want me. I'm no good for you." Then, he was gone.

Avery didn't know whether to scream or cry. "You don't know what I want, Isaac McCoy." This had been the best experience of her life and she wanted to have it again and again. Whirling around, she walked to the bed, her mind in turmoil. "Bankers and insurance salesmen leave me cold." Mustering her courage, she stood up straight, wiped her eyes and tossed her hair over her shoulder. "I want a Badass, Isaac. I want you. And I'm not taking no for an answer."

Chapter Four

Could he have made a bigger mess if he'd tried? Deciding not to go back to the bar, he headed out of town. Tonight, Isaac needed to be near his family. Riding toward home, he hit his hand on the handlebars. Hard. Was he crazy? He'd just walked away from the best sex of his life. But the urge to dominate her had been stronger than he'd ever felt before with any other woman. Isaac knew if they were ever together again, he would demand her complete submission and he couldn't do her that way. She would never understand. Hell! What a mess he'd made! His intention had only been to find her, make sure she was safe and caution her against putting herself in danger by coming into a place like Hardbodies alone. Okay, that wasn't exactly what he'd said. He essentially told her she wasn't welcome in his bar. But it wasn't because he didn't want her there. It was because he wanted her there too much.

As he headed out on the ranch road, he tried to analyze exactly what had happened. Flashes of the paradise he's just walked away from ate at him like acid. He hadn't had sex with her, but it was a wonder. What he'd done was bad enough, but God it had been good. Carved into his memory was how creamy her little sex had been as he swirled his fingers around her clit and how tight she clasped his fingers. And making her climax had been better than coming himself. Isaac had never felt anything like the thrill of giving her pleasure. Even the fulfillment he gained from dominating didn't even come close to this heaven. If only Avery could accept him as he really was, she would be his fantasy submissive. But that was asking for far too much. He knew that.

As their encounter played through his mind, detail by erotic detail, he realized he was trying to block out one critical image—Avery's eyes when he'd pushed her away. "Damn!" He'd been so intent on protecting her and worrying about his own shortcomings, he hadn't considered what his actions might have done to her. Isaac forced himself to remember her face and how those big amethyst eyes had filled with tears. He'd hurt her. After she had placed herself so sweetly and trustingly in his hands, after she had given him the incredible gift of that intimate kiss—he had hurt her. God, what had he done?

For a moment, he considered turning around, going right back to her, and trying to straighten this mess out. But what would he say? Lord, he needed to think about this. Everything within him said this was huge. Momentous. In other words, he couldn't afford to screw this up any more than he already had. Hell, he almost missed the turn off to the ranch house. Putting on his blinker, he turned onto Tebow property. It was getting late. Hopefully everyone had gone to bed and he wouldn't have to have a conversation with anyone.

Damn! Somebody was in his regular parking spot and he didn't recognize the car. Then he remembered. Joseph and Cady's engagement party was in a couple of days and her family would be joining them. It looked like some of them were already here. He wondered who? They'd never met Cady's mother or her grandmother Fontenot, so the rowdy McCoy brothers had to be on their best behavior, or face the wrath of an angry, hormonal Libby.

At least he could be thankful that all was relatively calm in his world. Keszey, the wire-cutting maniac was behind bars. The copycat crazy who had kidnapped Kane's fiancé had been apprehended. And for now, as far as they knew, no one was out to get, kidnap or ruin them.

The engagement party was going to be casual, per Joseph's request. A whole pig would be roasted all day, there would be plenty of BBQ, and tequila would flow like a river. Good times. That reminded him he needed to get the booze ready for the party. It was a good thing he'd ordered extra liquor, for the McCoy social schedule was full this month.

As he walked up to the wide front verandah, he was surprised to hear the porch swing squeaking. Someone was outside. Peering through the darkness, Isaac tried to see who it was. Geez! He knew who he hoped it wasn't! "Come sit by me, Bad-boy."

"Uh-oh." It was just who he was afraid it would be. This was one of Cady's favorites, a member of her extended family. "Nana Bogart, have broom will travel," he whispered.

"I heard that." There was no way in hell she'd heard his whisper. Damn magic. "Turn on the porch light, will you? I want to see you when I talk to you."

"Yes, Ma'am." What else could he say? He had to be polite. He didn't want to spend the rest of his life sitting on some lily pad out in the stock pond. Doing as she asked, he flipped on the switch and faced her. She was propped up in the swing, sipping on a big glass of tea. "It's good to see you, Nana. How have you been?" he asked nervously.

"Just fine. How 'bout yourself?" She patted the cushion next to her.

"I can't complain." At least they were meeting under more pleasant circumstances. The last time she and her family were here, Joseph had been paralyzed from the waist down. Of course, the Bogart witches had helped Cady perform a miracle. He still didn't understand how they'd done it, but knowing Joseph was walking and running and having sex again was worth any amount of discomfort he felt sitting down with a woman he was just a mite afraid of.

"Just a mite?" She laughed. "I'll have to work on my scare tactics."

"How do you do that?" he asked with all intentions of trying to keep his mind blank.

"Oh, Baby..." She patted his knee. "You're easy to read. The thoughts coming from your brain shine like a message on a neon sign."

"Great." Isaac could just envision what she was picking up from him. "That can't be good."

The old lady chuckled as she sipped her tea, one foot pushing the swing back and forth. "You have been a rambunctious rascal today, haven't you?"

Isaac leaned forward and put his head in his hands. "God, take me now." Some Dom Badass he was, a chubby little woman with better than average radar had him nervous as a whore in church.

Nana made a harrumph sound. "Chubby?"

"Oh, hell!"

Nana let loose a gale of laughter. "It's all right, Babe. I'm just messin' with you. What I wanted to talk to you about was more important than mind reading games." She sat forward and patted his knee. "First, I know you don't realize this, but you're the strong one in this family."

Being the fourth brother, he had always relied on Aron, Jacob and Joseph, and no way did he consider himself to be stronger in mind, body or will than those three. They were the Rocks of Gibraltar in his life. "I don't think so." He didn't know what he would've done without them, especially when they lost their parents in the flashflood.

"Oh yes, you are," she insisted. "That Dom nature of yours comes from a wellspring of strength." When he turned to look at her, she laughed. "I won't tell. Don't worry."

"Okay, so I'm strong. What are you getting at?" Surely, their troubles from varied psychos were over.

"You have the mistaken opinion that your value as a man is not as high as the others." At his look of protest, she whacked him on the back of the head. When his eyes widened in surprise, she roared in laughter. "Don't look like you want to backtalk me. Just because you've chosen a different path doesn't make you any less of a good man." She patted him on the back. "We're all different, Isaac. And you're one of the good ones despite what you believe in your head."

Isaac realized she wasn't saying all she knew, and God, he wished he could believe what she said. "My lifestyle is not understood by many, and accepted by even less." He was surprised that this well-dressed Southern lady was sitting here discussing his BDSM desires, but then, she was a witch. "Have you experienced much prejudice over your beliefs and practices?" He looked at her facial expression as he asked. She thought for a moment and a look of sadness briefly passed across her face.

Her hand on his back began to soothe him, rubbing up and down like his mama used to do when he was a boy. "You wouldn't believe what my family has withstood over the years. People judge those who are different and they fear what they don't understand. It's the same as with you." She gave him a quick hug. "What I'm telling you is that your penchant for being in control, especially with a partner who craves to submit, is no shame at all. No more so than those who prefer to drive a foreign car over a domestic." He knew she preferred foreign cars herself. "People are different, no harm no foul."

"Thank you, Nana." Isaac wanted to ask her other questions, but he sensed she had something more to tell him. Was he getting psychic?

"And one other thing," she began and Isaac wanted to say 'Whooo – ooo – ooo,' that 'I told-you-so' spooky sound. "It's just a feeling I have, but I'm rarely wrong."

"Self-confident, much?" He winked at the older lady, and she chuckled. Growing serious, he leaned back on the swing by her and helped her push them as they swung. "What can you tell me?"

"All right, Handsome, there's something you need to hear." As they sat, the crickets were chirping and in the distance a coyote howled. It was a perfect early October evening. "You're going to be tested, but don't let it get you down. You and the family will emerge stronger than ever before. Your strength of mind and character will be the key."

"Tested? What do you mean? I don't like tests." And then as if it had just registered about him being the key, he responded to that odd assertion. "The key?

Yeah, right. I don't think so." If there was an outsider in the family, a misfit, it was him.

"You are, and I plan on scrying for you on All Hallows Eve. I can feel things on the wind. This family is still in for big changes. Some will bring great joy and others, well, I can't see anything specific, not yet. But if I scry, maybe I'll be able to give you a little more guidance."

"Is scrying like looking into your crystal ball?"

"You just can't resist being a jackass, can you?" She elbowed him and he laughed.

"Halloween is my birthday. You wanna come back for my party? I plan on giving myself a shindig, here at the ranch."

"I knew there was some reason I liked you. Did you ever consider taking up magick?"

"I think I have enough trouble juggling all aspects of my personality as it is…cowboy, biker, Dom."

"Badass," Nana added dryly.

"Yeah." He didn't argue with her. "I'll be interested in knowing anything you might be able to tell me. Hell, I sure don't want anything to happen to my brothers, Libby, Jessie, Cady or the babies. And you probably already know this, but I have something going on in my life and it's weighing heavy on my heart. I'm struggling with it."

"Yes, you do. And she's almost more than you can handle. Isn't she, Mr. Dom?"

"You're damn right about that, Witchy Woman." He leaned over and kissed her on the cheek. "I'm heading in. Are you gonna stay out here and change into a black cat or something?"

As he stood up, she swatted him on the butt. "It's a bat, Bad-Boy. Ask Cady. She's always told me I'm part vampire." As Isaac headed toward the door, he couldn't help looking back, just to make sure she hadn't flown off into the night.

* * *

Glancing at his phone, he checked for messages. There was one from Levi. Isaac decided to check in with his employee. "Hey, did you get everything cleaned up?" Isaac asked as he climbed the stairs to his suite of rooms.

"Boss! Did you find Avery?"

Sometimes, Levi had a one-track mind. Isaac liked him for that. "Yeah, I found her. And that's all I have to say about that, for now. How's my bar? Is it still standing?"

Isaac could hear the jangle of glass as Levi dumped the dustpan in the garbage.

"Almost like new. Crowbar helped me put everything back together. Oh, and Madelyn left satisfied and happy."

"Good, that's good." If he closed his eyes, he could still hear Avery's moans of fulfillment. "Any more trouble after I left?"

"Nope, not a bit. Hold on, I'm setting the burglar alarm." The sounds of beeping could be heard clearly over the phone. "Isaac, I forgot to tell you earlier. I'm missing that collar I got back from my last girl. Keep your eye open for it. It cost me a pretty penny. I might have left it in your truck. Also, I got those flyers out and everything's a go for the dance contest tomorrow night."

"I'll watch for the collar. By the way, I have to hand it to you. You've come up with some good promotional events, Levi. You're bucking for a promotion, Bud." Laughter floated down the hall and Isaac couldn't resist going to see what the joyful racket was about. There was always something happening at Tebow.

"I don't need a promotion, but I'll sure take a raise." Levi didn't beat around the bush.

"If that dance contest packs them in tomorrow night, we'll talk about it. Okay?"

"Deal." Isaac closed his phone and put it in his pocket just as Cady came running down the hall with Joseph hot on her heels. There was no doubt about it. Seeing Joseph running and having a good time did his heart good. If anybody deserved happiness, it was these two. Just weeks ago, Cady had been electrocuted saving Joseph. Now, she was giggling like a schoolgirl. She'd found out she was pregnant during the chaos as well. Joseph was back in fine form—healthy, happy, and head over heels in love and anxious to be a father. No one who saw him now, would think he had ever been paralyzed and ready to give up on life.

"Hey! Hey! What is wrong with you two? People are trying to sleep in this house."

Cady slid to a stop in front of him. "I'm in trouble, Isaac. Save me." Joseph made a grab for her and she squealed and got behind Isaac, putting him in between her and her fiancé. "I'm sorry, Joseph. I didn't mean to insult your grand romantic gesture." Joseph growled and reached for her, but she dodged and he found himself face to face with his younger, but equally large, macho brother.

"Shall we dance?" Isaac asked with a straight face. When Joseph erupted in a loud guffaw, Isaac thought it was one of the best sounds he'd ever heard. "Do you two need a mediator or a referee?"

"Neither. I need to borrow one of your quirts. This little girl needs a spankin'."

"My quirt?" What the heck? Did everybody know his business?

Isaac started to ask Joseph how he knew about the quirts when Cady began to explain. "Listen to this, Isaac. Let me tell you what your silly brother did." She was still behind him, peeping around his shoulder at her beloved, both laughing so hard that Isaac couldn't help but smile. "He sent me flowers."

"Joseph, how could you?" So far, he didn't see the problem.

"Hey, you said you wanted big flowers, so I sent you big flowers."

Reaching around him, Joseph pulled a squirming Cady into his arms. She went, nestling up against him, laying her head on his chest, but she was still almost hiccupping from laughter. "Libby gets big flowers from Aron, birds of paradise and Asiatic lilies. You know, hunky flowers."

"Hey, aren't I hunky enough for you?" he teased her before finishing the tale. "I've been giving you flowers every week…roses, carnations, daisies. But you wanted something different." Looking to Isaac for support, he explained, "She asked for big flowers, so I sent them to her."

"You sent me a funeral arrangement!" She whacked him on the shoulder. "On a stand, with a big sash across it that said, 'I love you, Cady.'"

Isaac grinned. "What's wrong with that? You did want big flowers."

"And it wasn't a funeral spray. It was on a horseshoe and it was covered, literally covered in orchids. I thought I did a good job." Joseph looked so satisfied.

"So, you put a lot of thought into that, didn't you?" Isaac was about to crack up. "Were you serious? You sent your girl a racehorse wreath? You know, like the winner of the Kentucky Derby would wear?" This beat anything he'd ever heard.

Joseph looked offended. "Well, a horseshoe is sorta western, we have a ranch and it means good luck. Hell, I thought it was fittin', since I'm the luckiest man in the world to have Cady." He kissed her on the cheek, and then nearly choked with laughter as she punched him in the stomach.

"Where is this monstrosity?" Isaac had to see this.

Cady pulled away from Joseph and grabbed Isaac by the hand. "Come see." She leaned into Isaac's shoulder. "Actually, it's beautiful. I just love to give him a hard time." As they walked, he couldn't miss Joseph's eyes on Cady. He thought she was the beauty, not the flowers. And Isaac would have to agree. When Cady came to them, she was convinced she was plain. She had dressed plain, no make-up and no self-confidence. It had taken Joseph a while to see the real Cady, but when he had, she had bloomed. Love had made her beautiful and now she was so lovely, it almost hurt your eyes to look at her.

"Damn right, it's a masterpiece. I went to that new florist and designed it myself."

They stepped into Joseph's sitting room and Isaac had to suppress a cackle. "Well, uh, that's the most unique bouquet I've ever seen." Sure enough, just like Cady had said, it was a huge horseshoe covered with orchids sitting on a funeral spray stand. And across the expanse, like a Miss USA state designator, was a sash that proudly proclaimed, 'I LOVE YOU CADY'. He shook his head. Sometimes his brother didn't have enough sense to come out of the rain. But looking at the couple as they hugged one another close, he was relieved that Joseph had been wise enough to look beyond the unassuming surface to find the real beauty inside.

"I heard you had a wild night at Hardbodies." Joseph met his gaze over Cady's head.

"It was interesting." Word traveled fast in the McCoy clan. "Is there anything I can do to help with the party Saturday night?" It felt safer to change the topic. He wasn't ready to discuss Avery with the family. "I've already got the booze set aside. Do you need help setting up for the band? I could bring some more speakers and monitors."

"Libby is handling all the details. She'll let you know if she needs help. What I want you to bring to the party is you and a date." Cady winked at him as her cell phone started buzzing and Joseph reluctantly let her go to answer it.

"We've got everything we need, I think, but thank you." Joseph's eyes followed Cady and he had the most contented look on his face that Isaac had ever seen. Jealousy washed over him again, like a waterfall. Joseph continued, "I appreciate you getting the set-ups for the bar. Lance brought up those big metal tubs from storage so we could ice down a few cases of beer."

"No problem." Suddenly, he felt claustrophobic. "I'll see you guys in the morning. I'm dead on my feet." Isaac made his escape and wondered if he would ever find the happiness that his older brothers had found. The right woman made all the difference, it seemed. Isaac couldn't help but wonder if he was pushing the right woman away. And if he was, would she ever forgive him?

* * *

Avery yawned, rubbed her eyes, and held the piece of paper a bit closer. "Dance Contest at Hardbodies – Freestyle." The only limitations were no lap dances and no total nudity. "I think I can work with that." Avery felt a renewed sense of determination. She stared at the blue piece of cardstock which detailed the event. It would be ladies' night. Men had to pay a ten dollar cover charge and all drinks were half-price. The place would be packed. This would be another chance to prove to Isaac that she was his kind of woman.

Sitting back in the booth at the motel diner, she pushed her scrambled eggs from one side to the other. Why had she ordered this? Muffins were more her speed in the morning. Lifting the coffee cup, she took a sip. Blah! It had grown cold while she sat here and brooded. Apparently a waitress had seen her grimace, because she brought her a fresh cup. "Thanks," she smiled at the woman. 'Charla', as her nametag read, smiled back, but it was an odd smile. In fact when she looked around, everyone was sorta leering at her with that same knowing, goofy look on their faces. Avery glanced down to make sure her boobs weren't hanging out or something. They weren't. All the buttons were done and straight.

What was going on? It wasn't like she knew these people. Even though Kerrville wasn't a huge city, her path had not crossed with most of these folks. Feeling uncomfortable, she took one last drink of coffee, grabbed the flyer and made her way to the cashier where she was met with yet another smirk.

Relieved to get out of the restaurant, Avery made her way back to the room. Last night was still fresh in her mind. Sleep had been a long time coming. All Avery could see when she looked around the room was Isaac. The feel of his hands on her body was impossible to forget, and the look on his face when she had given him pleasure was burned into her memory forever. Avery wanted more. Was she just kidding herself? Could Isaac ever really want her in his life? Oh, he desired her, but what hurt the most was that he didn't want to want her. Lord, even the thought was as much of a brainteaser as it was a tongue twister. For some reason, she didn't appeal to him. And that hurt.

After he'd left her alone, she sat down, and in typical Avery fashion had jotted down a plan. Thank goodness, she didn't have to go to a typical nine-to-five job. Every time she thought about how wonderfully free her days were, it thrilled her. Avery had two careers that allowed her to be creative, sensual and made her a pretty decent living. Writing romance novels was fun as well as fulfilling. A tiny smile played over her lips. During the past year, she'd become a pro at promoting her books. With meticulous care, she had researched the markets and what types of books were selling and which ones weren't as popular. It amused her that the hottest, fastest growing market was erotic romances. Before she'd felt inadequate to pen stories with explicit sex, but now she had more information and even a tad of experience to fall back on. Just thinking of the tales she could spin with Isaac as the hero and her as the heroine made goose bumps rise on her skin. Soon, she promised herself, she would concoct another story so hot it would melt her fan's e-readers.

Sitting on the bed, she picked up the notebook where she'd detailed her game plan. Being fair to herself and Isaac, she put a time limit on her campaign. She would give it three weeks, just until the end of the month. If, by then, he was still pushing her away, she would go. The dance contest would fit perfectly within her strategy. And if her pole dance didn't work at convincing Isaac she was perfect for him, she still had two or three more ideas to try before she gave up.

Scooting back against the headboard, she twined one of her dark ringlets around her forefinger and considered the cosmopolitan-style list. First, she intended to show Isaac that she could fit into his world. Check. It wasn't a one-time feat, but last night was a good start, or at least a start. Second, she would try to tempt him. This would be a hard one. Avery knew she wasn't very tempting. Hmmmm, the clothes seemed to work, but the dance would have to be her piece de resistance. Making a few notes, she thought about what she would wear and what song she would dance to. Her safest bet would be to use the same songs Destiny had used when she taught her the one and only routine she knew. Glancing at the flyer, Avery decided to call and find out exactly what was expected of a contestant. "Please, just don't let Isaac answer the phone," she prayed. After two rings a male voice came on the phone,

BADASS

"Hardbodies, May I help you?" Thank God, it wasn't him.

"Yes, I was calling in reference to the dance contest you're hosting in your establishment tonight."

There was a pregnant pause, then a distinct chuckle. "All right, what would you like to know, Ma'am?"

"Should I bring a tape or CD of my song selection, or will you have some way of providing musical accompaniment for my dance number?"

"Uh, okay. What tune are you planning on performing to?"

"'Wild One' by Faith Hill and 'How Do I Live With You' by that...other girl. I can't think of her name."

"Trisha Yearwood and it's 'How Do I Live Without You'. Our band can play both of those songs."

"Oh, okay. Do you think they can play a medley? You know, go between the two?"

"I don't think that will be a problem. Any other questions?"

Why did this guy sound so amused? "Do I need to pay an entrance fee or register in some way?"

"No. Basically, you just show up and let us know when you arrive that you want to dance. We'll assign you a number and you're all set."

That surprised Avery. "You don't need to know my stage name?"

"Oh, I'd love to know your stage name. Tell me."

At his tone, Avery wondered if he was making fun of her. Gee, she wished she knew how these things worked. "My stage name is, uh, Rose. The Wild Rose." There, that sounded sexy. Didn't it?

"Well, Miss Wild, I'll be watching for you tonight. Good luck!" As the gentleman hung up, Avery could swear she heard him laughing. Men! She'd never understand them if she lived to be a hundred. Why couldn't things be simple? Over the years, she'd woven this elaborate daydream scenario of her life with Isaac. In her heart, Avery had imagined them dating, getting engaged and her walking down the aisle in white satin as her Dad and Isaac waited at the altar. After that, things had gotten a bit blurry. Would they live at Tebow? Would they have a little cottage with the proverbial white picket fence? She knew there would be children, dark haired babies with beautiful blue or violet eyes. Avery even had names for them. For a boy, Austin Isaac McCoy and a girl would be named Savannah Elise McCoy. Isaac would help her take care of them and they would take them to church and attend family gatherings. Oh, it was going to be wonderful.

Screech! Halt! Avery stopped her musings. Isaac was different and she had to be different, too. That was what this seduction campaign was all about—to prove to Isaac that she could be just what he needed. Back to the plan. The third phase in her mission would be to make him jealous. Now, that would take some thought. And the last item on the agenda was to make herself scarce so he would realize he missed her, and needed her. Sighing, she admitted to herself that she had a lot of work to do. And the first order of business was a trip to the Laundromat.

* * *

"Noah, I don't know who else to call?" Harper sounded desperate.

Noah closed his eyes and steeled himself to her pleas.

"I'll do anything, please. Just say you'll meet me. I only want to talk, that's all. Just talk."

Hanging his head, Noah debated what to do. "I can't condone your lifestyle, Harper. BDSM is not something that I could ever be involved in. You've ventured out way beyond my comfort zone. What you do, what you want done to you, it just turns my stomach." His voice betrayed his distaste, but he couldn't hide it. "I will never understand why you crave pain. I'm sorry, but I can't give you that."

"I know," she whispered thinly. "I'll try, Noah. I'll try to give it up, if you'll just help me. Please, say you'll meet with me tonight. Meet me at your brother's bar. Nothing will go on, except conversation. I promise."

Damn! Sadness and anger colored his thoughts. This was the woman he had built his dreams around, only to find that she'd thrown her life away in pursuit of kinky thrills and a sick desire to be tied up and whipped. "All right, Harper. But know this…I can't be with you when you're this way. It's like a disease. I'll never understand why you couldn't be satisfied with me and what I could give you." She'd hurt him. He was just now beginning to see a way out of the sorrow. His attraction to Skye was what he clung to now. There was life after Harper, and he didn't want to get drawn back into the torture of watching her try to hide the whip marks and the bruises. God, she even had started cutting herself. Seeing her addicted to pain was something he abhorred. "I'll meet you at nine at Hardbodies, but don't count on changing my mind. As long as you're involved in this scene, you and I are through." He hung up before she could say anything else. Hell, he wished he had someone to talk to, but he was too ashamed to tell anyone the truth.

***

"You've been busy." Isaac checked the receipts and notes Levi had given him. "These are some really good ideas," he complimented his employee.

"Tonight's dance contest will just be the beginning. Next week we have the wet T-shirt contest, and after that the Jell-O-wrestling, the pool tournament and a games night which will consist of darts, arm wrestling and a Texas-Hold'em poker night." Levi was excited. Isaac was pleased with the man. He was a good bartender. Plus, he had drive and determination, and no one could deny that the women loved his rugged good looks, and that never hurt. To top it off, he was becoming one of the finest Doms Isaac knew. Several other men had been asking to play in his dungeon, and Isaac was considering it. The only one he knew who wouldn't be joining them was Ajax; he was trouble waiting to happen.

"The mechanical bull will be here in a few days." Levi's comment brought Isaac back to the present, which was good. The less time he wasted thinking about Ajax the better. He was cruel, vindictive and blamed Isaac for getting thrown out of the BDSM clubs in Austin and San Antonio, and he was right. As long as Isaac had influence, a cruel Dom who mistreated his subs would be called down for their bad behavior.

"Good, I'm looking forward to trying that bull out myself."

"Boss, you need to see this." Doris walked into his office and laid the Kerrville Daily Times in front of him. "Everybody's talking about it." It took a second for

Isaac's eyes to focus on the photo and headline, but when he did he almost swallowed his tongue.

"What the hell?" Avery, his Avery, was standing in a line-up with several other women, all dolled-up in what could only be described as 'hooker attire'. The headline read, 'LOCAL PREACHER'S DAUGHTER JOINS A BROTHEL'. He stared, held it up close to his face and squinted, then stared some more. Was this a joke? Flashbacks of last night ran through his head, and his heart almost came to a halt as he remembered her words. 'I can do this, I've been practicing.' Practicing, be damned! She was turning tricks! Even though he was seeing it, Isaac didn't really believe it. There had to be some other explanation. Well, there was only one way to find out. "I'll be back." He stood and stalked out, paper in hand, leaving Doris and Levi standing there with their mouths open.

The Harley was a blur of metal and polished chrome as he tore down the street. Speed limits were irrelevant at the moment. Besides, he was in tight with the sheriff and this was an emergency. Whipping into Avery's motel, he bounded off his motorcycle, still clutching the newspaper. She had some explaining to do. He couldn't imagine what was going on. But, more importantly, he needed to make sure she was all right. Rapping on the door, he waited. And waited. Damn! Just the thought of being near Avery had his dick misbehaving. 'This isn't a damn social call,' he reprimanded his errant manhood. Damn! She either wasn't answering the door or she had checked out. What if something was wrong? There was only one-way to be sure. He knew Marvin, the owner, and he'd open the door and let Isaac in to see.

A few minutes later, he stood in the motel room and breathed a sigh of relief when he saw her childish suitcase still on the end of the bed. "I guess she's just out somewhere."

Marvin looked at him with a tired expression. "Suppose so. Do you want to leave a message?"

"No, no. I'll check back later." Getting back on his bike, Isaac tried to reason this out. First, there was that slip he'd made in full view of the whole town when he had kissed her on Main Street. Lord, how many times had he re-lived that moment? But that pleasure had been eclipsed forever by the hot lovin' he had enjoyed with her last night. What was he going to do? Every time he was with Avery, he hurt her. The first time had been the night in the bar when he had humiliated her by showing her the door, then lying to her about her sex appeal. The second time they were together, he had yelled in her face before the bar fight, and last night he had pushed her on the floor right after she'd given him the best oral sex of his life. Growling his displeasure, he headed back to Hardbodies once again, having no idea how to find Avery or what he'd say to her if he did.

Thankfully, the day passed swiftly. Avery was never far from his thoughts, but he had things to do that he couldn't put off. The article in the paper was another story. For now, as far as Isaac was concerned, it hadn't happened. He purposely refused to think about it. His mind was numb on that topic. But everyone that came in who knew Avery or knew that he knew Avery had something to say about the piece. The whole damn thing made him furious. People had no right to gossip about something when they didn't even know if it was true or not. Pictures could be photoshopped. Frankly, Isaac doubted the story. You couldn't believe everything you read anymore.

When night fell, people began pouring into the bar. The band was in fine form and the liquor was flowing like a fountain. There was no sweeter sound than the cash register ringing up sale after sale. It took both him and Levi to tend the bar, and the dance contest was in full swing by the time Isaac got around to focusing on it. Women of every form and fashion were putting on a show. Biker chicks, buckle bunnies, good-time girls, and a few regular hometown girls who didn't mind strutting their stuff. Hell, why hadn't he thought of it before? A night like this would be damn good for business. People loved to have a good time.

"Lord God Almighty," Levi breathed as he watched Doris announce the next number. "It's her."

"Everybody put their hands together and welcome Miss Wild Rose to our stage. Damn, I wish I had your hair, Honey. You're a hottie!" The crowd was going wild.

"Don't look, Isaac. I thought I was imagining things with that phone caller earlier, but I wasn't. Miss Wild Rose is your Miss Prim Rose." Joining them, Doris overheard Levi and cleared her throat. "Is that who I think it is?" She swallowed hard, an expression of disbelief on her face. "Lord, I feel like I've just announced the Pope would be buying the next round of drinks."

Telling Isaac not to look was like saying sic' em to a dog. With a run on the drums, the music the band was playing changed. Instead of just a pounding beat, it became playful and naughty. Every note screamed sex—thrusting, driving, toe-curling sex. And when the dancer came on stage, what he saw flipped his world.

Isaac stepped away from the bar and moved toward the stage like a man in a trance. Her body was encased in red leather: a form-fitting little bra, a bolero jacket and the shortest, sweetest little skirt he'd ever seen. Ye, gods! If he wasn't intimately acquainted with that treasure of a body, and if it wasn't for those damn sexy ringlets, he would've never believed this scene in a million years. Avery strutted out on his stage like she was born to it. Who knew little Miss Perfect would have that kind of rhythm? The way she moved was pure poetry, a sonnet written just for him that whispered of untold delights. Hell! Maybe, what he had read in that stupid article was true. Someone had shown her the ropes. That was for sure and certain. Isaac didn't know whether to be furious, aroused or just plain pissed.

Working his way through the crowd, he stood front and center. One idiot elbowed him, pointed down below Isaac's belt and then at his own meager package like it was something to be proud of. Yea, he was hard. "Back off, jerk." Pulling his shirt out of his pants to hide his burgeoning erection, Isaac felt funny. He didn't want to be aroused, but he was. All around him were sounds: wolf calls, whistles, and varied off-color phrases were being thrown into the air. Isaac barely comprehended them. He was too focused on what was happening on the raised dais in front of him.

Avery stepped close to the edge, wearing a pair of four inch stilettos that made her legs look like a stairway to heaven. Swinging her hips from left to right, she shimmed like a harem girl and Isaac's eyes followed every move she made like he was at a tennis match. And then…Lord Have Mercy! She started touching herself. Placing her little palms on her bare midriff, she caressed the silky, smooth skin and then let them glide downward. He heard moans and groans from the crowd, and it was all he could do to keep off the stage. His arms felt empty, his breathing was labored, and when she finally let one hand cup her mound, he almost went to his knees.

By God! He was mesmerized as her fingers teased the paradise between her legs. How did she know to do this stuff? Damn! What if it was all true? To think that other men had seen her do this, touched her, possessed her…that possibility was eating a hole in his very soul.

As she danced, Isaac knew Avery had every guy in the house straining their zippers. She tossed her head back, that amazing hair flowing behind her like a waterfall. Without a doubt, she was planting the idea in each man's head that her nipples were hard, her sex was creaming and she could bring herself to orgasm any time she chose. Isaac swallowed hard and sweat began to bead on his forehead. Dozens of bikers and cowboys alike were in the same shape he was, but Avery only had eyes for him. It was as if they were the only two in the room, and their bodies were connected by an electrical arc which acted like a magnet, seeming to awaken every cell in his body and all of them were screaming out for her.

Last night, after he'd gone to bed, he'd had a devil of a time going to sleep. Several times he'd awakened, stroking himself and begging Avery to give him another sweet release. Now he was cocked and primed, locked and loaded, and it wouldn't take much to set him off like a Roman candle. Isaac had never wanted sex as much as he did at this moment. His hips wanted to buck in time to the gyrations of her lithe, lush body. The song, 'Wild One' that she danced to was so damn true. This sweet baby was a good girl, a little doll who had been protected all her life from anything that could possibly taint her. Now, here she was—unbelievable, pure, unadulterated eroticism. Isaac couldn't reconcile the two images to save his life. Before morning, he promised himself, he would have answers—come hell or high water.

Moving seductively to the music, she lifted her hair and arched her neck while every man held his breath. As one, all of their hands itched to cup those twin peaks of delight swelling up over her bra, the thin material showing clearly the outline of nipples that looked exactly like the tops of baby bottles, all plumped up and ready to be sucked. Twisting and turning, she flirted with the crowd, peeling off the little jacket and letting it drop to the floor. Gasps were heard around the room, for now she wore nothing but a tiny bra and six inches of scarlet leather, which barely covered her pinchable bottom. Only hours before, he'd held that butt in his hands and caressed her sweet spot, spreading honey all up and down her slit. How he wished he'd tasted her. How delicious she must be. But no, he'd been weak and demanded her mouth on his erection. How was a man supposed to choose between so much delicious, intoxicating bounty?

Avery stepped over to the pole and, swear to God, everything went dead quiet. Even the band stopped playing for a few seconds. The musicians must have been in the throes of the same heat he was. Gripping the pole with both hands, she took it between her legs, humping it, undulating against the lucky metal. Isaac couldn't breathe, feeling every thrust of her hips as if he were buried deep within her. And what was most amazing, was that even though others were calling her name, even throwing money on stage, she only had eyes for him. There was no way he could miss her message. Avery was dancing for him.

The band smoothly changed numbers and eased into the provocative, sensual 'How Will I Live Without You?', and as the music swelled, Avery made love to the pole. Dammit! She didn't have to live without him! He was right here! As he stood there, totally captivated, she played with his mind and heart. Oh, she knew all the tricks, and how she'd learned them was eating him alive. Yet, he was hypnotized as she caressed her bottom lip with the tip of one finger, then began to suck on it, sensuously. Isaac felt every tug of those lips right on the head of his cock. God, he could still feel her mouth. He remembered how it had been last night and he wanted it again. He had to have it again.

Hell, he trembled with lust. How much more could he take? That question was answered when she swung around, held the pole with both hands over her head and began to slide up and down its length. And as the crowd cheered her on, she smoothed her hands up to her breasts and cupped them, lifting them up, offering them just to him. The expression on her face was undeniable. It was an explicit, erotic, engraved invitation to engage in ecstasy, in pure sweet sin, with her. Isaac was more than ready to accept that invitation.

All around the stage men were feeling their oats, and when one inebriated cowboy decided to climb on stage, Isaac knew it was time to put an end to this little show. Not only that, it was time to stake his claim.

This was kinda fun! At church, she'd sung specials in front of the congregation, regularly. Really, this wasn't a whole lot different. She used the same tactic then that she did now. As a coping mechanism, she just imagined everyone in their underwear and then they weren't nearly as intimidating.

Isaac didn't look happy. Well, that was just too dang bad. She was pouring her heart and soul into this dance, and by gosh, she was going to see it through. Was it affecting him? Heck, she didn't know. Her expertise at arousing a male was limited to him. And right now, he just looked mad. Crap! And here he came. As one poor tipsy man tried to make it on stage, Isaac charged like a rampaging bull. One moment, she was swinging around the pole, the next she was swinging over his shoulder. "Hey, I didn't get to do my big finish," she complained.

"Oh, you're finished, my little wet-dream." Stepping off the stage he was met by hoo-raws and backslaps. And then one slap landed right on her butt. With a huff, she tried to raise up. "Steady, baby. That was me. There ain't no other man who's gonna touch you, ever again, just me."

What other men? She didn't want other men. Yet, with those comforting words, he carried her out of the bar, down the hall, to where she didn't know.

"Where are we going?" She managed to ask. All she could see right now was his tight, gorgeous butt, and she wondered if he would notice if she copped a little feel. What the hell. It was there. Ooooh, she had thought the word 'hell' and the roof didn't cave in. That had to be a good sign. With both hands, she cupped his bottom, and squeezed. Pop! "Hey!"

"That's for playing with my tush." He swatted her again. Pop! She squealed, but it was full of laughter. "And that's for driving me crazy." He deftly opened a door and switched on a light and all Avery could see was beautiful Mexican tile.

"Where are we?"

"My apartment." He walked a bit farther. "Now, we're in my bedroom." He set her down and switched on the overhead light. "And now you can finish your dance."

Finish? Here? She didn't think so. But, then he said, "Please." And as Avery figured, she had no urge or will to deny him anything.

"I don't have any music."

"My heart's beating like a drum. Can you feel it?" He caught her hand and held it over his heart.

"Yes, so is mine." She took his other hand and placed it over her heart. "So, you want me to dance for you?" She wanted to skip the dancing and get right to the naughty stuff.

Isaac picked up the hand that lay on his chest and kissed the palm. "Yes, if you have an urge to strip, I'd rather you performed just for me. That way I can keep you safe." He was torn. He wanted to rail at her for being so foolish and at the same time, he wanted to lay her down and rail her till dawn in a different way. "Dance for me, Gypsy." He sat down on the bed to wait.

No music. "Okay, I'll try". Not that it mattered. Her blood was singing through her veins and the star of every fantasy she'd ever dreamed was sitting on this big, wide bed staring at her with dark, hooded, hungry eyes. Her body sought to obey. Avery didn't know where to look. He was so gorgeous. But, he made her nervous. Oh, Lord! He had a bulge in his pants! That observation made her smile. Okay, she knew what she'd be looking at. His penis would be like a barometer. The better she performed, the higher it would rise.

Okay, here goes. Avery turned her back to him, and bent over just a bit, looking back at him over one shoulder. She poured every bit of desire and longing into the stare she gave him. And if Isaac gripping the bedspread with both fists was any indication, it was working. "Do you know what you're doing to me, Avery? Have you any idea what it's costing me to sit here and watch you like this? When all I really want to do is pull you on this bed, flip you on your back, and bury myself as deep into you as I can get?" He sat there, a macho, alpha male dressed in black. Her dark knight.

"Who's stopping you?" God, she was getting bold.

"Don't, Avery. You have no idea what you're playing with."

No, she didn't know, but she wanted to. So she decided to see just how far she could push him and get away with it. The bra straps, they really needed to come down off her shoulders. And yes, she needed to bend over just a bit further, give him a glimpse of her bottom cheeks. The garters she had on were as red as the skirt, and beneath that was a thong, a thong! Her mom would have a cow if she knew her only daughter was wearing a thong. Oh yeah, she was getting into this. Her skin was smooth, and if she closed her eyes, she could pretend Isaac was touching her. As she danced to silent music, her palms teased their way up her thighs and under her skirt and before she could stop it, she moaned a little as her fingertips grazed her swollen nubbin. It wasn't her hand touching her. It was his. "Isaac," she gasped as her whole body tensed. A little giggle escaped. If she weren't careful, she was gonna make herself come.

'Come', that was a wonderful word. The girls had taught her it was cum, but she still thought about it the other way. So far, she hadn't been able to use the new spelling 'cum' in her writing. She'd have to practice some more. That thought made her smile. And Isaac had shown her how it felt. Glorious, stupendous, and she wanted to experience that rush again and again with him, only him. Pressing the issue, she picked up her skirt, unhooked the clasp and let it fall to the floor around her ankles.

"God be merciful," he growled as she cupped her own bottom and separated it just enough for him to see where the red string hid between her cheeks. One last move and she'd stop. After all, it wasn't as if he would see anything new, and this was her favorite part of the number. With arms over her head, she writhed to a rhythm as old as time. Turning, she moved toward him, hips swaying and pelvis gyrating. Did he like what he saw? Avery studied his face as she unhooked her bra. When he closed his eyes and threw his head back, did that mean he liked it?

"Open your eyes, Isaac," she almost begged. "I'm doing this for you." With that heartfelt confession, she let her breasts spill out. The nipples were hard and swollen. Lifting her breasts in her palms, she took a step closer to the bed. "How did I do?"

"Did you know there's a wet spot at the front of your thong?" he asked gruffly.

What? That wasn't the reaction she was expecting. Every bit of the bravado left her body. Cripes! "Sorry..." She crossed her arms over her breasts. Now, she was embarrassed. "I don't understand..."

"Well, I do," he nearly growled. "That wet spot means you want me. You're turned on, Avery, as much as I am. Are you always like this when you're with a man?"

"What?" She didn't understand what he was saying. She was only aware of his nearness. With a strong, but gentle tug he pulled her into his lap. Avery wanted to wrap herself around him, but she held back, not having enough self-assurance to pull that move off. What if he pushed her away again? He ran a big, warm hand over her back. Perhaps his intention had been to soothe her, but what he was doing was making her shake. "You're so beautiful," she whispered. With an outstretched hand, she touched his face, softly with just the tips of her fingers. If he jerked back, she would be up and off his lap and out the door in two shakes of a sheep's tail. Instead, he leaned into her caress, so she cupped his cheek, caressing his strong jaw. His face was almost perfect...that straight Greek nose, those killer cheekbones and a thoroughly kissable mouth. "If only you would smile for me." She tugged on his bottom lip with her thumb and then laughed when he tried to playfully bite her. "Hey!" Avery couldn't believe she was sitting here, actually getting to touch him, to play with him. It was hard to take. Isaac McCoy was intense, aroused and all of that heat and energy was, for a little while, focused on her. She couldn't help but praise him. "Your eyes are a mesmerizing blue, and this long, dark hair is the sexiest mane I've ever seen." As she ran her fingers through the almost shoulder length locks, it shocked her that he shuddered beneath her touch.

"Damn, you're good. I would have never dreamed you could become such a little vixen. I can't resist you another moment, Little Girl. I've tried. Whoever trained you, trained you well." All the happenings of the last twenty-four hours coalesced in his mind. "I don't know what you've been doing and I don't claim to understand what's going on, but if anybody else is going to have you, it's gonna be me."

Avery was having a hard time concentrating on his words. Instead, she was watching his expression and it told her one thing, clearly. Isaac wanted her. He wanted to make love to her and that was the grandest miracle of all. He set her gently aside, stood up and began to strip. "Lie right there, Avery. Flat on your back and don't move a muscle." There wasn't a moment's hesitation as she sought to obey, scooting back on the velvet bedspread. "Do you want me?" he asked her straight out.

"Yes, Sir."

Isaac had no idea why she used those exact words. Did she understand the significance? Did she know what that phrase did to him? Tossing his clothes to one side, he let his gaze slide over her hot little body.

"Are you wet for me?" His thought had been that she would dip her fingers between her legs to feel. God, no. Instead she bent her knees, spread her legs and opened for him so he could see for himself. God Almighty! She was pink, opened up like a flower, and as creamy as an erotic éclair. "Damn, honey. Avery, I want you in so many ways, I don't know where to start."

"Would you kiss me?" she asked in a hesitant voice. Holding up one hand, she beckoned him.

She had asked him this before. He remembered. God, he was grateful to get a second chance to fulfill that simple request. "Hell, yeah!" He covered her body like he was going to do push-ups over the top of her and began to devour her mouth.

She framed his face and opened for him. His tongue sliding against hers was heavenly. Isaac's hot male taste tantalized as he overwhelmed her with a grinding kiss that caused her to forget every doubt she had. They shared little bites and nibbles. He sucked at her lips and she tried to take over the kiss, demanding more.

"Uhuh, my rodeo," he teased, surprising her as he softened the kiss and made it sweet, licking her teeth, mapping her mouth with forays of that rough, velvet tongue.

Lord, he was softening her for the kill, brushing insistent, tender kisses at the corners of her quivering lips. Avery had never dreamed a kiss could be like this. And God, that was his manhood rubbing over her mound. Avery felt liquid heat pouring from her body. Her thong would be sopping at this rate.

"Never get enough," he moaned as his lips slid down her throat. "Can't pass these up," he whispered against her skin as he buried his face in her cleavage and began licking and nuzzling both breasts.

She was in heaven. Now, this is what she always knew lovemaking could be like. "Suck them, Isaac. I need to feel your lips on me. Please?"

Normally, he didn't take direction from his partner. He was always in charge. Tonight was different, because this woman was different. "Yes, Ma'am." Leaning on one elbow, he cupped one breast in his hand and molded it, squeezing until the nipple was poised for his lips. With the flat of his tongue, he licked it, tracing the nipple round and round like he was swirling ice cream on a cone. Avery whimpered and he latched on, sucking hard, using tongue and teeth, feasting, working his mouth down over her breast as if he were going to consume it whole.

"Oh, hell, yes," she whispered.

And when she did, Isaac chuckled around her flesh. "What did you say?"

"Sorry, it just feels so good. I wanna curse or something."

"I never heard you cuss before. Course, you've done a lot of growing up lately." Taking her nipple between his teeth, he chewed delicately. "Do you like that?" His answer came when she arched her back, pushing her chest into his face. "You do, don't you?"

"Uh-huh, I sure do. It's delicious."

"Why don't you let yourself go for me? Could you do that?" Not waiting for an answer, Isaac went back to work at her breasts, committed to bringing her ultimate pleasure. He massaged and kneaded, working one nipple between his fingers while sucking on the other.

"Harder," she begged.

Damn! His baby liked a little pain with her pleasure. So, he pulled at her nipples, twisting them just a little. A pinch, a nip, a bite of erotic fire, all coupled with long, sensuous pulls. Avery rubbed her thighs together, and she even put her hand on her own clitoris, desperately needing the friction.

"Let me." He pushed his leg between her, lifting it so his thigh was touching her mons. "Ride me," he instructed.

Avery was operating on pure instinct and erotic hunger. At first she didn't understand, but when his hard muscle touched her sensitive spot, she got it. Wrapping one leg over his, she rubbed herself up and down his leg, dragging her sex deliciously over his hair-roughened flesh. "Oh, yeah." This was what she needed. Holding him tightly, she let the feelings come. "Isaac, I can't stop," she whimpered as he ate at her breasts, suckling to the same rhythm as the blood that pulsed through her veins. "Isaac! God! Oh, baby. Yessssss!" Iridescent lights and colors flashed behind her lids as she climaxed. It was the second one of her life and this one felt better than the first. Isaac whispered in her ear, just soft praise words, endearments, bringing her down easy.

"God, you're beautiful when you climax. Did you like that?" He rubbed his face on her breasts, loving the voluptuousness of her body.

"Very much, thank you."

"Darlin', you're so polite and I'm so damn hard." He rose up over her. "I don't care how many men you've been with...tonight you're mine." He took a condom from his nightstand drawer and sheathed himself.

"I'm on birth control," she whispered.

Isaac didn't say anything. There was no use hurting her feelings, but pregnancy hadn't been his first thought. It was how many men she'd been with. "Spread your legs, I need to be inside of you before I explode." Taking his cock in his hand, he placed the head at her opening and pushed in—hard. Tight, Lord she was tight. He only had half of himself in her and he was going to have to work to get the rest in. She gave a tiny ragged whimper in the curve of his neck. He felt it more than heard it. "Avery?"

God, it hurt! Avery bit back a cry, not wanting him to know she was in pain. She had known that losing one's virginity could hurt, but she hadn't let herself dwell on it. Making love with Isaac was too important. "I'm okay, please. Don't stop," she urged him.

He started to pull out, but she tightened her hold on him and pushed upward. Her vagina was swollen and hot and plenty wet, so he pulled out and thrust back in, deeper. And then he felt it, resistance. Avery's whole body tensed. "Damn." She was a virgin! How in the world was that possible? Isaac felt like he was in the twilight zone. Nothing was making sense. The only thing he could process was that he was in heaven and he wasn't willing to call it a day.

"Make love to me, Isaac. Please." She wasn't willing to backtrack. This was the man she loved, and nothing he could do to her was wrong. Wrapping her legs around his waist and her arms around his neck, she tried to move her internal muscles the way the girls had taught her. Of course the Keigel exercises had felt different without Isaac's huge penis inside of her. God, he was big.

He couldn't stop. His whole body was clamoring for release. And when he felt her muscles working him, he gave in to his body's demands. "Angel, I don't understand, but I want you too much to stop now." One thing he could do was be gentle.

And the other thing he could do was to make sure she enjoyed it as much as he did. Hell, it was delicious. "Oh, Love, you'll never know how good this feels." She was so hot and so snug, and slick, and right. It was just so damn right. This was Avery. This was Avery. This was his Avery. His mind chanted the same litany, over and over again.

She felt him pull almost all the way out, and then slowly glide back in again. "Oh, that felt good." And it had. The shock had worn off and all that remained was a good burn and this incredible feeling of being stretched and filled. "More..." She raised her hips to meet his thrusts. Her request seemed to be what he needed to hear, because he let go. Avery had never dreamed that the connection between a man and a woman could be so complete and electric. As her father's wedding sermons always said, two became one. Isaac was inside of her, on top of her, wrapped around her and she felt like she wanted to stay that way forever. This was so much more than sex. To her this was everything.

"Are you okay?" His voice was hoarse with passion.

"God, yes. This is what I've wanted for so long."

Isaac stopped and was still.

"No! Why did you quit?" Avery clutched his shoulders and looked into his eyes. She couldn't read his expression. "What's wrong?"

Isaac dipped down and kissed her lips softly. His weight was pressing her into the bed and she couldn't believe how safe it made her feel. "Nothing's wrong, except I'm too excited."

He nuzzled her neck and sucked. Avery hoped it would leave a mark.

"You're squeezing me so tight and it feels so damn good. I don't want to come before you do."

Joy bubbled up inside of Avery. "I don't mind." She rubbed her lips on his shoulder. "I'm just happy to be here with you like this."

"Well, I mind. Give me your hands." He held up enough so he could take each of her hands in his and he held them on either side of her head. "Hold on, Love. I've about to make both of us feel really good." Her legs were spread wide with her knees bent and he was covering her completely. With her hands immobilized, she felt captured like an Arabian slave girl commanded to do her Master's bidding. Isaac was everything she'd ever wanted; caring, passionate and with a fierce edge which made her heart race. Somehow, he angled his body so that every thrust he made was giving her extreme pleasure. "Better?" He managed to ask through gritted teeth.

"Uh-huh," that was all she could manage. Something was building. She didn't know if it was due to how he was making her feel or the thrill of knowing that Isaac was enjoying her gift to him. "I love it."

"Avery, Sugar, God, this is good."

Yes, it was. Heat, light, and an electric fizz sizzled from deep within her and radiated out to every part of her body. "Isaac! Yes! God, yes!" she cried as her climax overwhelmed her.

When Avery came, he knew it. There was no way he could miss it. Her folds milked him like a velvet fist. And she lifted, her whole body arched up into him. With her legs around his waist and her arms around his neck, she came up to him, clinging like the sweetest vine. It was the most touching, erotic display he'd ever witnessed. When Avery climaxed, she gifted him with her whole body, her sweet cries and whispers a testimony to the rapture she was experiencing. If he hadn't been about to erupt anyway, her total euphoric reaction would have been enough to send him over the edge. The rush was so powerful and so sweet, Isaac shouted his release. "Avery! Sweet Baby! Yes! Yes!" Waves of ecstasy swept over his body, and all the while he held her tight, loving the little ripples of aftershocks around his erection as the orgasm swept over them both.

Coming down from that incredible high took a few minutes and he rolled over on his back and took her with him. Damn, she felt so good in his arms. With a shaky hand, he pushed a lock of hair back from her damp forehead, and planted a kiss there for good measure. His heart lurched when she exhaled a big satisfied sigh and nestled down in his embrace. What he wanted to do was stay like this forever, but there were things that needed to be said, and they just wouldn't wait another day. So with reluctance, he eased out from under her and sat up so he could see her face.

"Avery, I think it's about time you told me what the hell is going on. Don't you?"

Chapter Five

Avery lay in Isaac McCoy's bed, naked. That fact, in and of itself, was truly huge. Even better, Isaac was standing, heart-stoppingly nude, just a few feet away. What a pity he wanted to blow the mood by talking. "What do you mean? There's nothing going on." Avery felt a twinge of guilt. She didn't like to lie, and this was a form of fibbing, because she had a pretty good idea what he was talking about.

Isaac looked at her sternly. "Avery Rose, you know exactly what I mean."

She smiled at him. "Talking doesn't sound fun. We just made love and it was something that I'd like to repeat at the earliest opportunity." Jeepers. Why couldn't she be sexy? She made their rowdy bout of sex sound like a coffee klatch.

Isaac did his best not to smile. She had to be the sweetest thing in the world. For just a second he let himself look at her. She was his pin-up girl. Avery wasn't stick skinny like most of the women nowadays. She was curvy and soft, voluptuous and sexy-as-hell. Hell, he was getting hard again. He pushed it down with his hand and it bounced back up and Avery giggled.

"Lord, deliver me," he prayed.

"The Lord might not help you with that, but I can," she purred.

"Stop it, Avery Rose! Let's not piss off the Almighty. I think we have enough problems, as it is. This is serious." He didn't get dressed, but he did sit down and pull the bedspread over his adventurous appendage. She pouted, sticking that sweet bottom lip out, and he had to fight himself to keep from kissing it. "Now, explain yourself."

With a huff, she flounced on her back and pulled the other side of the bedspread across her middle, effectively covering her body from his hungry gaze.

"What do you want to know, exactly?" One did not cooperate with the enemy. She was almost tempted to just give him name, rank and serial number or in her case, name, age and tax number.

Isaac frowned. "I don't even know where to start." Thinking back over the last wild twenty-four hours, he started with the obvious. "What are you trying to accomplish by acting so out of character? And don't try making something up, I'll know." He used his best Dom tone, which was a miracle, since his body wanted to bow at her feet and grant her every wish.

Avery admitted defeat. She would never be able to pull the wool over his eyes. Scootching around, keeping herself covered, she managed to sit up and face him. "Isn't it obvious?" At his stern look, she let her shoulders slump. "Okay, I'll tell you. I was trying to convince you that I could be the type of woman you could be attracted to."

'Hot damn!' was his first thought, but then he pulled himself back on point, for her sake. "This isn't you, Avery. You can't force yourself to be something you're not." Isaac was trying to convince himself as well as her.

Avery clutched the blanket closer to her. How could he say that, after what they'd shared? Unless it meant more to her than it did to him. "I think we're perfect together. I love you, Isaac." She poured her whole heart into the words, and waited.

Torture, sheer soul-wrenching torture. It felt like he was turning his back on the greatest miracle of his life, but he couldn't stand to face a future where he was doomed to disappoint, perhaps horrify, this gentle, perfect woman. So, he played his ace. Reaching to the floor, he picked up his vest and took the newspaper article out of his pocket. "Explain this. Is there any chance this was photoshopped?"

"Oh, no!" She grabbed the offending piece of paper from his hand. "How did you get a copy of this? It only ran in the Nevada paper."

Nevada paper? Hell! "Sorry, this is the local rag."

Avery let out a screech and the sheet dropped without her even noticing. "Holy Crap!" Thoughts of the Women's Missionary Union and the Deacon Board and the Library Council and the Junior Service League kept running through her mind. "How did this happen?" She fell forward on the bed, hiding her face, not noticing that her heart-shaped rump was turned up right in front of Isaac.

He stared at the temptation in front of him. Lord, how he would love to mold and squeeze that darling behind of hers. His errant dick tented the bedspread and he had the devil of a time trying to arrange the covers to keep them from looking like a Ringling Bros. Big top.

"I don't know, but what in the name of goodness were you doing at a Brothel? Was that where you were all the time I was turning the world upside down trying to find you?"

"Yes," she answered with a muffled voice, her head still buried in the blankets. Then she bounced up. "Why were you turning the world upside down?" Hope lit her eyes.

Squash! "Because, I felt guilty. You disappeared right after I told you Hardbodies was not the best place for you to hang out."

Hanging her head, Avery confessed. "After you told me that I wasn't your type, I decided to try and change. I went to the brothel to acquire needed skills and knowledge."

Isaac jumped up, his pecker trying to be fully involved in the conversation. Grabbing one of the blankets, he wrapped it around his waist. "Do you know how stupid that was? Do you have any idea what could have happened to you? I ought to turn you over my lap and blister your butt!" When another hopeful gleam entered her eyes, he chided. "Stop that! Was this what you meant by the fact that you had been practicing? What did they make you do? Did strange men—"

Avery stopped him before he stroked. "Isaac, calm down, you look like a thundercloud." This wasn't going according to plan. "It was all academic, no hands-on contact. I practiced on a sex toy. Several of the girls gave me lessons on how to dress and walk and…well, you saw the dance."

"Why would you do that?" He knew why, but he needed to hear her say it. More self-torture.

Her voice was small and uncertain. "I went to Shady Lady's, because I wanted to learn how to please you. And I did, didn't I?"

"Yes, you did." He couldn't lie to her about that. "You pleased me more than you'll ever know. The problem is, that's just the tip of the iceberg. I want to do things to you that you've never dreamed of, that you'd never understand. My taste in sex is not what you deserve. You're a lady, Avery. And I'm into kink that would scare you to death."

"Try me," she challenged him. "I'll do anything for you."

"No," he argued, wishing it could be different. "You don't have any idea what you're talking about. Do you know what a Dom/sub relationship is?"

She was quiet a moment, as if deep in thought. Then her head popped up and she looked him square in the eye. "Maybe. But, it doesn't matter. If you like it and want it, then I want it, too."

"Avery, dammit!" Isaac was feeling things he had no right to feel. "You don't realize how tempting you are. I like you, I respect you. Lord knows, I want you. Hell, making love with you was beyond paradise. But it's not going to happen again, we're too different."

She sat there, dead still for a long moment. Admitting defeat was hard, but he couldn't make it any plainer than that. "Okay, my mistake." She got up, her heart breaking, and started to pick up her clothes to redress. Isaac looked like he had more to say, but she didn't think she could stand to hear more about how ill-suited they were for each other. All she knew was that she had offered herself to him on a silver platter, and he had rejected her gift. "I'll show myself out." As she started past him, he grabbed her arm, but both of them were taken by surprise by a loud banging and yelling at the door.

Isaac dropped the blanket and grabbed a towel as he went by the bathroom door. "Hold on! Give me a minute."

Avery grabbed her clothes and headed to the bathroom. But a very familiar, irate voice stopped her in her tracks. "Where is she, McCoy? There are 30 people out in that bar that say they saw you bring my little girl in here thrown over your shoulder like a sack of potatoes! If you think you're going to get away with besmirching her reputation, I'm here to tell you that you are dead wrong."

"Daddy?" Not thinking, she trailed into the living room wrapped only in a sheet to see her bald, gesticulating father step right into Isaac's face and shake his fist, menacingly.

"I blame you for all of this, McCoy! Have you any idea how people are talking? I've had dozens of phone calls, even one from the mayor. I may lose my church over this!" His face was so red that Avery was afraid he was having a heart attack.

"Daddy, are you all right? What are you doing here?" At her voice, Abe Sinclair wheeled around, still mad as a bull.

"There you are! Do you realize how big a disappointment to me you are? And look at the way you're dressed. I don't have to guess what you've been doing." Turning on Isaac again, he continued his tirade. "Our good name is in shreds. I don't see how we can hold our head up at the associational meetings. This..." He waved that dreaded newspaper article around. "...is being passed around among my friends like communion wafers."

"Daddy, Isaac had nothing to do with that. Besides, I did nothing wrong. No one laid a hand on me while I was in Vegas."

"Vegas!" Reverend Sinclair literally spat the word. "Can you say the same thing now? Has McCoy laid a hand on you?"

"That's my business, Papa." Avery stood as straight and dignified as she could in a taupe-colored, 800-thread count, Egyptian cotton sheet.

"That's where you're wrong. This is very much my business. What you do reflects directly on me and on the church."

He wheeled on Isaac, and Isaac, to give him credit, showed the older man only respect.

"I am terribly sorry that this happened, Sir. I wouldn't have hurt Avery or you for the world."

Avery began to see where Isaac had been coming from. This is what he'd feared. A heavy guilt began to weigh on her heart, not for her circumstances, but for her father and Isaac. She'd gotten them both in trouble. It was time she stepped back and put this into perspective. Avery had no desire to go back to being the boring person she was before, but she could put some distance between herself and these people she loved, for their sakes.

"You're going to do right by my daughter, McCoy." Preacher Sinclair glared at them both.

What did he mean by that? Avery began to have a distinctly uneasy feeling.

"Sir, if you'll give us a minute to get our clothes on, we'll be glad to sit down with you and have a civil conversation." He took Avery by the arm. "Come on, let's get dressed."

"What did he mean, do right by me?" Avery's head was spinning.

"I'm not sure." Isaac did have a pretty good inkling, and miraculously he was having a surprising reaction to what was running through his head. "Just pull on your clothes. No, don't, that will only make things worse." He snatched the red stripper outfit out of her hands.

Digging in his chest of drawers, he handed her a T-shirt and a pair of Longhorn lounge pants. "Put these on. They'll be big, but at least you'll be covered up."

She hurriedly pulled on the clothes. "Thanks, and I'm sorry about this. I'll get him out of your hair as quickly as I can. I'll just tell him that I'll go home with him and Mom for a few days. That will pacify him, I hope." She couldn't believe she was calmly discussing her father while standing semi-nude with Isaac. Perhaps her mission hadn't worked out as planned, but there was one thing for certain...her life would never be the same. The old boring, virginal Avery Rose Sinclair was a thing of the past.

Somehow, Isaac didn't think that was going to cut it. "Don't worry. Everything's going to be just fine." Funny, that's the way he felt. Everything was going to be just fine.

When they were both dressed, Isaac held out his hand. "Shall we face this together, Sugar?"

"All right." She put her hand in his, thinking this would probably be the last chance she got to touch him. "I'm sorry about all of this," she tried to apologize. "I never meant to cause you trouble. I just wanted a chance to show you how good it could be between us."

"Avery!" Her father's shout put an end to her speech.

"Coming, Daddy."

Together, they faced one very out-of-sorts Baptist preacher. "I'm glad to see you two have joined hands. That's the first thing I'll ask you to do in the wedding ceremony."

"Wedding!?!" Avery tore her hand from Isaac's. "Daddy, you can't be serious?" She didn't know whether to laugh or cry. Marrying Isaac was the dearest wish of her heart, but not like this.

"I'm dead serious, Girl." Her father looked at her with disdain, as if she was a piece of garbage that had stuck to his shoe. "McCoy, I expect you to marry my daughter as soon as possible. You've taken her innocence and led her down the path of sin. The least you can do is give her the McCoy name and a modicum of respectability. Your name isn't as good as your brothers, but a marriage certificate will go a long way in shutting up the gossips."

"Now, wait a minute..." Avery searched for words to say that would get her father off this absurd idea he had pulled straight from the dark ages. "There's no way that—"

"I think that's an excellent idea, Pastor." Isaac was calm, rational and more at peace than he had been in a long time. "It would be an honor for me to marry Avery. You can count this as my formal request for your daughter's hand in marriage."

Avery looked at Isaac and then at her father to be sure they hadn't lost their minds. "There's no way in hell I am going to marry you, Isaac McCoy."

"Avery Rose! Such language," her father sputtered.

A knife blade of uncertainty wounded him. Countless cuts from those who thought they knew better than he, began to bleed afresh. "Why not? Isn't marriage to me what you were after all along?"

His simplistic take on things hurt her. Avery wasn't ready to have a rational conversation. She was too shocked and horrified to think straight. No way was she going to let Isaac be forced to marry her. He didn't want her. And she had no desire to have a husband who wasn't desperately in love with her. "Not like this, it wasn't." She didn't think she had to say anymore. It was too humiliating to enunciate. What he must think of her? She had to get out of here before she cried in front of them both. "I'm not going to discuss this anymore, with either of you."

Turning on her heels, she went back to Isaac's room to gather her belongings. It only took a second. She couldn't wait to get out of there. It was time she found other things to occupy her mind besides the mindless pursuit of Isaac McCoy. As she passed Isaac and her father on the way out the door, she stopped to put in one last plug for sanity. "Father, I have lived my entire life to please you, and that's over. Isaac, all my life I dreamed that you could come to love me as much as I love you, but you can't. Dad, tell Mother I'll call. Isaac, I won't be bothering you anymore."

Avery walked away and left the two men in her life standing side-by-side, speechless.

* * *

"Don't worry, sir. I won't let her leave town." Isaac walked Avery's father to his car. "I'll handle it. Your daughter will be protected and sheltered by everything the McCoys have to offer."

Abe huffed and puffed just a bit more. He had worked himself into such a lather, expecting Isaac to refuse to do the right thing that it was hard to let all that angst go. "Well, you see that you do. Avery is a good girl and she wouldn't be in this mess if she hadn't set her sights on the likes of you."

Isaac didn't try to defend himself. There just wasn't any use. He agreed with the reverend. Who would have ever thought he would be joining forces with Reverend Sinclair for a common cause? Or that said cause would be to bind himself in the bonds of matrimony to the angel of Kerrville County. At the moment, his angel's halo was slightly tarnished, but he knew better than anyone how truly perfect she was. It had never been Avery's intention to do anything but win his love, and if he wasn't mistaken, she might very well have accomplished that feat.

As he stood there, waiting for the rotund reverend to get in his car, Isaac tested his feelings. No remorse, no uncertainty, no hesitation. He smiled. It was as if her father's demands had freed Isaac to do exactly what he'd wanted to do all along. He wanted Avery. Standing in front of Hardbodies, he watched the preacher leave and considered what his next step should be. There were a lot of things to get done, from big to small, but his first order of business was to go and persuade his errant fiancé-to-be to move in with him.

* * *

"It's not as bad as you make it out to be." Harper gazed at Noah McCoy with longing in her eyes. "We could make this work. I won't go to any of the clubs, if you'll just work with me. I'll try to change, but maybe you could change too. If you would just give me a little of what I need."

"No." The word was flat. There was no room for argument. Noah hardened himself to the beautiful blonde who sat in front of him. She was shaking like a leaf. If he wasn't fooled, she was high on something. How could such a promising life go down the drain so quickly? "You're asking me to do something that I can't do." He laid down the law. "I will not have anything to do with the BDSM lifestyle. I will not raise my hand to you. Hitting someone during sex is sick, and I can't be a part of it."

A hardened expression came over Harper's delicate features. "Don't get high and mighty with me, Noah McCoy. You have no idea how close to home this is to you."

"What do you mean?"

She pursed her lips as if she would say more. "My kind of people don't rat on each other."

She stood up and put a hand on her hip. Noah could see black marks on her arms and a red lash mark on her neck. It made him want to throw up. "I don't want to know your kind of people," he replied stoically.

Harper reeled back as if she'd been slapped. "Don't worry, I'll find what I need elsewhere. And you…" She jabbed a finger in his chest. "…you will never know what you're missing. We could have taken pleasure to a whole new realm. You're an idiot, Noah McCoy, a strait-laced, conservative, no-imagination idiot." With that, she flounced off.

What in the hell had she meant, 'close to home'? Noah got up from the corner booth and spotted Joseph and Jacob walking across the bar.

"Where's Isaac?" Joseph asked, taking a beer off of Doris's tray.

"In the back with Avery," Noah volunteered. "There was a dance contest, tonight. You should have seen the show."

"Oh, we saw it." Joseph stated nonchalantly as he looked out over the crowd.

"You did? Were you as surprised as I was?" Noah asked with a touch of humor in his tone. He was trying to put Harper and everything she'd said behind him. But it wasn't easy. Making small talk with his brothers helped.

"Avery Sinclair danced in a bar," Jacob said with wonder. "That little girl is just full of surprises. I saw what was in the paper. Of course, I'm not judging. I'm sure there's more to the story than what we read."

"Did you catch Isaac's number?" Noah laughed. "I've never seen him so determined in my life. He carted her off that stage and into the back like a pillaging Viking."

"Look, there she goes, and she doesn't look happy." Jacob and Noah joined Joseph as they observed Avery leaving the bar. She moved quickly across the floor, her eyes looking nowhere but straight ahead.

"I don't see Isaac. This doesn't seem to be ending well." Jacob sat down at the booth. "Let's just wait here. I'm sure he'll be out soon. Then we can get the whole story."

"May I join you gentleman?" The brothers were surprised to see Zane Saucier standing by them.

Joseph almost jumped. "Man, you're quiet on your feet. If I didn't know you were Cajun, I'd swear you had Indian blood."

Speaking of Native Americans reminded Noah of Skye. "You think Lance's sister would be my date for the party tomorrow night?"

"Waitin' till the last minute there, aren't you brother?" Jacob surmised. "You know how women are. They like to be prepared for these things. No girl wants to think she's an afterthought or second choice."

"She's not second choice," Noah said quietly.

"What about Harper? Didn't I see her leaving your table a minute ago?" Zane asked and the others got amused.

"You see more than any blind man I've ever known." Joseph patted his friend on the back. "You got some of them psychic powers like my Cady's family has?"

"No." Zane grinned as he sipped his beer. "I heard her voice, I smelled her perfume…she's the only woman in town who wears Midnight Poison by Dior and Terence sent me over here to see about you. He said it looked like she was giving you trouble."

"Not anymore. Harper and I are through. We don't see eye-to-eye on some major issues." Noah's face closed off and the others backed down. They could tell when a man was hurting.

* * *

It was almost closing time and the crowd was beginning to thin down. Isaac made his way back into the bar to check on things and get his motorcycle keys. As he opened the door, he heard familiar voices and knew his brothers had come to call. Sauntering in, he saw Joseph, Jacob and Noah sitting at a table with Zane Saucier. "There he is." Joseph lifted a longneck in salute. "We've been waiting on you."

"What's up?" He didn't sit down. He couldn't afford to let Avery get too far ahead of him.

"We walked in on the performance of the decade." Jacob smiled a gotcha grin. "I thought you intended to keep your distance from that little preacher's daughter."

"Shoot, he's got it bad for Avery. You'd have to be blind to miss that," Zane drawled.

Isaac held up his hands in surrender. "You're not going to get any argument from me. I'm tired of fighting what I want. I want that little preacher's daughter. Only trouble is, I think I waited too long. I hate to run out on ya'll, but she's on the move and I've got to catch her."

"As the world turns," Noah commented dryly. "You've certainly changed your tune. What happened?"

"No time to explain. If I have my way, she'll be at Joseph and Cady's party tomorrow, as my fiancé. But mums the word, and I mean it."

Doris was standing there with her tray at her side when Isaac turned to make his exit. "Make sure those deadbeats pay their tab before leaving, Doris," Isaac said with a wink.

"Yeah, right. Gotcha, boss," Doris agreed. No McCoy or Saucier would ever have to pay for a drink in his bar. She could read Isaac like a book.

* * *

He looked for her everywhere. When Isaac arrived at the motel, she was nowhere in sight. Marvin didn't know anything. He said she'd left the key on the dresser and if he hadn't been taking the trash out to the dumpster, he wouldn't have seen her leaving on her Roadster. All he could tell him was that she had turned left. Left could lead a lot of places, but the next thing he had tried, logically, was her house in the modest subdivision behind the park. She wasn't there. He had even peered into the garage, just in case. It had been empty. Isaac was just relieved no one had called the cops and reported him for snooping around. Where in the hell was she? Isaac was worried that she could've left town. Damn! Climbing back on his Harley, he had no choice but to leave it till morning, which wasn't very far off. Tomorrow was Joseph's party, so he couldn't leave town to look for her. If she didn't show that cute little butt of hers by noon, he'd call her Dad and see if he had a clue to where she might have gone. As Isaac turned toward Tebow, he couldn't help but smile at the memory of Avery and how incredible loving her had been. "This isn't over, my Wild Rose," he promised her. "I'll make you mine, or I'm not a real McCoy."

* * *

"What on earth happened to you?" Tricia Yeager pulled Avery into her living room. "Do you realize it's three o'clock in the morning?"

Sniffles were all she could manage to get out.

Suddenly, there was light as Tricia flipped a switch. "Are you crying? Are you hurt?"

"One question at a time, please. Can I crash here, just for tonight?" Forlorn, she felt deserted, and she didn't want to be alone.

Concern colored her friend's face. "Of course you can, Hon. You know that. Let me help you."

She'd left the motel and couldn't face going to her house, not tonight. Isaac probably wouldn't follow her, but in case he did, she didn't think she could face him.

"I'm not hurt. Well, just my heart. But, I don't think that's fatal." She let Tricia take her bag and lead her to the couch.

"What are you dressed in?" Never one to mince words, the stacked blonde crossed her arms and surveyed Avery. "Do you know you look like a bag lady?"

Avery fell face forward on the couch in a pitiful lump of self-pity. "Yes, but these clothes belong to him and I'm never taking them off again. I love him."

"I'll put on coffee. Why don't you wash your face and straighten that rat's nest of hair. You look like Rapunzel after she stuck her finger into an electric socket."

Yes, this was her friend, Miss Honest. Avery grumbled all the way to the bathroom and then shrieked a little when she looked in the mirror. "I guess safety isn't the only reason one should wear a helmet." After taming her locks, she dabbed her face with a washcloth, trying to get a handle on her emotions. What was she going to do? Maybe Isaac would just let this crazy marriage idea go. He might, but her Dad wouldn't. "Holy Hell, I'm in a mess," she moaned.

"I can tell you're upset. You're cussing, Miss Church Lady. Want to fix your own cup, or do you trust me?" Tricia leaned against the doorjamb and handed her a towel.

"I trust you," she breathed. "If you have any alcoholic libations, feel free to add them to the mix."

Tricia whacked her upside the head as she left the room. "That's the last thing you need. Meet me on the couch and blow your nose."

"Okay." She blew her nose, made a pit stop, then stood and smoothed the clothes she was wearing. As she ran her hands down them, she wished she didn't have to give them back. Tricia was waiting for her, so she went to join her. Accepting the big mug of fragrant brew, she sat down easy so as not to slosh hot coffee on either of them.

"So, tell me what's got you so stirred up."

Tricia was so pretty and had such stunning blonde hair. Watching her, Avery wished she were taller and thinner. "Isaac."

"McCoy, yes I know you've been in love with him your whole life." She waited, pinning Avery with a stare.

"He wants to marry me."

Tricia choked, setting her coffee down on the table in front of her. Avery had to smack her on the back. "What did you say?"

Avery rephrased the information. "Well, he didn't ask me to marry him. He told me we were getting married."

Tricia coughed. "Isn't that your fondest dream?" Apparently, she didn't see the problem.

"It's complicated. Did you get a newspaper today?"

Tricia spoke slowly, as if speaking to a child. "Yes, I always do. But, I haven't read it yet. Today was a busy day at the shop, and my partner hasn't been keeping regular work hours."

Avery made a face at her. Glancing around the room, she spied the Kerrville Daily News and got up to fetch it. Folding it to highlight the photo, she handed the damning evidence to her friend. "You'd better read this. You might not want to be in business with me anymore."

Taking it without looking down, Tricia grinned at her. "What did you do, rob a bank?"

Avery just stood there. Tricia looked, pulled the paper closer and looked again.

Wait for it, wait for it.

"Holy Mother of God!"

There it is.

"You're a hooker! When did you become Pretty Woman?"

Avery almost laughed at the horror on her friend's face. "I didn't turn any tricks. What I did was stay at the Shady Lady Ranch for a few weeks, but I was only there to learn how to please Isaac."

"You what?" Tricia cracked up. She held her sides, she was laughing so hard. "You, Avery Rose Sinclair, Miss Perfect, took sex lessons from prostitutes? I don't believe it." She paused, and then asked with a straight face. "Are you any good?"

Avery threw a pillow at the amused girl.

"Actually, I might be. Isaac seemed pleased." She couldn't help but smirk.

"You, Dawg!" Tricia pushed Avery on her butt. "You had sex with hunky Isaac McCoy? And he wants to marry you?" Her mouth was wide open in surprise. "You must be good."

Avery's skin flushed. She muttered something under her breath, but Tricia didn't stop talking.

"I don't understand why you aren't looking at bridal magazines. I expect to be maid of honor, by the way."

Sitting on the floor in front of the couch where she had landed, Avery rested her head on her knees and confessed with a more somber tone. "He only wants to marry me because Daddy saw the article and blamed him for the whole thing. My father showed up at the bar today to confront Isaac and caught me and him, you know, almost naked."

"Shit!" The off color word was said with a wealth of emotion. "What did you do? I can't imagine. Your dad, the preacher, almost caught you doing the dirty!"

A fresh groan escaped Avery's lips. "I know!" She'd been so focused on Isaac, she hadn't given her father much thought. "The shock could have killed him."

Tricia recovered before she did. "I want to know more about the whorehouse. How did your DIY sex-experiment happen to make the papers?"

Avery got up and sat down beside her. "The women were good to me and gave me the run of the place. I got to sit in when customers came, just like I was one of the girls and they taught me all sorts of dances, and uh, techniques. But I always practiced with toys, so no man ever touched me. One day, someone from here came to the ranch and recognized me. Madam said that this mystery man kept asking questions about me and I guess, obviously, he took my photograph with his phone. He must have had local contacts, because it made the Nevada paper, but I never dreamed it would ever run here. Guess I was wrong, huh?"

"Looks like it." Tricia stared at the image. "Why didn't you wear a wig or contacts, or do something to disguise yourself?"

"I don't know, I didn't think about it. My motivation was pure, so I was just happy being myself."

Turning to glare at her with a wicked grin, Tricia teased. "Lord, I bet this spreads like wildfire. Are you ready to be a celebrity?"

"Oh, God. Kill me now." Avery sighed and suffered, aloud. "I just hope it doesn't get out that I write racy romance novels."

This time Tricia almost fell off the couch. "What did you say? Are you trying to kill me? Do I even know you?"

Avery frowned, not happy that her friend was having such a good time over her problems. "I write love stories. Most of them are mild, but the last one was a bit risqué. But don't worry, only the girls know my pen name, Sable Hunter."

"You told them your pen name? What if they happened to mention that information to the mystery guy…the one from here? This could come back to bite you in the ass." It was obvious Tricia was excited; the ugly words were coming easier.

Avery hadn't thought of that. "Why would anyone care what I do?"

"Because it would be the most luscious piece of news to hit the Hill Country since LBJ was sworn in as President, that's why." Tricia got up and started pacing, waving the paper around. Avery watched her, helplessly. "You're well known in these parts. Everybody thinks you're just about perfect, your reputation WAS sterling and now everybody finds out you've spent time at a brothel AND you write smut?!? Are you kidding me? We're lucky CNN hasn't arrived to interview you!"

"Well…" Avery paused, looking perturbed. "Well, hell." Her disgust made Tricia laugh. "Since you put it like that, Dad will have a stroke if he finds out I'm writing erotic romances."

"I can't believe you told those women your business, talk about letting the cat out of the bag. You have a big mouth, you know? Huge. I could probably put a saucer in there sideways." She was joking, but Avery got her point.

"I'm too trusting, aren't I? I'm naïve."

"Yes, to put it simply. So, explain about Isaac again. When did he propose? And why did you turn him down?" Tricia calmed a bit and the two girls sat cross-legged, facing one another on the couch.

"I went to Hardbodies decked out in leather, riding my new motorcycle." Her friend's eyes grew big. The next part of the explanation, she said fast. "A bar fight started over me and the pole dance I did, according to Isaac—"

"You did a pole dance?"

Avery didn't even hear her friend's question. "After Isaac carted me off stage, we had sex. Dad found out. And, like I said before, he blamed Isaac because I tried to change everything about me so Isaac would think I could fit into his world."

There was a thick silence. Finally, Tricia answered, all amusement gone from her voice. "You don't seem different to me, you seem happy. Isaac makes you happy. Period."

Avery thought for a moment. She picked at the hem of Isaac's T-shirt, raising it to inhale the scent of his laundry detergent. How she wished he had recently worn it, although she had no trouble remembering his clean, sexy smell. "You may be right. I've always lived to please others, burying my dreams and desires, even my personality, to be what my family and friends thought I should be. Only when I thought about Isaac and how much I wanted him I could let the real me come out."

"So the pole dancing and motorcycle leather is you and the good-girl was a front?" There was a bit of skepticism on her face.

Avery's face fell. "No, I wouldn't say that. What am I doing Tricia? I don't think I'm either one, not really."

"You, Avery Sinclair are a wonderful person, that's what you are. Maybe, you're a mix. The real Avery can be whatever she wants to be, a biker babe or an angel. That's what I think."

The events of the day bore down on her heart and mind. Avery felt raw. Her very heart was chafed. Despite her disquiet, she yawned big. Reading the situation, Tricia got up and held out her hand. "Girl, you are dead on your feet. We need to get a few hours' sleep. Tomorrow, I have to open the shop at ten, and you're going to make my deliveries. And guess what? One of them goes to Tebow for Joseph and Cady's engagement party. They liked the prank flower arrangement we made per Joseph's request so much, we got the booking for the party and we already had the double wedding. We, Miss Wild Child, are on a roll!"

A look of panic came over Avery's face. The only thing she had garnered from Tricia's speech was that she expected her to make a delivery into McCoy territory. "No, no. I don't think so."

With a sly smile, her friend ignored Avery's trepidation. "Don't be such a chicken! It'll be early. Isaac won't be around the pavilion before noon. You'll be in and out of there as quick as a wink," Tricia assured her as she showed her to the spare bedroom. "Sleep well, now. I'll wake you up by eight."

"Funny, I'm not sleepy anymore. I can't believe you'd send me into the lion's den!" Chunking her Hello Kitty duffel off to one side, Avery knelt on the bed and began pulling back the covers. "Knowing how my luck's been running, Isaac will be standing guard at the gate."

"It seems to me your luck has been pretty good, future Mrs. McCoy." Tricia laughed as Avery stuck her tongue out. "Just keep your lips pressed together. Remember, you don't have to tell everybody everything, you know?"

"Yes, Mother." With a wink, Tricia left her alone. As Avery lay down to sleep, she couldn't keep Isaac off her mind. Lord, she loved him. Saying her prayers was a nightly ritual, and tonight was no different. And when she prayed, Avery couldn't lie. The truth always came out. So, tonight's prayer ended this way, "Lord, if there's any way you can let me have Isaac that would make him happy, please, let it happen. And keep him safe and in your care. Amen."

* * *

"Who's the pretty little blonde?" Ajax asked as he took a swig of the longneck. The bike rally at Luckenbach had attracted lots of hot babes, but Ajax was having trouble hooking up with one. Spitting on the ground, he cursed Isaac McCoy. That damn cowpoke had almost ruined him. Since he'd been blackballed, Ajax wasn't welcome at any of his regular hangouts. Being accused of 'excessive cruelty' to his subs was the last straw as far as he was concerned. The fact that the charge was true was of no consequence. Isaac McCoy was going to pay.

Jethro Diaz stood by the hulking bald man and eyed the delicate woman who was laughing way too loud and flirting with everything in pants. "That's a little girl named Harper. Now, she's exactly what you've been looking for, Ajax. From what I've heard, she can give you exactly what you need. You love to dish out pain and she is a pain junkie, if there ever was one."

"Who is she? Do I know any of the Dom's she's subbed for?" His cousin Crowbar was supposed to be keeping him informed of any hot honeys that came to town. Ajax scratched his balls and imagined how good it would feel to make that bitch scream.

"I don't know how you've missed her. She's caused quite a ruckus in the underground. Can't seem to make up her mind. Harper has fought who she is and what she wants. What I do know is that she used to keep company with one of those McCoy brothers. You know, the ones that own that big ranch out of Kerrville." Jethro threw the comment out there, not knowing he'd just said the magic word that sealed the deal for Ajax.

So, this was the rich boy's play-pretty. How friggin' perfect could you get? Fate was smiling on poor ole' Ajax Neal. Now, he had a new goal, to give McCoy's sub more pain than she could handle. How sweet it would be to play rough with something that belonged to that jerk McCoy. Ajax intended to break Isaac's toy and enjoy every scream he could beat out of her.

* * *

"What do you need me to do?" Isaac asked patiently. Libby was in a tizzy and he'd been instructed by Aron to consider himself at her disposal. People were scurrying right and left. The whole McCoy household was spinning in circles. Good thing, he had Levi to take up the slack at the bar. He wanted to help. Today was a red-letter day at Tebow and he needed to do his part. It was as simple as that. There was no way he could tell Libby that every cell in his body was screaming to go find Avery.

Isaac knew Aron would have been taking care of his fiancé's to-do list, but several of his prize cows had decided to calve early this morning. They had learned the hard way that it was better if one of them attended the birth. Last year, one of the big Beefmasters had suffered from a uterine prolapse. Sometimes when the calf was big, they would actually have to get a tractor and hook it to the calf and pull it out. The whole process sounded brutal, but every once in a while, it was necessary. But last time, the strain had been too much and the cow's uterus had come out with the calf and Aron had been forced to call in a vet to put the uterus back in place. If the cow received immediate attention, they didn't have to be culled and could be bred again. These registered cows were so valuable that he couldn't afford to risk their lives or the lives of their offspring, so duty called, and Isaac understood.

"I need you to go down to the pavilion and supervise everything. The party event and tent rental…people will be here by ten and I want you to make sure the tables and chairs and bar are set up the way they should be. Remember, the last time we had a gathering at the pavilion, the main tent collapsed and Mrs. Reynolds nearly had a heart attack."

Libby looked tired, Isaac thought. "You're trying to do too much, Libby. The house is full of people. Why don't you put everybody to work?" Pulling out a dining table chair, he guided her down into it.

She crossed her hands over her baby bump, a typical pregnant woman's gesture. Isaac thought it was sweet. How would Avery look pregnant? Libby's words brought him back to the present. "Everybody has offered to help. I've delegated almost everything. The only thing I can't get anybody to do is carry me around."

"My brother will do that for you, gladly." Isaac had no doubt. He cherished Libby. When she'd had her cancer scare, Aron had been scared to death. "There's nothing he wouldn't do for you."

"I can't wait to marry your brother, you know?" She took the glass of water that Isaac had handed her. "Although, as far as I'm concerned, we're a family, right now. A piece of paper isn't going to make me love any of you, including him, one bit more." She pulled Isaac down and kissed him on the cheek. "Thanks for helping me today. I want Joseph and Cady to have the best party two engaged people ever had. Just think how scared we were the first night after Joseph was paralyzed, and tonight, he'll dance with his beloved in his arms. Not every family is as blessed as ours, Isaac."

"That is the gospel truth, Libby." He knelt in front of her and hugged her tight. "Let me get out there and do what needs to be done. You take it easy. Promise?"

"Promise."

* * *

Isaac took his truck and set out. Before heading to the pavilion, he checked on Jacob who was watching a surveyor mark off the spot where he hoped to build Jessie a new house. The blueprints were to be her wedding present. While he was there, they had strolled over to the place where their parents and grandparents were buried. It was a peaceful spot. "Do you think they'd be proud of us?" Isaac asked. Even though he'd made great strides in his life, there were days when he questioned himself.

"I have no doubt about it, Brother." As they stood there looking at the pink granite headstone, Jacob held his hat in his hand and let out a long sigh. "You know, I've been meaning to tell you how proud I am of you. Sometimes, Aron and I have come down hard on you. We didn't mean anything by it. We just wanted you to grow up and be the man Daddy always said you'd be. Do you remember what he called us?"

Isaac smiled. "Yeah, he and Mom referred to us as 'the wrecking crew'. We were pretty rowdy, weren't we? I can still see Mom's face the day that she found me under the neighbor's house with all those hound puppies. I thought she'd never get through yelling at me."

"You know why, don't you?" Isaac shook his head. They hadn't reminisced like this in a long time. "She thought for sure you had fallen in that old uncovered well right over yonder. This spot was always one of our favorite places to play. I don't know how many times she asked Dad to fill it in, but he never did get around to it. That's one of the reasons we've never kept cows out here. That and all these damn stickers. Have you ever seen the like?" He pulled some of the Velcro like seedpods off of his pants.

"I guess we ought to fill in the well now. It's still an accident waiting to happen."

"Yes, I saw Crowbar peeking over in it a few minutes ago. I didn't know he was working with the surveyor during the day. He helps you and Levi out at night, doesn't he?"

"Yeah." Isaac looked up and waved at Levi's friend. "He does a lot of odd jobs for us."

"I'm glad the people of the community are giving him a chance. You know, he isn't really retarded, he's just slow. The word is that his birth was hard and the doctor had to use forceps, damaging his brain. Why they didn't do a Caesarian is a mystery to me."

Isaac knew Crowbar was fascinated with his playroom. He often wondered if the man had ever been with a woman. Thinking of being with a woman drove his mind right to Avery. Lord, he needed to hunt for her. He wished it was him breaking ground to build Avery a house. "Are the surveyors doing a good job for you?" This was something the brothers had discussed. The big house was getting crowded and as soon as all the babies were born, all of them living together would be almost impossible. However, no one wanted to move too far from the fold. The McCoys were a close-knit family and they wanted it to stay that way.

"Seem to be. Jessie loves this spot. She's going to be so happy here. It's not so far from the main house that we can't walk over, plus it's close to the hunting cabin. I couldn't ask for a prettier location."

"Tebow will be overrun with children soon. I wonder if they'll be as rambunctious as we were." Isaac couldn't help but imagine what a son of his would be like, or a daughter, one with violet eyes and big fat ringlets. A warm feeling came over his heart.

"I can almost guarantee they'll be just as mischievous as we were. Remember the time you drilled all the holes in the basement wall with that electric drill?"

"Hell!" Isaac rubbed his hand over his backside. "I can still feel the burn after all this time. Dad whaled the tar out of me."

Jacob chuckled. "Rightly so. You do realize that you missed electric wires by mere millimeters." He measured with his fingers the minute distance.

Isaac smiled. "They loved us, didn't they?"

"That they did, that they did." Jacob slapped Isaac on the back. "Where are you headed? I know you didn't come all the way out here just to check on me." He looked at Isaac's expression and whistled. "You pulled the short straw didn't you? Do the women have you jumping through their hoops?"

"Pretty much." Isaac headed back toward the truck. "Speaking of, I guess I'd better head out. What are your plans for the rest of the day?"

"I'll be heading over that way to check the grub. Cady requested that I make my famous Jack Daniel's sauce for the pulled pork."

"Sounds good. I'll see you there." He left his brother studying blueprints for the big log home he was determined to build for Jessie and the baby. Driving the short distance to the pavilion, Isaac noticed there were some dark clouds on the horizon. Crap! He hoped no rainstorms came to put a damper on the festivities. The 'gathering place' as his Mom had called it was set in a grove of oak and pecan trees, and a picturesque stream bubbled nearby. A few of the cowhands had been called over to do whatever they were told. Lance and Skye were tending the huge BBQ smoker where the briskets and pork shoulders were smoking and the whole pig roasted slowly in a special pit that had been dug in the ground. Parking, he checked with everyone and passed on a few messages from Libby. Thankfully, he didn't have to wait very long before the panel trucks arrived with all the stuff they'd rented—serving tables, round tables, chairs, tents, staging and audio equipment, plus all the stemware, plates and linens. The event planners had brought a crew, but Isaac instructed several of their men to pitch in and soon everything was set up. Now, all that was lacking were the decorations, and that wasn't his problem. Flowers and balloons were not his forte. But the very thought of all that frivolity seemed to conjure up the florist van. He was just about to go ask if he could help unload when one of his men called his name.

"Isaac, what do you want me to do with this portable PA system? It doesn't go with the band's stuff, does it?" Trace, Lance's right hand man was new, but he was working out well. He'd been hired to take the place of Morton, who had been arrested for kidnapping the sheriff's fiancé. From now on, Roscoe would do a background check before hiring anyone. Trace was a keeper. Isaac was impressed with his willingness to pitch in and his easy-going personality.

"It goes up here on the main table. That's where the toasts will be made. After you hook it up, just lay that microphone on the table. I'll find the stand in a minute." He signed a delivery receipt, handed it to the bored truck driver and gave Trace a hand as he helped a couple of teenagers set up the steam tables where the food would be kept warm for the buffet. When he came back to the pavilion, there were centerpieces on some of the tables, and up on the stage there was a figure. Isaac took a second look. What in the hell was going on? "Avery?" He couldn't believe his eyes. "Hell, yeah!" Things were looking up!

* * *

There was a God, and he was mad at her. This, Avery knew to be fact. Why, o why, had she let Tricia talk her into delivering the flowers to Tebow? 'Oh, you'll be out of there long before Isaac shows up, I'm sure he sleeps late. It'll be a breeze,' she'd said. Tricia's ass was grass. Hell, it was her own fault, she knew it. Isaac McCoy wasn't helping matters either, that was for certain. At this very moment, she was so mad at him she could spit. But unfortunately, her mouth was otherwise occupied.

Her tall, broad-shouldered bad-boy was laughing at her.

"How did you get your lips stretched around that big old thang, Darlin?" He looked at her with a twinkle in his sapphire blue eyes.

There was no way she could talk with the broad, round head in her mouth, so she glared at Isaac for all she was worth. He was having entirely too much fun at her expense. It wouldn't be so bad, if she could just forget how they'd parted. He had proposed and she had turned him down. Yes, she was certifiable. Great! They were beginning to attract an audience. Several of the ranch hands and deliverymen were gathering around to stare at her. That's all she needed! Now her reputation was permanently in the toilet. Oh, yeah, that's right, it had already been in the toilet. Everyone thought she was a loose woman. 'Somebody flush, already!'

Good gravy, he was trying to help her. Avery felt her face flame. "Can you open your mouth any wider, Baby? I can't seem to pull it out." A loud guffaw from behind him made Avery clamp her teeth down on the smooth surface instead of trying to let go. It was obvious that Isaac's double entendres were not going unnoticed.

"Now, don't you bite down on my Peavey, Sugar." Titters of amusement floated across the stage and Avery growled, making Isaac laugh all the harder. "What kind of engagement party can we have if you swallow the microphone, Doll?"

That was it! Avery planned his demise as the man of her dreams had the audacity to chuff her under the chin and even kiss her on the nose! Sheesh! Any other time, she would have given her Elvis Presley record collection to feel his mouth on her skin. And the humiliation wasn't over, oh, no. It just kept getting better. "You know, there are better things you could have between these lips. All you had to do was ask."

A knowing look from him told her that he knew exactly how pissed off he was making her. Arrgghh! With a gasp of indignation, her jaws opened just wide enough for Isaac to pull the microphone free. "That's my girl," he praised her.

"Well, I never," she sputtered, ready to make mince-meat out of the male chauvinist who looked like a million dollars in his tight black jeans and cowboy boots.

"Not exactly true, Miss Sinclair, if my memory serves me correctly. Something tells me, that if you play your cards right, you might just get the chance to please me again. In fact, I'm counting on it."

Do it again? She could be persuaded to pleasure him again, that is, if she didn't murder him first. His swagger was infuriating, his sexual prowess was legendary and her eyes were drawn to the speed bump in his jeans like a bee to pollen.

"See anything you like, Cupcake?"

Folding her arms over her chest, Avery sought to erect a barrier of protection between them. "Don't be so egotistical, Isaac." Today wasn't working out anything like she'd planned. All she wanted to do was get in to the ranch, deliver the fresh flower arrangements, and make it out before anybody saw her or could ask about that blasted newspaper article. "I wasn't looking at your groin." She choked the last word out. "You have a cocklebur on your – uh – coc – uh – fly." Hell, she needed to get out of here before she died from chronic mortification.

With a wicked, sexy grin, he removed the prickly little seedpod from the front of his pants. "I've been out playing in the bushes. Shucks, I thought you were checking out my package." He winked at her, making her blood pressure spike to new levels. "Just for my peace of mind, Precious, explain to me how the microphone got in your mouth in the first place."

Lord Have Mercy! Would the humiliation ever end? Avery couldn't think of a believable lie, so she stuck with the unbelievable truth. "Before I came over, Tricia had teased me about how big my mouth was. She said I couldn't keep my mouth shut to save my life." What she wouldn't tell him was the secret Tricia warned her to keep, about her erotic romance writing. Maybe if she didn't dwell on it, nothing else bad would happen to her. When Isaac's amusement brought his beautiful dimples into view, she almost lost her train of thought. Now, where was she? "And when I put the flowers on the head table, that microphone was just lying there and I got to wondering..." Her words trailed off. Why wouldn't the floor open up and swallow her when she needed it to?

Much to Avery's surprise, Isaac pushed a strand of her hair behind one ear. God, if he started to touch her, she would probably jump him. "Let me guess…" Isaac offered dryly. "…you wondered if your mouth was big enough to manage the handheld?" His fingers traced down her face, caressing her cheek and tugging at her lower lip. Avery trembled. "Did you get those pretty little white teeth hung up behind the guard band?" He picked up the mic and rubbed his finger on the rim. "Do you have any idea how sexy that was, seeing those plump pink lips in that provocative position?"

He was turning her on. It was time to leave before she did something she'd regret later. Enough. "Thanks for making me mad, Isaac. If you hadn't baited me like that, I might still be wired to the sound system. Excuse me." She turned to leave.

"Uh, no way." Isaac grabbed her by the wrist. "Stay. You just saved me a trip. I was about to come looking for you. I want you to be my date for the party."

Avery stared up at him. If he'd wanted her to be his date, why hadn't he asked her before? Nope, not gonna happen. She'd made up her mind to leave him alone, and being near him now was just sweet torture. "Thank you, but no. I have some more deliveries to make." With a small smile, Avery pulled her hand from his and fled like the devil himself was after her.

Well, hell! Isaac watched the adorable doll take off like a ruptured redbug. At least he knew she was still in town. He was sorry to see her go, but he sure enjoyed watching her leave. Damn she had a fine ass! Isaac didn't do much business in a flower shop, but he guessed he would start. The women he used to keep company with weren't interested in him for the posies he could purchase. They were more into the pleasure he could provide.

* * *

"Isaac!" Lance motioned him to join a few of the men at the bar. "It's too early to drink. How about some coffee?"

"I think I'll pass." Isaac held up a hand in greeting. "I just got a better offer." Pushing his hat down on his head, he took off to follow Avery. He remembered the name on the van. Heart Strings. Yep, he knew right where that little shop was located, right across from the Fire Department. And the delivery van had been red, so it should be easy to spot. Isaac kept his eyes out for it as he headed down the road toward town. God, he was relieved to see her.

The drive into Kerrville only took about fifteen minutes. First, he drove past the florist shop, but there were no vans parked there. Hoping to get lucky, he made a few blocks and let out a breath of relief as he saw her pull into the Baptist church parking lot and walk to the back of the van. She was dressed all in pink—pink jeans, a pink camisole top, pink tennis shoes and a pink sparkly ribbon braided into her hair. Avery looked like cotton candy, and he couldn't wait to have another sweet taste. Pulling in beside her, he arrived at the rear of her vehicle as she pulled out a red and white basket of roses. "Are these for me?" When she turned, he had to catch the basket as she tossed it up in the air with fright.

"Land sakes! Isaac, what are you doing here?" He got transfixed watching her chest rise and fall as she panted. Avery didn't miss his ogling, and threw his earlier comment back at him. "See something you like, Stud-Muffin?"

Her tart little retort tickled him to death. "Yes, Ma'am, I certainly do." God, he was going to enjoy being married to her. Just a few days ago, this thought would have shocked him, but now, it seemed to be the most natural thing in the world.

"Why are you following me?" She huffed the sweetest little protest, retrieved the flowers from his grasp and edged around him. "Did you forget to buy flowers for your latest flame? You know, just because we slept together yesterday, doesn't mean you can't buy flowers for your girlfriends. Do you want me to run back to the shop and get you a dozen roses?" Not giving him a chance to respond, she set out toward the side door of the sanctuary and slipped into the house of God.

Isaac was right behind her. The church might fall to the ground. He hadn't made a practice of attending too many worship services. "No, Prissy Pants. Not unless you're hankering for some roses. I'll be glad to buy you some. There's no other girlfriend, single or plural. You and I are practically engaged. Why would I want to buy presents for some other girl?"

At the word engaged, she whirled around. "I ***don't*** want any roses. I'm ***not*** your girlfriend and we ***aren't*** practically engaged. We're in a church, Isaac. Aren't you afraid of getting struck by lightning for telling a lie?"

Chapter Six

'Me thinks the lady doth protest too much', or at least that's what he hoped. His Avery was something. He even liked to watch her fuss. She had the most beautiful face. He didn't know which feature he liked best—those high cheek bones, soft violet eyes, dark long lashes or plump pink lips. No, he knew, his favorite part was her nose that tilted up the tiniest bit. There were so many places he wanted to trail kisses, beginning with the soft skin on her neck and following the line of her graceful sloping shoulders. Avery was a soft, curvy woman that was shaped the way God intended a woman to be shaped. And he knew several things he wanted to do with that braid. Wrap it around his fist while he took her from behind was the first thing that came to mind.

Avery shuffled her feet. She could almost hear the thoughts in Isaac's mind as he catalogued her assets, and it unnerved her. She dropped her gaze and turned to straighten the bottom of the lace runner. As she stooped over, he was sorely tempted to run his palms over that heart-shaped rump. God, he would love to hold those cheeks apart and ram home. "No, Baby, the Lord knows I ain't tellin' no fibs. If he's omnipotent, he can hear my every thought, and what I'm thinking right now is what a lovely job he did creating your sweet little tush."

"We are in a holy place, Isaac." She turned and shushed him like they were in a library. "Have some respect!" Her hands on her hips brought his attention to the narrowness of her waist. Yea, he couldn't wait to tug her close again.

"Yes, we are in a holy place." Isaac licked his lips. "If I remember my Sunday school lessons correctly, didn't God tell Moses to take off his shoes on that holy ground? Why don't we show more respect and take off that little pink top you have on? I swear, you look good enough to eat. I don't know if I ever told you, but you have the most beautiful body. I can promise you one thing. I'm going to give you a honeymoon you will never forget. And it don't matter where we go, 'cause I ain't gonna let you get out of the bed."

Avery closed her eyes, wishing he would just disappear. "Why are you being this way? Are you determined to break my heart?"

The pain in her voice got his attention, damned quick. His tone totally changed. "Avery, look at me. Now."

Reluctantly she met his gaze. "Do I need to remind you that just a couple of days ago you couldn't wait to see the last of me? Do you think I'm stupid?" she huffed incredulously. "It doesn't take a genius to know the only reason you want to marry me is because you feel guilty."

Seeing the hurt on her face, he whispered a word that shouldn't be repeated in church. What a fiasco! Making a grab for her, she frustrated him by stepping quickly out of his clasp. Her lack of self-confidence tore at his heart. Walking to the table in front of the pulpit, he placed his hand on the Bible. "This is just one, but I'd swear on a stack of Bibles that I didn't lie to you. I'm not ready to give up on us. I want to be with you, more than you'll ever know, Avery Rose Sinclair. Let me explain. Hear me out, that's all I ask. Please?"

Avery looked at his face. It was confusing. He sounded so sincere. She dug her fingernails in her palm as a reminder to stay strong. Because he was sincere, sincerely trying to do the right thing. There was no way she could be rude to him. Belonging to Isaac was her fondest dream. Just because it was slipping through her fingers didn't give her the right to be mean. "Okay, we can talk. I'm not agreeing to anything, but I've always enjoyed spending time with you. Now is no different."

Not exactly the level of enthusiasm he was hoping for, but he'd take any time with her he could get. All he wanted was a chance to change her mind. "Is that your last delivery?"

"Yes, but I rode to work with Tricia. I spent the night at her house last night. So I don't have my motorcycle."

"Remind me to speak to you about your *ride*," he emphasized the last word. "I know you didn't go home, or to the motel."

"How'd you know I didn't go home?"

"I went looking for you after the ruckus at the bar. I was worried about you."

Avery's heart swelled at this revelation, but she stifled a smile for her own good so he wouldn't see how his concern had affected her. He was staring at her with such heat that she had to look away. "Come on, let's go." He took her by the hand. "I'll follow you to the shop. Then you're going to spend the rest of the day with me at the ranch. Joseph and Cady's party is tonight, and I want you to be my date. We have some serious talking to do."

Avery pulled her hand from Isaac's grip. This was just too much. "How about if I fix you some lunch at my house and we have a civilized conversation? I don't think the party is a good place to discuss this."

"I'll change your mind."

"You can try."

Damn, she was sassy. As she sashayed by him, he reached and grabbed her, pulling her hard against his body for a quick kiss which stole the air from her lungs.

"No fair," she whimpered. "You know I crave you more than chocolate." Was there any use pretending?

Chuckling, he let her go. "That's what I'm counting on. Consider that kiss a down-payment on what I plan to collect later."

In a daze, she left the church, locking it carefully behind them. He helped her in the van, fastened her seat belt and gave her the most tender, most luscious kiss she'd ever fantasized. Nothing she'd ever written in any of her books even came close. He shut the door and walked off to his truck, starting the engine before she opened her eyes and remembered what planet she was living on. "Wow." Was all she could say as she drove to the shop and took time to tell Tricia what was going on. "Remind me to tell you the microphone story."

"The what story?" Her friend was about to ask questions, but when she looked up and saw Isaac standing in the door waiting for Avery, Tricia pushed her toward him. "You can tell me later. Go." So, she did.

Isaac's King Ranch had bench seats. He led her to the driver's side door, opened it and before she could squirm, squeal or skedaddle he picked her and placed her gently in the seat. And when he'd settled behind the wheel, he instructed, "Sit close, I want to snuggle." She hesitated, but when he curled his big hand around her thigh and pulled her toward him, she followed his instructions. This was going to kill her. So, she'd inched up close, trying to keep a little distance. But he made a game of it, tugging and tickling her till he had her giggling. And when he tucked his fingers underneath her leg, there was no way he could miss how she trembled. "Now, lay your head on my shoulder and let's talk." Avery tentatively placed her head on his shoulder and when he turned and kissed her forehead, she couldn't help it. She wrapped both hands around his muscular arm. Her death must have been quick and painless, because she was in heaven.

"Why don't you already have a date for the party tonight?" Whoops! She hadn't intended to ask that question. It just popped out on its own.

Isaac didn't answer right away. Instead he took off his Stetson and tossed it in the back seat. She didn't often see him in a cowboy hat. God, this was a whole new level of sexy.

"I can't do any proper kissing with my hat on. Now, to answer your question, I don't date much. In case you haven't heard, my reputation is in sore need of repair." When he put on his blinker, Avery peeked out of the truck to try and see where they were. They certainly hadn't made it to her house. As far as she could tell, he had pulled down a side street into somebody's pasture access road. "I can't wait to get my hands on you, Avery. Your house is just too damn far away." Parking, he adjusted his seat until it was pushed all the way back. "Come here, Baby. Straddle me."

Avery thought about it, but only for a moment. She didn't understand this. It seemed more like a dream than reality. But she wanted it, God, how she wanted Isaac McCoy. "All right, Isaac. Are you sure I'm not too heavy?" She couldn't miss the confusion on his face.

"What are you talking about? I am six-five and weigh over two-forty. Next to me, you're just a little bit of a thing."

Facing him, she was partially standing with one knee on the seat, when he took her by the waist and pulled her over and on top of him. Her legs fit neatly, one by the door and one folded down beside his hip. The really intriguing part was that her sex settled perfectly over the swell in his jeans.

"Now, doesn't that feel good?"

"Yes." She sighed. Her body softened and even though there were two layers of material between their bodies, it seemed like she could feel his heat. Avery had to bite her lip to keep from groaning.

"Now," Isaac said with a growl. "In case nobody ever told you, it's not a good idea to go biting your lip around an already overheated male like the one you're on top of right now." He bucked his hips off the seat and his throbbing bulge pressed firmly into Avery. Her entire body shuddered with ecstasy and she couldn't miss the fire blazing behind his blue eyes. "See how good we fit together, like two pieces of a puzzle." Isaac began rubbing her back and down her arms as if he was gentling a skittish little animal.

She bit down on her lip again and luxuriated in the bliss when Isaac bucked his hips. She wasn't sure if she would be able to keep from chewing her lips right off if this was the action it elicited from the hunk underneath her at the moment. "You're making me crazy," she admitted with a whimper. Lord, she couldn't breathe. There was no way she could draw air into her lungs. This was just insane. Isaac was looking at her so intently, she felt trapped in his gaze. It was wild. There was so much heat and hunger in his eyes. Avery tried to reason this all out, but she couldn't think straight. All she wanted was to feel his lips on hers one more time. She was tempted to lean forward and just take what she wanted. God, she wanted him so much. "Kiss me now, please. Don't make me wait."

Damn! She wanted him enough to ask. That was so hot. With shaking hands, he framed her face

"Look at you," he whispered. "I don't know where you came from. Heaven, I guess." Reverently, he kissed her eyelids and her soft, smooth cheeks. And when she turned her mouth and sought his, he thought he would shout from sheer happiness. She fit her mouth over his and the tip of her tongue played along the seam. "Kiss me, Baby," he begged and when she opened her mouth to let him in, he thought he would come in his shorts. God, she was like honey. Hot. Velvet. The sweetest thing he'd ever tasted in his life. A little whimper of need came from her throat and he tightened his arms around her, feasting at her lips, making up for the lost years, lonely nights, and the broken dreams of a lifetime of wanting something he never thought he'd be lucky enough to have.

Isaac bit at her lips, licking them, sucking them, loving the fact that she held nothing back. Sliding his mouth to her cheek, he gasped for breath.

"You're a really good kisser," she whispered and followed him, seeking to meld their mouths back together.

"I'm glad," he said between kisses. "Can I touch you?" Asking was new to him, but Isaac didn't want to do anything to scare his angel. She was breathing so hard, he felt guilty. "Do you feel okay? Do you want to stop?"

"No, please no. Don't stop. Touch me." She picked up his hands and put them on her breasts. There was no doubt where she wanted to be touched. Happy to oblige, he cupped her breasts. The first touch was so soft, and she pushed her bounty into his hands, begging for more.

"Steady, we'll get there." He nibbled and sucked at her lips, first the top and then the bottom.

Everything within her wanted to cry out for what she wanted. While Tricia had prepared breakfast this morning, she'd made use of her partner's laptop. Her curiosity had gotten the best of her. Avery wanted to know everything she could about the Dom/sub relationship Isaac had mentioned to her. Now that she knew what turned him on, she ached to know more. What little she'd learned affected her in ways she never expected. Avery wanted to submit. She needed to submit. "Isaac, I need you to..." she started to just ask, but would it sound dumb? "Would you let me sub—"

The blowing of a car horn startled them both. "Damn." He was so hard, he was afraid it would break off if anything bumped it. "What were you about to say?"

"We need to go, Isaac. That truck wants to drive by us." She maneuvered herself off his lap, embarrassed to be caught by the occupants of the other vehicle. Had the proverbial bell saved her?

"I want to know what you were going to say." He bit out the words as he backed over to one side to let the annoying driver pass.

Her courage had faded fast. Could she ask him to teach her submission? Would that be like asking for a commitment from him? It wasn't marriage, but it was a type of commitment, nevertheless. Just the thought of her Dad trying to force him to marry her sent a fresh wave of humiliation over her. She'd better give this a little bit more thought. "Nothing."

"It didn't sound like nothing," Isaac pressed.

Avery turned to look out the window. Damn! The moment had passed. "It was nothing important. We should get going."

"We'll talk about it when we get to your house. I won't forget." He didn't sound angry. What he sounded was desperate. And that she didn't understand. Even though, he held out his hand for her to draw closer, Avery politely turned him down. She had to get a handle on herself before they got to her house. The last thing she needed was to just fall into bed with him without both of them knowing exactly what they were doing.

"Sitting over there by yourself isn't going to solve anything."

No, but it did help her think. When he pulled into her driveway, she used her garage door opener to let them in. By the time he shut his driver's side door, she was out of the truck and going in the kitchen door of her small cottage. "Come in, please," said the fly to the spider.

"You ought to lock your doors, Sweet Cheeks. If you don't, there's no telling who'll walk in on you." She didn't argue with him. Perhaps he was right. She was too trusting. "I guess it's a good thing you won't be living by yourself any longer." He walked around her little house as if he were looking for something. Maybe he was looking for evidence of the real her. If that were the case, he was out of luck. Her house didn't hold any secrets. They were all in her heart.

"Stop that, Isaac, I'm not moving in with you." She had walked into her kitchen and went right to the refrigerator. The cool air felt good to her overheated body. "I don't have a lot to choose from. Perhaps we should have stopped for take-out." Inspiration struck. "I know. We'll have macaroni and cheese. I think I have some canned milk for it. That's fast and filling." Hooking her foot under the leg of the kitchen stool, she pulled it over and agilely climbed up and stood on tiptoe, straining to reach the very top shelf.

"Dammit! Avery, what do you think you're doing?"

Avery jumped at the sudden voice, lost her footing and fell right into Isaac's arms. "What did you yell at me for? You scared me. I was just trying to reach the box so I could fix you some lunch, you behemoth! I keep it up high, because it's fattening. I won't eat it so often if it's hard to reach. Put me down," she demanded. Her heart was beating so hard, she was afraid it would pop out of her chest.

He didn't put her down. Instead he backed up and sat down in a dining table chair, with her still in his arms. "Don't do that. You might fall and hurt yourself, and that won't ever do. You belong to me. I want to take you home with me. Did you know that?" Isaac spoke so matter-of-factly, that Avery was momentarily at a loss for words. Lord, it felt good to be held close. His chest was so broad and his arms so strong that she felt completely protected and safe from the world. But, she had to keep reminding herself this was an illusion. Isaac had no real interest in her. He was only feeling guilty for taking her virginity.

Wiggling until he released her, Avery put the width of the room between them. "Please, don't talk like that. I'm not moving in with you. You know that." Oh, this was going to be harder than she thought. It was like turning down a huge lottery win after having spent your life savings on the ticket. Isaac could move fast for a big man. Before she knew it she was caught up against him. He held her hands gently behind her back and she was totally at his mercy. Thrills shot through her. She knew what he was doing. This was classic Dom behavior. He made her feel helpless, and helpless before Isaac was heady, indeed. His eyes searched her face, as if for any sign of panic, then he claimed her lips, giving her a long, soft, consuming kiss. When he drew back, Avery was dazed with pleasure. With her eyes closed she instinctively leaned forward, wanting more pleasure.

"Feel, Avery. Feel what I do to you." He bucked his hips, pressing his cock into her softness. "Feel what you do to me." Nudging her forward, she couldn't help but rub her breasts against his chest. Dang, she was like a cat and he was a huge hunk of catnip. Intoxicating.

"Do you know how rare this is? How can we turn our backs on this? I thought you said you loved me?"

Wiggling anew, she tried in vain to get loose. "I was acting crazy. Besides, you don't love me, Isaac. You are only willing to marry because you feel sorry for me and you think you've contributed to my fall from grace."

Her huffy little speech was pushing her breasts against him and Isaac was having a hard time concentrating. So, he let her go and paced to the other side of the room. It was time to come clean. This was just too important. "You want the truth? I've been attracted, infatuated—hell, almost obsessed with you for years." Avery looked at him with disbelief. "Remember what I said to you in front of the drug store?"

How could she forget? She remembered every moment her eyes had been privileged to feast on Isaac

McCoy, but she didn't believe him. "Yes, but when I came to you at the bar, you said—"

With hands on hip, he studied her, weighing his words. "I never said I was smart. In my own stupid way I was trying to protect you."

"And now that I've contaminated myself at the brothel, and thrown myself at you...it's okay?"

Isaac stepped right up to her, taking her by the shoulders. "Don't you dare say a word against yourself, not a word. You hear me?" He was angered by her insinuation that she was anything less than perfect. "The only man who has been lucky enough to touch you has been me, and you are exquisite."

His conviction took her breath away. "So, what are you proposing?"

"I am proposing. That's exactly what I'm doing."

Not that she was considering it, but she couldn't help but be curious. It was like a child being let loose in FAO Schwartz. "How would that work, our being married? Would it be a real marriage or just until the hoopla dies down?"

Isaac paused, thinking. What was she saying? Didn't she want a real marriage? Better focus on the image instead of the physical. "You'll be a McCoy. We're involved with all kinds of benevolent organizations. Hell, we have a few of our own. You won't just be a barkeep's wife."

That just made Avery mad. She pulled out of his arms and put at least three feet between them. It was hard. He was everything she'd ever wanted. Being near him like this just made her ache. "But it's you I wanted, not the McCoy name or the McCoy land or the McCoy money. Wherever you were, whatever you were doing, that's what I wanted to be a part of—you. And I know all about your benevolent activities, you know that. I was usually right there with you."

"Wanted?" Past tense? If he hadn't been so pissed, he would have appreciated the color in her cheeks, the way her nose turned up and how she slung that sexy hair back over one shoulder. Avery was hot. There was just no two ways about it.

Her heart dipped down and a sinking feeling hit her in the pit of the stomach. This was so final. Was she nuts? No, she was being brave and generous. And smart. "Shot-gun weddings went out with the demise of the wagon train. People don't get married to salvage reputations nowadays." Or at least she didn't. She wanted Isaac, but not against his will.

"Are you turning me down, Avery?" He literally growled at her. "I promised your father that I'd take care of you."

"I can take care of myself, Isaac. The flower business is blooming and I have a side job that I'm quite good at." Seeing his skeptical look, she nearly spilled the beans, but the news that she wrote racy romances would only add to the confusion. "And as far as love and sex are concerned, you've given me a great gift and I'll cherish the memories forever."

That didn't seem to satisfy him. "You're going to make bouquets with Tricia Yaeger? That's what you want to do with your life? You'd rather do that than be with me?" Even though he fought it, Isaac knew that, deep down, he questioned his value as a man. That was one of the reasons he gave so freely. There was always this doubt that he deserved to be loved.

She walked up to a chair and held on to the back of it, tightly. If she didn't grab on to something, she was going to grab on to him. "It's not that I don't want to be with you. You know better than that. It was me who pursued you, not vice-versa. This whole thing isn't fair to you, and I want no part of it." Now, she needed a quick subject change to get his mind off of their involvement. "And, as far as the flower shop goes? Tricia is doing a great job. She believes in going the extra mile. Did you see what she made up for Cady from Joseph? I helped her come up with the idea. It turned out real cute." Certainly, working with Tricia wasn't all she wanted to do with her life. Isaac just didn't understand how hungry she was to do something for herself.

Isaac grumbled under his breath. "I should have known you were behind that. But, back to the more important things you said." A wicked little smile escaped his lips. "You just said you want to be with me. That's all I was waiting to hear." He began to slowly walk toward her. "I'm not giving up, Avery. And as for this great gift I gave you, if you mean the passion we shared, that's just the first installment, Doll-Face. I mean to make love to you over and over again. Bottom line, I'm not taking no for an answer. You will marry me, Young Lady."

Hearing her own words thrown back at her, she now knew the futility of trying to force one's will upon another person. "We'll see." Her mother always said that, and it was always her way of saying 'no' without saying it. Surely, it would work with Isaac. She had no doubt he would come to his senses. Her father would back off once the gossip dissipated, and they could just resume life as normal. "Lunch wasn't a good idea. I'm not really hungry. No hard feelings, but I'd like for you to leave now." How hard it was to request that of him. She looked at his beautiful face, his proud, hard, powerful body and knew that when she went to bed tonight and turned off the lights, she would regret she hadn't rushed to his arms and accepted his proposition. As far as marriage proposals went, it was unique, but she knew it couldn't be heartfelt. Isaac was suffering from a case of misplaced chivalry. He was trying to be her knight in shining armor. Little did he know, she didn't want a knight on a shining white steed, she just wanted her motorcycle riding warrior in black leather. He was all the man she had ever wanted, but couldn't have.

"You know what you need?" Watching her clutch that chair like it was a lifeline made him want to rip it out of her grasp and chunk it against the wall. It was all Isaac could do to keep his hands off of her. "I ought to turn you over my knee and warm your butt till it's rosy red." Right before he slid into her as deep as he could go.

Avery was about to insist, again, that he left, until she looked at him closely. By all standards, she was still fairly innocent, but she wasn't stupid. Isaac was aroused. He wanted her. He craved her. Okay. Now, this she could deal with. Could she risk it? She might never have a wedding veil and orange blossoms, but she could have untold nights of bliss. For as long as he wanted her, Avery could be his. There would be pain when it was over, but if this was all of Isaac she could ever have, she wanted it. Calling upon all that the girls had taught her, Avery proceeded to flirt. "Promises, promises." With that she moved by him, putting a little wiggle in her walk.

Isaac watched her parading her curvy little rear right by him. What was she trying to do? Drive him insane? "What the hell do you mean by that?" As he devoured her with his eyes, his jaw dropped as she skimmed her shirt over her head, right in front of him.

"God, it's hot in here. When I get my stuff from Tricia's, I'll wash your clothes and return them to you. I enjoyed wearing those lounge pants. I think I'll order me some." She was chattering like a magpie, totally oblivious to what she was doing to him. The sexy little minx just walked right out of the room. Isaac followed with his mouth open. His tongue would have been hanging out, but he managed to hold on to some decorum. He couldn't believe it. She rummaged around in her closet, seemingly oblivious to what she was doing to him. God, she had a beautiful back. There was this lickable indention down her spine that ended in the sexiest pair of dimples just over her crease. He remembered that much from having his hands all over her last night. Damn, he wanted her again. Now.

Finding what she was looking for, she pulled out a T-shirt that had seen better days, and began to shuck her pink jeans. Holy Jesus! She didn't have a damn thing on under them. Clearing his throat, he held on to the bedstead to keep from grabbing her. "Answer my question, love. What did you mean by 'promises, promises?'"

Tossing the clothes into a hamper, she pulled on a pair of bikini panties. "Honestly, the idea of a spanking turns me on. I didn't have a whole lot of time this morning, but I checked out what it means to be submissive."

Turning to face him, she lifted her arms over her head to loosen the braid, which lifted those luscious breasts of her up. Isaac's rod rose with them as if it were attached by a lead line.

"What I read turned me on. If you had decided to, you know, explore that with me, I think I would have liked it. The idea of you dominating me made me wet."

Isaac couldn't believe the words that were coming out of her mouth. "Do you know what you're saying, Avery? You think you would enjoy me controlling you in bed?"

She caught her bottom lip in her small white teeth and smiled dreamily…the thought of Isaac's bucking hips dancing through her already foggy mind. "Oh, yeah. I would have liked that a lot." She closed her eyes and made the sexiest little whimpering noise he'd ever heard. "I would love for you to push me to my knees, command me to suck you, holding my hair in your fist as I make you feel good. But what I would like most is for you to push me on the bed, face down and command me to be still while you mounted me. Oh, God!" She ran her hands down her body as Isaac stood mesmerized, stone-hard, frozen in lust. "What I wouldn't have given to experience that with you, Isaac." She sighed.

His voice hoarse, Isaac answered, "It's not too damn late. We're standing right here by a perfectly good bed." His sex was hugely erect, throbbing and leaking pre-cum.

She bit back a grin. Her plan was working nicely. There was no denying it. They were both aroused, and the very air between them was electric. "No, it's not too late," she agreed. "I want you, more than you know."

Isaac started toward her. "So, you'll marry me?"

Remembering what she had read in the very basic article on BDSM, Avery sank down in a classic slave position, on her knees, hands behind her back and head bowed. "No, sir, I can't marry you. But, I will do my best to make your every dream come true." Despite her brave words, Avery realized there were still vestiges of hope in her heart. Maybe she still had a chance to make him love her, if she proved to him they were totally compatible.

Relief washed over Isaac. It wasn't over. He still had a chance. "God, you're beautiful in that position. Give me your hand." She did and he drew her to her feet. Taking her chin in his hand, he rubbed his lips over her mouth, marking her. Kissing the corner of her mouth, he whispered, "I want you so much."

"You can have me," she stated simply. "I only want to please you."

"You're speaking my language, Baby." Avery was his dream. His greatest fantasy. He pulled her to him and she cuddled into his arms, like she was seeking comfort as well as pleasure. Slipping his hands in the sides of her panties, he pushed down, dropping to his knees in front of her.

"Get up off your knees. What are you doing?"

"I'm getting my sub ready to take to bed. There's a lot you don't understand, yet. Here's your first lesson." He looked deep into her eyes. "You belong to me. As long as I'm your Dom, I take care of you."

'As long as', she heard him use that clarification. "Oh." Oh well, she understood that. And she could live with it. His touch made tingles of awareness shoot over her body. He rubbed her arms, his palms gliding from her forearms, up to her shoulders, where he tenderly pulled down her bra straps. Reaching behind her, he unfastened it. Goosebumps rose over her whole body. Being the object of Isaac's intense scrutiny was heady, indeed. This bra was nothing like the others he'd seen. It was just a plain white one with a little rosette in the deep vee of her cleavage. So when he leaned over and placed a kiss right over that little bud, she jumped.

"Easy, honey. I wouldn't hurt you for the world. Even when I paddle that sweet bottom, it's going to be all about the pleasure."

Avery started unbuttoning his shirt. Isaac smiled. Now wasn't the time to tell her to keep her hands at her sides. He wanted them on him too damn bad.

"Are we going to make love again?" She hoped so. Her body was going haywire at his slightest touch.

At her suggestion, his manhood stood up even higher, as if answering roll call. "Yes, my near-virgin girl. But, we've got to take it slow. I want to give that little treasure of yours a chance to rest. I don't want you to be sore. There are other things we can do." As he talked to her tenderly, he pulled down the cups of the bra and slipped it off, kissing each nipple, pulling them into his mouth like pieces of candy. "We're gonna kiss and cuddle and talk." He was teasing her. "And if you're good, I'm gonna kiss and cuddle your pussy, lick your cream and make you purr like a kitten."

"Heavenly. I'm ready to get to the purring part," she assured him. He shed his clothes as she watched. In her writing, there had been several times that she had said the hero had a magnificent body. It was accepted romance novel phraseology, but until Isaac, she'd never been privileged to see one in real life. He was ripped, and all she could do was stare and lick her lips.

She let him pull her down in the bed. This time she swore she was going to remember every touch, every kiss, every whisper. Being with Isaac like this was amazing. The other two times they'd been together, she'd been too nervous to focus on the sheer wonder of it all. Avery had never shared a bed with anyone. Well, not since her last slumber party in junior high. And being cradled in Isaac's strong arms was nothing like sleeping next to bony Janice Richards. He pulled her up tight against him. "How's this? Comfy?"

She was completely surrounded. His arm was over her waist and one leg flung over hers, anchoring her down. And Lord help her, he was buck-naked. How was she supposed to listen and respond coherently when his erect penis was nestled against her bottom? "Yes, Sir."

Immediately, teeth sank into the tender skin of her neck, the slightest, softest nip.

"What did you do that for?"

It hadn't hurt. In fact, she wanted to press her bottom back against that baseball bat nudging her backside. As she thought about how it would feel, she couldn't resist. Pressing her legs together, she pushed backward. As she did, she tightened her inner muscles, and then gasped at how good it felt. If he didn't touch her soon, she would die.

"You have no idea what it does to me when you call me Sir," he growled in her ear. Stroking the soft skin of her waist, Isaac wanted nothing more than to sink into her heat and stroke himself to paradise and back.

"You like that better than this?" She pushed her rump into his erection again just to hear him grunt.

Isaac let out a breathy gasp after a chuckle. "God, you're sweet. If you're not careful, I'm going to spread those cheeks and give you a preview of attractions to come." Stopping to give her a squeeze, he sobered. She had gone perfectly still. Had he scared her with the talk of taboo sex? "What are you thinking?"

Avery shivered at the thrill the idea gave her, and as he rubbed his hand up and down her arm, she answered, "I'm thinking I might like that."

Stunned. Damn! "Avery, you're shocking me. And I think it was supposed to be the other way around." The very idea that she might welcome anal sex was mind-blowing. His Avery? But back to the original topic, they had some things to iron out. This was just too important. "Twice you have answered me with 'yes, Sir.' Are you doing that on purpose? Cause, that's music to a Dom's ears. To hear you calling me 'Sir' or 'Master' is a bigger turn-on than you could possibly know."

Avery scooted on her back so she could see his face. "I'm glad you like it. I said it the first time because I respect you and, I don't know, I wanted to please you. When I was researching the topic, I saw how big a part that plays in it all, and I wanted to show you I can be what you want me to be."

A low moan rumbled through Isaac's chest. She had a true, loving submissive nature, an instinctual desire to please, an amazingly hot body, a gorgeous face and the tastiest lips in the world. In other words, she was perfect. "You just made me a very happy man. But, there's a whole lot more to it than that. We'll take it slow. Okay?"

"Do you want me to call you 'Sir'?"

"Only when we're in bed." As he answered her, it hit him. Sex with Avery was going to be different than with an ordinary sub. His whole spirit went still. Hearing his name on her lips…'Isaac'…was going to be the most precious sound he'd ever heard. His world was changing, and Isaac was having a hard time keeping up with it. "Let's play it by ear, okay?" Moving his thumb up to caress the arch of her cheekbone, he marveled at the wonder of being in this woman's bed. Only in his wildest fantasies had he allowed himself to dream about this possibility. He wanted to cherish her, be so careful with her. "Lord, Baby, I want you so much. It's going to be damn hard to hold back."

"But, I'm—" She stopped, blushing. Dare she ask? He filled her bed. How she wished she could get up and grab her camera and record this moment for posterity. Isaac McCoy in her bed. Would wonders never cease?

"You're what?"

He narrowed his eyes and moved closer, and as he did a thousand muscles rippled. Sweet Mary, the man looked commanding. Even lounging nonchalantly in her bed he looked to be completely in charge. "I'm…in need. Please? I don't want to wait. I'm not sore, at all."

Her cheeks were flushed, and she was chewing on that suckable lower lip. "Jesus," he groaned. With near trembling fingers he felt between her legs. "I love that you keep yourself bare. It's so tender and soft and pink, and very, very wet. You do want me, don't you?"

"Oh, yes," she cooed, and when she held out her arms he could deny her nothing.

Sitting up against the headboard, he pulled her to him. "This time you're on top."

"But, I don't know how," she protested.

"Have you ever ridden a horse?"

His twinkling blue eyes let her know he was enjoying this as much as she was. "No, but I'd like to learn."

"You will, I promise." He arranged her luscious body on top of him. "Straddle me, Sugar." When she slapped at him playfully, he held one breast up to his lips and kissed the pink, puffy tip. "That's my girl. Today you ride me. Lift up."

She rose on her knees and he rubbed the head of his erection from one end of her slit to the other, making her whimper with anticipation. Her whole body fizzed, which wasn't surprising. Every part of her was desperate to surrender to his raw magnetism. "You're so big and hard. You wanted me, too."

"You sound surprised. You shouldn't be. I've always wanted you. Now ease yourself down, as slow as you want. Are you sure you aren't too sore?" In answer, she began to sink down on his stiffness. The movement took his breath away. This time there was no rubber to dull the sensation. Isaac had no idea what he'd been missing. "God, that feels fantastic."

Avery held her breath, relishing the burning and stretching, welcoming the invasion of his manhood into her body. Face it, she loved everything about him, even that take-charge, blustering macho attitude that he loved to display at every opportunity. Grabbing for his hands, she wove their fingers together. "God, there's a lot of you, Isaac. If we hadn't done this before, I'd swear it was never gonna fit inside me."

"Does it hurt, Avery?"

Avery's heart swelled at his concern. "It hurts really, really good," she purred.

"I'm gonna take care of you, I promise. Just turn yourself over to me. I'll give you everything you didn't know you needed, in bed and out." The lust raging in his blue eyes almost startled her. Would she be able to be what he wanted? Lord knew she was going to try. With a snap of his hips, he filled her to the brim, fully seating himself inside of her.

"Isaac," she gasped, throwing her head back and arching her neck. She couldn't be still. She was on fire and he was the only source of relief. Placing her hands on his chest, she began to rock, rising up and down, impaling herself over and over again on his hardness. "Oh, I like this."

Wanting to touch even more of her, he maneuvered farther into the bed. "Now wrap your legs around my waist and your arms around my neck, and rub those hard nipples on my chest." She didn't quibble, but followed his directions to a tee. Isaac slid his hands to her behind and rocked into her. When she was on top like this he couldn't pull himself out, but there was something incredibly sexy about staying connected while hands ventured over warm skin and mouths explored wherever they could reach. Avery might be new to this, but she was a fast learner. The sweet doll kissed, licked and nibbled his jaw, down his neck and across his pecs, scraping her teeth across his nipple, all the while making the cutest, most satisfied kitten noises. Hell, she was something else. Isaac loved the way her nipples were poking into him, rubbing the hair on his chest when she moved on to kiss another spot on his hungry skin. God, he was loving this—all of it. Every time he lifted his hips and drove into her a little deeper, she let the sweetest puff of air tickle his skin. It would be heaven to stay right here, his erection being milked by the object of his desire, but his body couldn't wait. It needed release. "Kiss me," he demanded, urgently. Knowing how close they both were, he cupped her perky butt, lifted her high enough so that he could pull out and then ram back in—hard. Avery nipped his lip, pulled her mouth from his and arched in absolute ecstasy. And when she did, she clamped down on him for all she was worth. "Damn, yes. Milk me, Doll. That's it." Isaac buried his face in her neck and sucked hard enough to mark.

"Yes! Yes! Oh my God!"

Avery held him tight, everywhere. Isaac exploded with a roar, pulsing inside of her with every beat of his heart. The world stopped spinning and the most magical quiet of his life settled around him. He kissed the spot over her heart and she kissed the side of his face. And when he pulled out, his seed mixed with her cream and covered the proof of his desire for her. Being inside Avery bareback was the most amazing thing he'd ever experienced. No more condoms for Isaac McCoy. His manhood had found a home and it wanted no other.

He laid her back on the bed. "Remember the first lesson, Sub. A Master takes care of what belongs to him." Going to the bathroom, he ran the water till it was warm, wet a washcloth and returned to clean her tenderly. Patting her dry with a towel, he cleaned himself, threw the linens in a hamper and crawled back in the bed.

"Thank you, Isaac." They returned to the position they were in before the lovin' started. Only this time, he cupped one of her breasts like it belonged to him.

"For what, Sugar?" He couldn't resist planting a kiss on her shoulder.

"Thank you for the best time of my life." She let out a perfectly happy, satisfied sigh and it was the sweetest sound he had ever heard.

She had only intended to close her eyes for a moment, but when she opened them, Avery could smell bacon frying. Odd. Coming awake, she started to move and at least fifteen muscles protested. Oh yeah, she smiled—Isaac. With a careful move, she rolled over and buried her head in the pillow he had slept on. Yes, there it was, that mix of clean ocean breezes and leather. "Get up, Pumpkin. We need to eat. I went to the store while you were napping. I made us BLTs for lunch. We've got things to do and people to see."

Bouncing up, she faced him with an almost guilty look on her face. "Yes, I was...uh, just remembering what we did together." Lord, she looked like an advertisement pitching the joys of an afternoon delight. Her hair was mussed, those ringlets had a mind of their own, and all that cuddly softness made him want to run his fingers through those curls and kiss her till she begged for mercy.

"What am I waiting for? Now she belongs to me," he said, as if to himself. With one knee on the bed, he tugged her to him and took the kiss he craved. Bringing his mouth down slowly, it sent spirals of satisfaction through him when her lips parted right away and her tongue met his in a fiery mating. Isaac groaned, lost in the pulse pounding passion. Somehow, he pulled back, finishing the kiss with sweet smooches and little licks. He held her face in his hands and wiped the sleep from her eyes with his thumbs. "You are so damn cute."

Avery stared at him, lifting a finger to her lips and tracing their swollen wetness. "I want to remember everything." She'd heard what he said. For now she belonged to him—'for now'. If this was only temporary, she planned on wringing every moment of joy out of it that she could. She reached up, and let her fingertips trail over his cheek. "You've shaved; I like how smooth you are."

Realizing he had been scruffy as hell earlier, he pushed back her hair and looked for the telltale signs of his rough beard on her skin. Yeah, there was a red rash on her neck and the upper swell of her breast. "I used one of the disposable razors in your bathroom. Damn, I'm sorry, Kitten."

She cocked her head, glanced down and put her hand over his. "Stop, I wasn't complaining. I don't care about the redness. I loved the way your whiskers felt rasping against my skin, especially my nipples." A blush flashed over her skin. She had embarrassed herself.

"I'll be more careful in the future. Get up and get dressed, we've got a helluva lot to do." Opening her closet, he thumbed through her clothes and selected a pair of blue jeans, a crisp white shirt and a denim vest. "Put these on, we're going to be out in the pasture. And these..." He chose a swirly skirt and matching top. "...will be perfect for the party tonight." He fully intended to buy her new clothes, some things that were in between ultra-conservative and the all-out seduction wear that he had seen her in the last few days. A tiny giggle made him face her. "What's so funny?"

"In all of the fantasies I've had about you, not once did I ever picture you digging through my wardrobe and finding something for me to wear." He wore only his jeans and a tank top, and Lord was he fine. "I like what you have on. You look sexy." Good grief! Where was all this moxie coming from? Give a girl a little sex and she becomes Braveheart.

Isaac decided the bacon could wait. "You think I'm sexy, huh?" Pushing her back, he climbed into the bed, straddled her hips and whipped the tank top over his head.

"Mercy, mercy, mercy," she intoned. "It should be a law that you have to go naked. A chest like that should never be covered up."

Her praise pleased Isaac. In fact, he ate it up. She was looking at him like he was a sirloin steak and she hadn't eaten in a week. He was about to let her feast, until his damned cell phone went off. "Hell!" He answered, and she took advantage of the situation and began to play. "Hello?"

"I can't resist you," she teased as the palms of her hands massaged the muscles of his chest.

He couldn't concentrate. Her body was too beautiful, and she was making him harder with every caress she gave him. Trying to quell her exploration, he placed a strong hand over one of hers, but she had two hands, and a lot of determination. And when she cupped his bulge, he damn near lost it. "Hold on, Libby. I have a wild filly here that ain't been saddle broke yet."

"Oh, sorry." Avery covered her mouth to stifle a laugh.

Pressing the phone to his thigh, he glared at her, but a smile played around his lips. "Is there something I can do for you? You do realize I'm talking to your future sister-in-law here. Do you want her to know you're a sex maniac?"

"No, Sir, I'll be good." She tried to ignore the future sister-in-law remark, but her heart wouldn't let her.

When she put her hands behind her back in a classically submissive pose, Isaac's heart lurched. If it hadn't been Libby on the phone he would have hung up and ravished her.

"Good girl. Now, keep your hands there till I finish talking." He kissed her on the end of the nose. "And that's your second lesson in loving for the afternoon.

Loving obedience." Isaac had a hard time keeping his mind on the conversation, as he'd much rather watch Avery. But Libby had some things she wanted him to pick up from the store. "I'll be glad to get everything you need, and tell Cady I'm bringing that guest we talked about." He cupped the side of Avery's head as he listened to Libby's rapid-fire questions. "I'll explain it all when I get there. Be patient, Libster. You two have fun at your doctor's appointment."

He rung off and pocketed his cell phone. Avery watched him grab his shirt and slip it back on. Drats, playtime must be over. "Do you have to go?"

"Yes, I have to go. But you're coming with me, of course. Aron's taking Libby to her gynecologist appointment and we're going to take up the slack. She had let this check-up slip her mind and my brother refuses to let her skip it, party or no party. Come on." He held out his hand and waited until she took it. "Go get dressed, we'll eat our BLTs and be on our way."

* * *

Avery pinched herself to see if she was dreaming. Surely this whole day was a figment of her overactive imagination. Isaac had hand-fed her a bacon sandwich, punctuated with kisses. While she had slept, he had gone to the market. She had to admit, he was surprising her. And while they had eaten he had begun to explain to her about the Dom/sub lifestyle. "For the most part, all of this will only apply to the bedroom. I have no desire for you to be anything but my equal in all other areas of life. But if you're in danger and you hear that tone in my voice, you'll follow my directions to the letter. I will never have a motive other than to protect you or give us pleasure, that's it. You can trust me. Do you trust me, Avery?"

To trust in Isaac was not a major leap of faith for her. Over the years she had watched him, and she knew he was a good man. And the revelation of his affinity for being in total charge in the bedroom didn't scare her one bit. What did scare her was how he made her feel. Before, she had just thought she was in love. The better term would have been infatuation. Now, after having felt his hands on her body, his lips on her skin, after having slept in his arms, she knew the difference. Loving Isaac would be the easiest thing she'd ever done.

After eating, he had helped her gather her things. Even though she still had a qualm or two, Avery was determined to see where this would end up. If she walked away now, she would never know. Happiness was too sparse of a commodity to squander a chance like this. And everything was going along great until they got in the argument over her motorcycle. "We can race," she said, with a hint of mischievous adventure in her voice.

"Over my dead body." Isaac laid down the law. "You will ride behind me, holding on to me as tight as you can. Later, after I've seen you ride around the ranch, we'll see about riding somewhere together."

"You realize I rode that bike here from Nevada."

"Don't remind me. Anything could have happened to you. That's over 1200 miles." He rubbed his hand across his face in exasperation. "How many times had you ridden it before you took off on that trip?"

"A few...the guys at the Shady Lady helped me practice with it." When she used the word 'practice' his expression turned thunderous.

"If you want to practice anything, anytime, anywhere, you come to me. Got it?" He probably thought he was intimidating the crap out of her, but all he was succeeding at was giving her a thrill. Since they weren't even riding the bikes today, Avery thought it was a moot point, but she did like that he was concerned about her. Loading up in his pickup they headed west.

When they rolled under the big arch proclaiming McCoy land, she felt chill bumps go over her body. Oh, she'd been here before, for one such function or another, but this time she was here in a far different capacity. For now, she belonged. Pulling into a parking spot, Isaac stopped his King Ranch and helped Avery out. Taking the small duffle that held her clothes, he announced, "We'll get the rest of your things later."

"I'm just here for the day," she reminded him. "We're just playing. Remember?" Even though it hurt her to say it, she wanted to make him understand that they weren't getting married. Not yet, anyway. Now, if he fell in love with her, for real...well, that would be another story.

Her protest didn't faze him. It was as if she hadn't said anything. "Okay, Doll-Face. You're in for a grilling. There's gonna be questions. Do you want me to deal with it?" He put his arm around her, fitted her next to him as they walked.

"No, I can handle myself."

Isaac looked down at his perfect armful. She wasn't lying. Lord, she knew how to handle herself, and him too. "How about we handle it together?" He couldn't resist kissing her.

"Help me, help me, help me." A slightly panicked female voice sounded from the far end of the porch. As they climbed the wide front steps, Isaac spotted Jessie teetering on a low stepstool. Both he and Avery rushed to her rescue.

"Lord help, Girl. Are you trying to give me a heart attack?" Isaac ran over and grabbed the young woman and set her carefully on her feet.

Avery knew Libby, but she had never met Jessie. The fact that the girl was very pregnant did not escape her attention. A lot had happened back in Kerrville while she'd been caught up in her own drama in Nevada. "Are you all right? Do you need a drink of water or something?"

"That would be nice. I'm Jessie." She smiled over Isaac's shoulder. "I just refilled the hummingbird feeder and was trying to rehang it."

Isaac looked at Jessie with a broad smile. "This is Avery. She's with me."

Jessie nodded, recognizing the name right away. "Avery, of course, I've heard so much about you. I'm so glad you're here. Granny Fontenot said you were coming."

At that revelation, Isaac winked at Avery. "I can't wait for you to meet that lady. Hold the door, Sugar, and let's get her inside." Avery smiled as she stepped over and opened the wide wooden door and held it as Isaac carried Jessie in. "Jessie is Jacob's fiancé," he explained.

Hearing her beloved's name, she clasped her hands together. "Please don't tell Jacob I was doing something so foolish. He didn't want to leave me as it is. He's trying to finish with the surveyor before he and Joseph have to take the pig off the grill." Directing her next comment to Avery, "I'll have to show you the house plans and the spot we've picked out. It's where Jacob's grandparents used to live. Jacob is going to build us a beautiful log house."

"When's your baby due?" Avery asked as she followed Isaac through the beautiful entrance hall and into the kitchen. She couldn't help but glance around. It had been years since she'd been in the Tebow main house.

"The doctor says eight weeks, but I don't think I'll make it that long." She patted her stomach. "At least we'll be able to say 'I do' before Bowie Travis comes."

"They're getting hitched on the 16th along with Libby and Aron. Jacob's naming the baby after his childhood best friend," Isaac explained.

Avery pulled out the dining table chair and started hunting a glass. "I know, Heart Strings is doing the flowers." Isaac sat Jessie down gently. Watching him with his family just tugged at her heart strings. If only the rest of the world knew the Isaac that she knew.

"Eloping would've been fine with me, but you know how sentimental and traditional Jacob is. I swear this wedding means so much to him, and he's been so good to me. I mean..." She rubbed her swollen belly softly. "...considering that this baby isn't even his."

Finding a cupboard full of glassware, Avery filled a glass and handed it to the pale girl. She was becoming ill at ease. "Do I need to leave?"

"No, no," Jessie assured her as she sipped the water. "None of this is secret from the family." Avery didn't miss that she had just been classified as family.

Isaac pulled a chair over near Jessie and straddled it so he could look her in the eye. "Jess, you listen to me. Jacob is the father of that baby in every way that counts. Marrying you is the most important thing to Jacob, not how or when or where. You and that baby are his highest priorities."

Avery couldn't keep her eyes off of Jessie. She was so beautiful. Pregnancy agreed with her, and it was true what they said, she glowed. A jolt of jealousy pierced Avery's heart. Oh, to be pregnant with Isaac's baby. What a joy that would be.

A commotion in the other room made them look toward the door. Leaving the two women, Isaac went to see what was going on. There was a wizened little woman with skin the color of an aged magnolia. She was standing at the foot of the stairs looking up, and if Isaac wasn't mistaken, she had a pair of panties on her head. She didn't see him, and he didn't linger. He backed back in the kitchen and just stood there, and then he peeped back around and looked again. Jessie noticed him and laughed. "I bet I know what you see. That's Granny Fontenot."

"Okay," Isaac spoke slowly. "Why is she wearing underwear on her head?"

Avery couldn't pass that up. "I bet I know, let me see." She crept over and peeped out the door and sure enough, there was a small lady all decked out in cream-colored lace with a pair of baby blue, satin granny panties fitted over her head like a helmet. "Yep, I've seen that syndrome before. It's common in churchwomen. They get their hair fixed every week. It's called a standing appointment. And that hairdo has to last for seven days, so to preserve it they wear a pair of satin drawers on their head to prevent it from getting messed up."

She spoke with such assurance that Isaac almost cracked up. "Are you serious?"

"I can see that." Jessie struggled to sit straighter. Clearly her back was bothering her. "Makes sense to me. Right now, my head is the only place where my panties still fit."

"Oh, Lord," Isaac grumped. "TMI! Women! Although, I do remember when Joseph would wear Mom's bra on his head when we were like five or six years old. He thought he looked like Mickey Mouse."

"Awww, I bet he was cute." Jessie rubbed her tummy again.

"May I have a word with you, Miss Jessie?" The fragile little voice caused them all to turn around. There stood Granny Fontenot. She had removed the drawers from her head, but Isaac smiled a little to see that she still held them in her hand. When she realized they were all looking at them she grinned a semi-toothless smile. She had front teeth, but that was all. "I'm not crazy, Children. Wearing my skivvies keeps my do pretty."

Avery elbowed Isaac, telling him 'I told you so.'

Jessie straightened in her chair. "Of course, please sit down."

Isaac pulled out her chair. "Should we leave?" He held his hand out to Avery. "We have a lot of things to do, anyway."

"No, please stay. This is important to all the family." Sitting down heavily, the old matriarch folded her hands on the table and looked at Jessie. "I understand you are planning a double wedding with the eldest and his bride."

Jessie glanced at Avery, as if for support, then back to Granny Fontenot. "Yes, that was the plan. All the arrangements have been made. Is there something wrong?"

"Don't do it."

"What?" Jessie looked completely taken aback. "I don't understand."

"Why not?" Isaac took the chair on the other side of the old lady. He dwarfed her. Avery didn't know what was going on. What did this woman have against Jacob?"

"I'm trying to protect you," she stated simply. "With all the excitement and worry over Cady's Joseph, she neglected to tell Honoria or any of our family that you were considering celebrating two weddings on the same day. In New Orleans, we know not to do this. To be fair, Cady may not even know about this belief. She has always been so focused on healing that we have not trained her in all aspects of our ways. Cady is special. Until Joseph, she has not ventured into realms of the heart."

Jessie looked near to tears and Isaac appeared concerned, but he didn't refute Granny Fontenot's words or ask her to refrain from upsetting his future sister-in-law. Little snippets of information came back to her, including Jessie's statement that this woman had known she would be arriving. Surely not.

"Have you seen something?" Jessie put her hand over Cady's grandmother's wrinkled, arthritic fingers and held them gently. "Tell me, please."

"No, no, I have seen nothing. Neither have any of the others. Nothing specific. But it is a common belief among my people that if two couples willingly share the moment of matrimony, a double wedding, one of the grooms will die an early death. Marry him any other day, before or after the other wedding, but not together. In fact, one should never even plan for such an event."

"Isn't that just a superstition?" Avery couldn't help but ask.

Isaac grabbed her by the hand and pulled her on his knee. "We've learned to respect Cady and her family's gifts," he spoke softly. "I'll explain later."

Pushing up from her chair, Jessie stabilized herself and walked over to look out the window. "I've seen what you and the others can do and what you know. Only recently did I learn that it was Cady who told the Sheriff where to find me when Kevin McCay was torturing me in that little shack." She turned around to face the others. "If you say it's unwise, I'll heed your advice. Jacob will be disappointed, but he'll understand. His life or the life of Aron is not worth the risk. We'll elope." As soon as she said the words, a look of relief came over her face. "Libby will have her big day all to herself."

A surreal feeling filled the air. Too much had happened. Avery was having a hard time taking it all in. She looked at Isaac who sat there so confident, so serene. There was no qualm in his expression, and he had no fear of the strange behavior of his houseguest. All of her dad's reservations and the church's teachings flowed in her mind, but she weighed them against what she knew of this family and what they stood for in the community and she was amazed to realize that her faith and trust in Isaac outweighed any fear she had of the unknown. In fact, she wanted to know more. "How did you come by this information, Ma'am?"

Granny Fontenot let out a peal of laughter. "Ancient knowledge, my Dear. Did you know that most of the modern day wedding ceremony that is held as so sacred and so holy is full of customs that originated in magical beliefs? For example, in hoodoo and voodoo, crossroads and thresholds are favorite haunts of evil spirits. That is why the groom carries the bride into his home, to protect her. A new bride always seems to attract the attention of the spirit world, perhaps because of the high emotions that are created by the love and lust of the happy couple."

"Better to be safe than sorry," Isaac mused as he offered his hand to the elderly lady. "I'm Isaac by the way. I don't think we've met. And this beautiful woman on my lap is my Avery. Avery Sinclair, meet…I'm sorry, all I know is Granny Fontenot. I'm sure you have another name."

"Adele is my name." She placed her hand in his. "It is my pleasure to meet all of you. To see my Cady so happy in your midst is the answer to a lifetime of prayers." Turning her attention to Avery, Adele gave her a saucy wink. "I like women with spunk and this man will have the devil of a time keeping you in line."

Her announcement disturbed Avery. "Causing trouble is not my goal." Had she disrupted Isaac's life? Maybe she had. With a little tug, she tried to stand, but Isaac's arm was like a band of steel around her waist.

"Don't you try to get away from me," he growled in her ear. "I've got you right where I want you."

Aron's laughter pealing through the house followed by Libby's trying to shush him announced their return from the doctor. "Where is everybody?" he yelled.

"Kitchen," Isaac answered.

"Excuse us, Adele." Jessie smiled. "These men lived without female companionship in their home up until a few months ago. Libby and I are still trying to instill some manners into them. In many ways they are sadly lacking."

Avery felt Isaac's chest rumble as he chuckled. "Do you think I'm lacking, Baby-Doll?" Just his whispered teasing made her body tingle.

"Be good," she playfully chastised.

"I thought I was." He gave her bottom a soft pinch. She jumped in his arms about the time Aron and Libby walked into the kitchen.

"Avery!" Libby hugged them both as a unit. "I'm so glad you're here. And I see you've met Adele. Isn't she a character?"

"That she is," Isaac agreed.

"Libby, I need—" Jessie spoke up, obviously wanting to confer with her friend. But Aron had something to say, and he couldn't wait to say it.

"Ya'll will never guess what Libby did." No sooner had he said the word 'did', Libby whirled on him and ruffled every feather she had.

"If you tell that story in mixed company, Aron, you will wake up tomorrow with your manhood all dressed up and nowhere to go. Do you understand me?" She meant business too. Aron actually backed up about six inches and Isaac hoorawed. "I think that you and Isaac need to go find something productive to do while I make myself and these ladies a cup of tea."

Isaac gave Avery a peck on the cheek as he helped her up. "Meet me outside in fifteen minutes and we'll escape this madhouse." She gave him a warm smile. It sounded like a good idea to her.

Aron good-naturedly grumbled all the way out, but he left with Isaac. As soon as they were alone, Jessie grabbed Libby by the hand. "What did you do?" As the men left, Cady and her mom joined the ladies. "Come in, you two. We're about to make tea."

"Let me do it, please." Making tea was something that Avery was good at. Fitting into the excitement at Tebow, not so much. She didn't get very far, before Cady spied her.

"Avery?" Cady asked just to be sure.

"Yes," Avery answered, tentatively. She had been around some spiritual powerhouses in her times, people who were connected to the very gates of heaven through the power of prayer, but never had she felt such an aura of peace and…yes, power…that emanated from this one small woman. "I'm Avery. You must be Cady." She fully expected for the handshake they shared to shock her, but it didn't. The smile Cady gave her, literally, lit up the room.

"I am so glad you're here. Isaac has needed you, so much." Without preamble, Avery was clasped in Cady's arms and she felt like she had been enveloped in pure love. There was something about this woman that exuded joy.

"Thank you." Was all Avery could think to say.

Cady pulled back and took the other woman's hand. "This is my Mom, Celeste Renaud. Mom, this is Avery Sinclair. She belongs to Isaac. And I presume you've already met Granny Fontenot, sitting there with her underwear in her hand. Have you had those things on your head again, Boss Lady?"

Avery was entranced with Cady. And mystified that everyone kept saying she belonged to Isaac. "Hello, Mrs. Renaud. It's a pleasure to meet you both, and yes, I've been chatting with your grandmother. She is a character."

"I'm waiting to hear the story of what you did, Libby." Jessie had sat patiently while the niceties had been taken care of.

"Me, too," Avery admitted shyly. She sat out cups and arranged tea bags and sugar and cream for everyone to help themselves.

As the kettle hissed, Libby entertained them. "I made a fool out of myself, that's what. Cady, this party is going to be great, but I've gone overboard, I guess. You know I was making those individual place cards with everybody's name done in glitter."

"I told you that you were going to too much trouble." Cady was emphatic. "I'm the happiest woman in the world to be marrying Joseph. I didn't need any fancy decorations."

Jessie shooed Cady. "We know, we know, Joseph is a sex god. They all are. Let her finish the story." Granny Fontenot whooped at the sex part. She might be old, but she wasn't dead.

"Anyway..." Libby continued. "I'd been working down in the craft room and I'd scattered glitter everywhere. As I was trying to clean up, the phone rang. I'd been wiping down the counters and when I ran to our bedroom to get this checklist for the caterer, I had that washrag in my hand. I laid it down on the vanity counter next to the sink. When Aron got it in his head that I had to keep the doctor's appointment, I did a quick wash up just to make sure I was clean..." Her face fell, and she looked sheepish. "I used the wrong rag."

"Oh, no," Jessie yelped. "I can see where this is going."

"Yes." Libby leaned over and held her head in her hands. "When the doctor got me all spread out like a filleted pork chop, he cracked up and said 'Well, hello there. This is the first time anyone's ever decorated it for me.' I had glitter everywhere."

"You were Vajazzeled!" Avery laughed. "When I was out at the Vegas cathouse, I heard all about it." Now all eyes had turned on Avery.

"What were you doing in a cathouse, pray tell?" Jessie was having the time of her life. She loved being in this family. There was never a dull moment. The giggles and the titters grew to mammoth proportions as Avery explained what she had been up to and Libby continued describing the doctor's red face and Aron's shock that she had presented her lady parts in full glitter glory.

"You people are crazy." Granny Fontenot passed a smiling judgment. "Cady is going to be in good hands."

"And look at this." Libby pulled out a package from her purse. "This is going to be his wedding present." They all crowded around to look. "The sonogram today didn't show this miracle clear enough for Aron to pick up on it. But the doctor slipped these to me as I was leaving."

"Twins," Avery breathed, reverently. "Libby, you're having twins!"

"That's wonderful, Libs." Jessie hugged her first, before she was passed around. "But, we need to talk. It's important." As Jessie sat Libby down to tell her that their wedding plans would have to be changed, Avery slipped out to find Isaac. They had some things to work out. Besides, she missed him.

* * *

Isaac helped Aron load his pickup with the gifts that had been delivered for Joseph and Cady. "I like your gift, and they're going to love it." It was a sculpture, one that would have special meaning for the couple. Aron was a western artist of some renown and had pieces in galleries and museums around the country.

"I hope so. So, what's up with you and Avery?"

As they stood there, Nathan's dog ran up to greet Isaac and he knelt to scratch the eager pup he had rescued and brought home. "We're getting married, if I have any say in the matter."

This information stunned his big brother. "Aren't you rushing things a mite?"

Immediately, Isaac got his back up. The days of Aron's questioning everything he did were too fresh in his mind. "Maybe, but that's my business. I'm man enough to stand by my decisions and try to make the best of my mistakes." He wasn't talking about Avery. He was talking about the bar, his reputation, and the tendency his brothers had of thinking they knew how to handle his life better than he did.

All Avery heard was 'mistake'. And she knew what mistake he was talking about. Her. She stopped dead in her tracks. He had fooled her. Almost, he had convinced her that he wanted her. Almost. She turned and walked away, but not before Aron saw her go. "Your little mistake just heard what you said and high-tailed it toward the front yard."

Chapter Seven

"Dammit, Aron! I wasn't talking about Avery! Hell!" She couldn't leave. She didn't have a vehicle. Unless. Sure enough, he heard his Harley start up with a growl. That bike was way too big for her. Plus, she was upset. By the time he rounded the corner of the main house and hurdled over Libby's rose bushes, Avery was headed down the driveway at too fast of a speed, with no helmet. "If she hurts herself, I'm gonna kill her." He went right to his pick-up, switched it on and gunned it after her.

Why? Why go through this charade? She could handle her dad. What she couldn't handle was Isaac toying with her like this. The bike was big, but once she got it started, her determination kept it between the ditches. Tears streamed down her cheeks, but she couldn't take the chance to wipe them off. Isaac was going to be pissed that she took his hog, but there was no way she could stay at the ranch another moment. She hadn't gotten her purse! Crap! She considered turning around, but she couldn't face him. Maybe Libby or Jessie would meet her somewhere with her stuff. The motorcycle was loud, but it couldn't drown out the sound of 350 horsepower staying right with her. Glancing over and up, she saw Isaac looking at her with a thundercloud expression. God, he was probably going to have her arrested for grand theft Harley. "Pull over, now!" He mouthed at her and pointed to the side of the road.

She considered her options, and decided to do what he asked. He would follow her all the way and probably make her so nervous that she would wreck. So, she eased off the gas, downshifted and pulled on the handbrakes until she brought the monster bike to a standstill. Isaac whipped open the door, stalked over to her and for a moment, she thought he might hit her. Instead, he caught her by the shoulders, lifted her off the Harley and into his arms. Without a word, he covered his mouth with hers and kissed the breath out of her. It wasn't a gentle kiss, and as mad and hurt as she was, it didn't go a long way in helping her feelings. So, she pushed against his chest, to no avail. It was like pushing against a brick wall. His mouth ate at hers like he was starving to death. And a girl can only resist so much, but by God, she tried. When he pulled back for a breath, she tore away. "Stop it!"

"Don't you ever, ever dare put yourself in danger like that again. That bike is too big for you, and you know better than to go off without a helmet. Why, I ought to turn you over my lap and paddle your behind!" He took the keys from the ignition, and before she could protest, he picked her up and tossed her over his shoulder.

"Put me down! I want to go home. I heard what you said. You said I was a mistake. You don't want me, Isaac. Let me go." Spank! He didn't hit her behind hard, but a sob escaped just the same. Her pride was stung and her heart was aching. "Isaac, I swear to God. If you don't put me down, I'm going to scream." He flung open his truck door and sat her down.

"There, you're down." He was breathing hard, and she noticed a pulse point by his sexy mouth that was throbbing with every beat of his heart. "I know what you heard and I'm here to tell you that you misunderstood. There was no way in hell that I was talking about you. I want to be with you, I've wanted to be with you for years." He was sincere. It was as if Avery could see into his very heart. With a small cry, she launched herself into his arms, and he wrapped himself around her and held her tight. "I'm so sorry. I wouldn't hurt you for the world."

She shut her eyes, and surrendered. "I want you, Isaac. I love you. I'm sorry."

Isaac whooped, he actually whooped. He picked her up and swung her in a circle. "Thank God! So, you'll marry me? When?"

Avery wasn't a gambler, usually. But, this was important. Avery wanted Isaac's heart and she was willing to risk everything in order to have a chance at the big prize. She'd said she loved him, but there had been no return of the sentiment. That's what she wanted. Avery wanted Isaac's love. "Listen to me. I have a proposition for you." He stilled and let her slide down his body. She didn't miss the bulge of his erection, and it made her second guess herself, almost.

"Proposition? What are you saying, Avery? I offer you a proposal and you offer me a proposition? Who's the badass in this relationship?" He was teasing, a little. There was a hint of vulnerability in his voice. Steeling herself against it, she sought to be strong. This was too important.

"Yes." She placed both palms on his chest. It was wide, strong—a place of comfort, protection and strength. "I'll marry you." His muscles tightened. "Wait." He relaxed and listened. "I'll think about marrying you, if I can learn to please you." He started to speak and she put her fingers over his lips. "No. This is non-negotiable. I'll consider marrying you if I can become the type of submissive you've always dreamed about."

Isaac wanted to curse. Didn't she understand? "You Please Me Now." He ground out the words one at a time.

She refused to give in. "I want you to train me. I want you to show me the ropes—literally," she said with a wink. "If you have a playroom like in the articles, I want you to take me there. Anything that you've ever wanted, desired or longed for, that's what I want to be for you. And if I can't, I'll walk away."

Isaac was amazed. He was simply amazed. Someone had given him the world on a silver platter, yet he wanted more. "There will be no walking away. Like I said, you please me now. You don't have to be a perfect sub. Do you know why?" She shook her head. "Because, you're my perfect Avery." He laid his forehead against hers. "We'll play it by your rules, for now. But the end game belongs to me, love. You don't have to fit in some mold to make me happy. All you have to do is breathe, Sugar." How could he make her understand? One more shot. "The only thing that ever held me back, Avery, was because I thought I wasn't good enough for you."

At that admission, Avery tightened her arms around him, buried her face in his neck and vowed, "Give me a chance. I know I can make you happy. I just know it."

"Ah, Darling, that's a done deal."

* * *

"So, you can give me what I need?" Harper looked the big man up and down. Tremors of anticipation made her whole body quake. God, she needed a fix. Her drug of choice wasn't synthetic, nor was it a pill or drink. Harper craved pain. It was the only way she could get off, and she needed some relief more than anything.

"I guarantee it. Put yourself in my capable hands and you won't ever want another man. I'm the best. I can bring you to your knees and you'll beg to stay there."

Ajax sounded confident. But the stakes were higher this time. It wasn't just a hook-up or a scene. No, this was revenge and it was gonna taste sweet.

"I agree, Master. Take me. I'm yours."

Ajax licked his lips as the too-skinny blonde bowed her head and gave complete control over to him. He started to say, 'You won't be sorry', but that's wasn't necessarily true.

"Somebody hand me my bullwhip."

* * *

"I'm not a very good dancer," Avery apologized as Isaac pulled her close.

"What?" He laughed out loud. "You put Gypsy Rose Lee to shame, Sugar. That pole dance was the hottest I've ever witnessed."

"Destiny and Desiree spent hours going over that routine with me. But they didn't spend much time on two-stepping." She let out a contented sigh as she nestled close to his big body. Little quivers of excitement radiated through her as he rubbed soft circles on her back.

"We're not two-stepping. This is a waltz."

"It doesn't matter, I'm just floating." Truthfully, she hadn't been to very many parties like this. As the sun had set, the tiny white lights and the lanterns which hung from the big spreading oaks had entranced her. No short cuts had been taken. The McCoys definitely knew how to throw a party. "Will you teach me how to ride?"

Horse. She was talking about riding a horse. Isaac's brain comprehended that fact, but his cock had other ideas. "Sure, I'd love to. Have you ever ridden before?" He cleared his throat, trying to get a grip.

Not even an inch separated them, so Avery felt his excitement growing. "Only the one time with you today, but I enjoyed myself immensely." When he nipped her earlobe, she giggled. "Perhaps, you can teach me some trick riding."

A muted groan made his breath ruffle the hair on her neck. "Let's see, Reverse Cowgirl comes to mind."

"What's that?" She had some idea, but she wanted to hear his husky voice whisper it in her ear. Already, her body was responding to his arousal.

"You sit on my lap, with your back to my front and my hands can play with your bottom or rub your little pleasure button. Does that sound like something you'd like to try?" Thank goodness it was dark. Isaac was setting himself up. He could feel Avery trembling in his arms. She was turned on, but he was as hard as a rock. And there was no way they could leave the party, not yet.

"Yeah, I want to try that." Her breath hitched with erotic anticipation. "I want to try everything with you. Sex standing up, against the wall, from behind, 69, all of it. I want you to tie me up and spank me and—"

"Hush!" Isaac hugged her harder than ever. "You're killing me." He humped up against her, rubbing his erection against her softness. "I promise you, we'll do it all. Just as soon as we can, we're outta here. I'll take you back to the bar and show you my playroom."

"When can we leave?" she whispered.

Was she real? "Soon, after we eat and after Joseph and Cady make their talks. Don't worry. We won't stay one moment longer than necessary. I set all this up. Jacob or Noah can help take it down."

The music came to a stop and Aron called for everybody to take their seats. Avery admired how beautiful everything looked and couldn't help but be pleased that the centerpieces of mums and other fresh flowers made everything perfect. "If everyone will make themselves comfortable and begin to help themselves to the food, we've got four buffet tables to serve you. You'll find roast pork, brisket, chickens, potato salad, baked beans and all the trimmings. And the best banana puddin' you've ever wrapped your lips around. We've got a lot to celebrate tonight, so have a good time."

The crowd began to file to the four corners of the pavilion where the food was spread out. "Would you like me to fix your plate?" Avery asked as Isaac escorted her to a spot at the head table.

"No, you aren't my slave. I want you to be my partner, my friend, my lover...only in the bedroom do I want control." He was whispering, but he did look around to see if anyone could hear them. It hadn't escaped his notice that several people had been surprised to see them together. There had been whispers and sly glances.

"Mom always filled Dad's plate for him and I don't think they were into BDSM."

"Thank you, Love. But we'll go together, how's that?" She followed him through the food line, filling their plates with fragrant BBQ and sides. Isaac stopped by the bar and Doris handed him a longneck with a knowing smile. "What would you like, Avery?"

"A diet Coke, please." Beer didn't appeal to her and she wanted to keep a clear head to enjoy every moment of the night with Isaac. He escorted her back to the table and they sat between Cady and Noah. It was a bit nerve wracking to look out in the crowd and see so many curious eyes watching her. She didn't know what they were thinking about, the photo in the paper or how unsuited she was for him. Isaac dwelled on his supposed faults, but she couldn't forget how awkward and unsophisticated she was. Her hair was plain, no designer cuts, and her clothes didn't bear a fancy brand. Face it, she was rubbing shoulders with society and her background would be woefully lacking in their eyes.

"Stop it." Cady nudged her. "I can hear your thoughts as plain as day. Look at me. Do I look like I fit in with these people? I'm an ugly duckling in the midst of a bunch of swans. Yet, I belong. Do you know why? Because Joseph loves me. I'm not blind, I can see with two sets of eyes, physical and spiritual. And I can tell you...you have nothing to worry about. Isaac is totally into you, and from what I have heard, he has been for a long time."

Pushing her food from one side of the plate to another, Avery listened and marveled at what Joseph's fiancé said to her. "What are you talking about? You're gorgeous. And as for me and Isaac, I pray to God that your insight is correct."

"What are you two talking about?"

"Girl-talk," she informed Isaac with a smile.

"Did you hear about Ronny Joe McGraw's girlfriend? What's her name?" Noah asked between bites.

"Tammy?" Isaac licked sauce from his fingers. "Damn, you smoke the best meat in the state."

"All I did was season it up and give the boys the directions."

"Yea, but it's your recipe. What about Tammy?"

Noah lowered his voice and looked around. "I heard that she was over there at the Longbranch and after Ronny Joe and his men had finished branding they all got drunk. The story is that she pulled down her jeans and demanded he put his brand on her, and he did. They say she won't be able to sit down for a month. Can you believe that?"

Isaac chuckled. "So, that's why she's standing up to eat."

"They're here?" Noah craned his neck. "Hell, I didn't know Joseph invited him. What do they have in common, or do I want to know?"

"Quit being so damn judgmental," Isaac gently chided his brother. "You need to learn how to enjoy life. Not everybody is as straight-laced as you are."

"I'm not straight-laced."

"You're tied up in a knot half the time. Enjoy life, man. It's too short not to." Noah stiffened. "If there's something on your mind, just say it," Isaac challenged him.

"Nothing, it's just your reference to being tied up. Harper's into that kinky stuff and I hate it. We could have had a relationship, but she wallows in that sick, twisted lifestyle and I can't understand it."

Isaac didn't know what to say. But, he had to say something. "Don't judge her too harshly. Food is good, but gluttony is bad. Beer is good, but an alcoholic's life is miserable. The relationship between two people who enjoy a power exchange may be more beautiful than you realize, but even that can have its dark side. Any form of addiction or extreme overuse can be dangerous. Harper may not be able to control her craving for domination, but that doesn't mean she's beyond help." Noah was looking at him so closely, that he wondered if he'd said too much. Keeping his involvement in the BDSM world from his brothers hadn't been easy. Often he'd wondered if it wouldn't have all been easier if he had just been honest. Hiding the truth from them had taken a heck of a lot of energy and needless subterfuge.

"Know a lot about this, do you?"

Alarm bells went off in Isaac's head. Time to back off. "Hey, I read."

"Ladies and Gentlemen..." Aron's voice was a welcome intrusion in a conversation which had gotten a tad out of hand.

"I want to thank all of you for coming and helping to celebrate the love of two people who have found one another in the midst of a miracle. To stand here before you and know that he's happy is worth more to me than I can tell you. Joseph, Cady, if you'll come up here, I have a little gift for you." They joined him at the podium and he picked up an object about the size of a computer monitor. Setting it on the table in front of them, he removed the veil. Cady's gasp could be heard over the whole room. "I call it The Guardian."

"Aron, I don't know what to say." Joseph's voice was hoarse with emotion and Cady threw her arms around Aron and hugged him for all she was worth.

"I love it and I love you," she whispered, but her voice carried easily through the microphone. Joseph held the statue up so everyone could see it. There were two figures, one was a proud stallion, his mane waving in the wind and he was galloping freely, his head thrown up and his neck arched powerfully. Hovering over the stallion was a winged angel, a beautiful woman with the most perfect look of love on her face.

"You're the stallion, Joseph." Aron didn't have to explain, but he did for the benefit of all the people who looked on. "That was the name you were given in college when you so proudly played for The University of Texas. You have always had the same proud, wild spirit of a stallion. And Cady is your angel, looking over you, looking out for you, always loving you." The audience had no idea how true to the mark he was. Cady was Joseph's angel, in every way that counted.

"May I say something, Brother?" Joseph asked. Aron sat down, giving the podium over to Joseph. Cady looked at him with adoration on her face. "My Cady asked me to speak for both of us, to tell you what it means that you have chosen to spend these happy moments with us. But, I want to speak, not only to you, but also to her. Tonight, I celebrate the best thing that has ever happened to me. Those of you who know me might think that the blue ribbons, the championship rings, and the gold purses are the best things that have happened to me, but you'd be wrong. When I was paralyzed, I thought that if I could just run again, hell—walk again—if I could race again, drive again, play football again, I would be happy. I prayed for a miracle, ladies and gentlemen, and God sent me an angel. He sent me Cady. And she and her family gave me back my health and my ability to function. They gave me back my life. Now, you might think that is what I celebrate tonight. While this has been one of the greatest blessings I could ever hope to experience, it is not the best thing. The best thing, my miracle is Cady. She is my reason for living. She is..." He took her by the hand and drew her close. "...the one who I love above all things."

When Joseph finished his speech there wasn't a dry eye in the house. Scores of people got up and approached the head table. Many of them had gifts of their own. People continued eating and some got up to dance. Isaac touched Avery's arm. "Let's get out of here."

"Now?"

"I can't wait to get you alone." There was something in his voice, a predatory quality that made Avery's nipples throb.

"Let's go. I want to be alone with you, too."

* * *

Noah's cell phone vibrated in his pants pocket, so he slipped away from the table to stand under a lamppost to better see who was calling. It was Harper. Torn, he hesitated, then finally answered, "Hello."

"Noah, I need you," she cried. Huge wracking sobs tore through the receiver. "Please, please, I don't have anyone else to call."

"Where are you?"

"I'm at a gas station just outside of Luckenbach." Noah could hear the pain in her voice as she spoke. "I'm hurt."

"Why haven't you called an ambulance?" Her voice was scaring the shit out of him. He wasn't in love with Harper any longer, but he couldn't stand for anything bad to happen to her either. They shared too much history for him to turn his back on her completely.

"I'm not dressed," she sobbed, almost incoherently.

"Do you have a mile marker?" She gave it to him. "I'm on my way. For God's sake be careful."

* * *

The bar was dark when Isaac let Avery in the back door ahead of him. He had disabled the burglar alarm as soon as they walked in and the security lights were the only illumination they had. Holding her by the hand, he was well aware she was trembling, and it wasn't all from excitement. Stopping, he decided to alleviate any reservations she might have. "Honey, hold up."

"No, I'm ready." But there was a slight hitch in her voice. "I want to do this more than anything. Are we going to your apartment?"

"No, I built a special room for times like this." He kissed her on her forehead, and then sought to reassure her. "Nothing will happen unless you wish it. All power will be yours."

"But, I thought..." she began.

"Many believe as you do, and that's a misconception. The submissive is the one with the power and the Dom seeks only to give pleasure and in so doing, they receive pleasure themselves. When we go behind these doors, I will take control of your very being, your movements, your joy, and your orgasms. They will belong to me. But when you place them into my hands, I commit myself to you. Your pleasure and well-being is my greatest concern."

This was what she wanted. So much. The only thing that was giving her pause was his previous experience. "Have you done this with many women?"

"Oh, Honey." He pulled her close and enveloped her in a hug. "There are a lot of things in my life I regret. But I can tell you this. From the moment I realized how I felt about you, I haven't had sex with any woman. I couldn't do it." Admitting this gave Isaac such freedom. "Before that, I participated in safe, consenting scenes. I served as the Dom and I trained subs and other Doms. Rarely, did I have a relationship, but when I did it was handled with respect."

Avery pressed her face to his chest and kissed him through his shirt. "I trust you. Show me what it means to belong to you." The hitch in her voice was gone. Now, it was Isaac who trembled. The depth of his responsibility was not lost on him. Taking her by the hand he led her to his sanctuary and opened the door.

Her eyes had a hard time adjusting to the darkness and when he flipped on the light, Avery stared, eyes wide and jaw dropped. "My stars and garters!"

"Intimidating, isn't it?" He sounded a bit contrite. "Don't be. There's not a thing in this place that I would allow to cause you one moment of pain, unless you wanted it." She looked around at him and he smiled. "Avery, my love, nothing awaits you here but multiple orgasms." And love. But, he didn't say that part out loud.

A dozen different things battled for her attention as they stepped deeper into Isaac's domain. "I don't know what any of this stuff is even for. It looks medieval." And exciting. There were tables with restraints, a circular object which reminded her of a miniature Ferris wheel and devices on the walls that looked like places to chain people up, but when she got close enough, she saw the cuffs were made for comfort. That eased her mind somewhat. The one thing her eye finally settled on was a hood and a cape. Seeing her confusion, Isaac explained, "Sometimes we take part in scenes, and I've been known to wear a hood and a cape and gloves. It does make it rather medieval. Except if you look closely, the McCoy brand is in the middle of the forehead." They walked on. This was all so new and foreign to Avery, she wanted to see everything. On the walls were cabinets filled with who knows what and there were mirrors everywhere. Speakers and TV screens blanketed one wall and there was a bar with a mini fridge and a full array of wine and glasses. It was elegant and mysterious, but at the same time—edgy. But the most amazing thing was the way her body was reacting. Avery was wet.

"Come here, Avery." Isaac guided her to a padded table. "Now, let me tell you what I want to do. The goal of this exercise is not only to give us both a full measure of ecstasy, but also to get you used to giving yourself over to me." Slowly and gently, he began to undress her. "I want you to trust me, yield to my voice, yield to my will. I want you to be so focused on me so that your body obeys my every command." With measured movements, he revealed her nakedness inch by inch. She didn't help. She allowed him to do with her as he willed. "That's my girl." His touch was warm, tender, yet she quivered with anxious anticipation.

Never before had he been so at the mercy of a woman, she had no idea of the power she wielded over him. Isaac had the urge to drop to his knees in front of her and ask what she would have him do. That wasn't what she needed, however. Avery desired him to be strong and sure, and that was exactly what he would be. There was nothing more important to him than pleasing her. 'New territory, McCoy,' he thought, 'new territory'. As he drew the material down, he revealed smooth, creamy shoulders. Her neck was graceful and drew his lips like a magnet. "You have no idea how beautiful you are. Look how your breasts respond to me." The dress fell to her waist and he rubbed a finger across one swollen nipple. It poked out through the shear lace of her bra, hard and aroused. She moaned as he teased the swollen nubbin. "Turn around, Sweet." As she did, he swept her hair over one shoulder and unfastened her bra. The tiny panties were no barrier to his appreciation of the perfect pale globes of her behind. Cupping one, he squeezed and she rose on tiptoe, but she didn't step away. "You're going to love it when I take you here. If everyone knew how good it felt, this taboo would be tradition." Taking the top of the panties in his fingertips, he stripped them down, moving onto his knees to get them all the way down and kissing a trail down the back of Avery's leg as he went. "Step out, Treasure." While he was down there, he slipped off her sandals and peppered kisses all the way back up to the silky skin of her derriere.

"Isaac, you are making me so nervous," she admitted.

"Nervous excited or nervous scared?"

"Not scared."

"Good. The curve of your back is delectable." To prove it, he licked a trail up the indentation of her spine, and rose to his feet without missing a taste. "Now turn around." He pulled the bra from her hands and let his eyes feast on her tits. Taking them in his hands, he massaged them, rubbing his thumbs over the tips and making her squirm a little. "I'm going to be here, real soon," he promised. "I've been dreaming about thrusting up between these beauties. "Now, up you go." He picked her up and laid her flat on the table. "Arms to each side." She obeyed and he fastened each wrist in the attached cuffs. "God, you're perfect, that's what you are."

Before he could ask, she moved her legs apart so he could fasten her ankles. "You sure you haven't done this before?" He asked with a wink.

"I guess I'm just a natural."

Isaac didn't argue with her. After he had buckled the soft bindings, he stepped back to look at her. She was exquisite.

"Now, what?" She asked in a husky little voice.

"We don't need to rush." He ran a hand up one leg from ankle to knee, his fingers lightly rubbing the velvet expanse. "I just want to look at you right now." He drank in every inch of her quivering body with his hungry eyes. Avery's skin was electric under his gaze. Isaac noted every subtle movement of her body. "Did you know that your tongue keeps coming out to wet your lips?"

Avery felt the tip of her tongue on her bottom lip and it sent a chill down her spine. He saw all of her.

Isaac moved around the table. The sound of his heavy leather boots hitting the floor shattered the silence of the room. He leaned into her ear. "Can you hear it, Avery? In the still of the room. Listen."

She shook her head. She didn't know what he was referring to.

Isaac moved across to her other ear and licked the lobe. "Your breath, Baby," he whispered in her ear. "Your excitement has you breathing harder. Your chest keeps rising and falling and the way your breasts move has got me throbbing in my jeans."

"What are we going to do?" She couldn't help but ask.

"I'm going to play." He moved back in front of her. "And you're going to feel. Your body will learn to crave my touch. It is my wish that you be so in tune with me that you'll climax at my command. Do you think you could do that?" As he talked he reached for a glass flask on a nearby table.

"I want to try."

"Tonight, you won't need a safe word. In fact, I don't know that we'll ever worry with one, for you will never, ever have anything to fear from me." Holding the bottle high, he let a stream of warm oil pool on the trembling muscles of her abdomen. "You're shaking."

"With desire," she offered without hesitation. "I need your hands on me. I need your mouth, too." Standing over her, his shoulders looked a yard wide. "Will you take off your clothes? You have the most beautiful body of any man in the world."

Isaac wanted to smile, but he forced his face into a stern expression. His heart was turning to mush around this doll. If he wasn't careful, he would lose his Dom card. "I'm in charge, Miss Avery. It will be my pleasure to give you anything and everything you need, when the time is right."

"Oh, I see." Then, "oh, my!" she groaned as he stood at the edge of the table and began his sensual massage. Both palms covered her abdomen, rubbing in circular motion. He let his hands dance down near to her sex, but no further. He skated north to her breasts, but not quite. Every pass, he edged closer to the places where she needed him most and each time he made the fire burn brighter and the heat rise higher inside of her.

"Now, for an experiment. No talking, not unless I give you permission. You may groan, but no conversation. Your job is to just feel. Close your eyes, and feel."

Avery did as he asked and, immediately, she understood why. Everything magnified. In the darkness, his hands on her body became her world. It seemed as if her breasts were growing, swelling, and begging for his touch. She had no desire to get away, yet her body undulated. Her hips wanted to rise, seeking a caress in just that necessary spot. "Hmmmm," she started to speak, but held back. Praise, she yearned to praise him as he worked his magic.

God, he was beyond any state of arousal his body had ever known. Isaac couldn't remember being this hard. His manhood was so heavy with need that he would be surprised if it could stand upright. She was pleasing him. Not once did she open her eyes, not once did she speak, but her body's response told him volumes. Her nipples were like diamond chips, the areolas puffy and distended. With broader strokes, he let his fingers skate the underside of her breast and as he expected, she arched her back asking for more.

A shuddering sob broke from her lips. If he didn't touch her breasts soon she was going to do unspeakable things to him. Come to think of it, she might do that anyway. But there would be repercussions. Was that a chuckle? Without opening her eyes to see his face, she couldn't be sure. A tiny whimper of begging escaped, and she wanted to laugh. Tricia had a puppy that made this same noise when he wanted a treat. But it worked. She heard an answering growl and his palms covered her breasts and began an erotic assault.

Control was about to slip through his fingers. She was totally turned on, and he couldn't keep his eyes off her slit, which glistened with her cream. And the sounds she was making were the most arousing of all. God, he needed a kiss. Without taking his hands off of her, he moved to the head of the table so he could bend over her and take her lips while he played with her nipples. For just a second, he let her go to get in position and one tiny word gave away her desperation. "No."

"Shhhh," he reminded her as he covered her lips. Sweet, she was so sweet. God, he loved to rub her breasts. Taking her nipples between his thumb and first fingers, he milked them. The intensity of her kiss increased, and she sucked on his tongue while moaning one little hungry moan after another. Avery shook the table with the pumping of her hips. His baby was hungry. "Easy, I'll make us both feel good." Stepping back, he stripped. "Open your eyes."

Immediately she sought his gaze, her teeth biting down on her lower lip. She was holding herself back, following his directions. Good. "Damn, I wonder if it will always be like this with you. I'm too freakin' excited to prolong this like I should." The look of trust on her face gave him strength to push forward. Going to her feet, he set out to push her limits. He began kissing and licking her skin, memorizing the texture, what parts made her squirm and the places that, when he nipped, made her pant. This was the first time he would have his mouth on her sex, and he planned on blowing her mind.

Lord Have Mercy, she prayed. Isaac McCoy was worshiping her body. There was no other way to think about it. His lips, his tongue, his teeth, his hands, they were everywhere. No square inch of her flesh was going unattended. Her hips undulated as he was giving her more rapture than she had ever known existed. God, he was kissing, licking, sucking between her thighs and it was driving her mad! She tried to rise up enough to watch him and it was a sight to behold. His eyes were shut and his mouth was busy, but his left hand had strayed to her breast and he was kneading it, hiking her blood pressure to dangerous levels. She wanted to scream, she wanted to beg. But her most sincere desire was to please him, so she gave herself over to the euphoria and floated in a daze of bliss.

"I want you to come for me, Love. And I want you to shout out one word. It doesn't matter what that word is, whatever comes to mind." She was so close, he could feel it. If he were a betting man, he would say that as soon as he took her clitoris between his lips…

"Isaac!" she screamed as a rampaging orgasm threw her body into an electric storm of sensation.

His name. She chose his name to herald her release.

Oh, yeah! Every muscle in her body contracted and he held her down, determined to give her an orgasm she would never forget. Running two fingers into her channel, he sought out the spongy sweet spot and worked it, ensuring every pleasure circuit she had went into immediate overload. Isaac wasn't immune. He was sexually incensed and eager to join her in the pleasure.

Like a predatory panther, he moved over her, kissing a path up her body. The table was sturdy, and it was a good thing, because he wasn't a small man. Straddling her body, he reached for the bottle of oil and filled his palms with it. Rubbing them together, he gave her a knowing smile. "You enjoyed that, didn't you?" She gave him a tremulous smile and nodded her head, maintaining her agreed upon silence. "I own your orgasms now, Avery. You're mine to pleasure. You're mine to take my pleasure in." First, he rubbed his cock up and down with an oiled palm. It felt so good that his body wanted more, but he knew the treat that awaited him would be like heaven. Next, he cupped her breasts and massaged the oil in them. She grunted, enjoying his touch. "I would rather play with you than eat. And I love to eat, but you're stacked, Sugar-Doll." When he had them coated with the vanilla scented rub, he pushed them together. "God, look at you. You're hotter than any pin-up girl ever thought about being. And you're all mine, my own private play-toy. My Avery." Pushing his erection into the valley of her cleavage, he groaned, "Damn, that's good. Do you like that? Answer me, and keep your eyes locked with mine. I want to know you."

"I love it. I love everything you do to me," she offered, breathlessly.

He pulled out and worked his hips, his eyes closing with how good it felt. "Mmmmm…oh, yeah." Unfastening her hands, he gave her further instructions. "Push those perfect mounds together and hold them. I need my hands for other things. She did as he asked, and was glad she had when she found out what he was up to.

Pumping between her breasts, he reached behind him and cupped her mound, massaging the whole vulva.

"Damn!" Avery gasped and Isaac burst out laughing.

"I'll take that as a compliment, Church-Girl," he picked at her. "Now, look at me, Babe. Your eyes are glazing over with passion. I need for you to put the icing on the cake for me." When he had her attention, he continued, "When I push up through the Valley of Delight, I want you to have that mouth open and lick and suck the head, every time I thrust, you reward me. Okay?"

"Yes, Sir." She let her eyes drop from his to the swollen purple head, the object of her desire. She was enjoying everything, but God, she hoped he f*cked her soon. Surprising herself by giggling, she looked back at Isaac. "I just used the F-word in my thoughts. It had an asterisk in place of one of the letters, but it's a start," Avery announced proudly as if she had achieved a milestone.

"I love it. But don't change too much, Treasure. I love you just the way you are."

From between her breasts, the swollen head emerged and she lovingly took it in her mouth and sucked. Swirling her tongue around and around, she made the most of the time that she got to keep him in her mouth. When he pulled out, she whimpered, but in the next moment, she had him again. Who was enjoying it more was a toss-up, and that was how it should be, she thought. To give him credit, he didn't lose his concentration. He played her body like a fine instrument, pushing between her breasts and at the same time working magic between her thighs. Avery didn't know what to do first, count her blessings or pray this wasn't a dream. He'd said he loved her just the way she was. But did he mean it, or was it just something to say in the heat of the moment? Time would tell.

Too good, too good. Isaac picked up the pace, knowing he was about to erupt. But, like any male animal, he had an irresistible urge to mark his territory. "You're mine, Avery. Every last luscious inch of you belongs to me." Standing up on his knees, he took his cock in his hand and pumped it—once, twice, three times and exulted as streams of his seed decorated her chest, her neck, and even her lips. And what did his doll do? She licked every bit she could reach and beckoned him with welcoming eyes, so he slid his still throbbing member back into her mouth and she swallowed the last pulsing drops, and licked him clean for good measure. Home. At last, Isaac McCoy was home.

* * *

"My God, Harper! What happened to you?" Noah was horrified to find a shaking, badly bruised woman standing shivering in the night air with only a beat-up leather jacket wrapped around her naked body. She was huddled behind a dumpster, and he wouldn't have found her at all if he hadn't heard her sobbing.

"A scene went bad on me," she hiccupped, as she let him wrap his coat around her waist to cover up her nudity. Even in the light that the security lamp gave off, Noah could see whip marks all over her body—red whelps, blood stripes. The sour taste of disgust nearly made him throw up.

Leading her to his truck, he was torn between wanting to help her and wanting to get as far away from her as he could. "Who did this to you?"

"Ajax is what he called himself." She sniffed loudly as he helped her up into the shelter of his truck. "I think I need to go to the doctor, Noah."

"That's where I was headed." He sighed loudly. This wasn't the way he had wanted the night to end. Skye had stopped him on the way out of the pavilion area and invited him on a moonlight walk, and it had torn him up to have to tell her he had somewhere else to be. She had smiled at him when he asked for a rain check, and he fully intended to pursue her, that is if he could get loose from the entangling tendrils of his past. "Where did you meet this asshole?" he asked as soon he got around to his side and climbed in.

Harper doubled-over in the seat, burying her head in her hands. "At a biker's rally in Lukenbach." Her shoulders began to shake. "I'm so miserable, Noah. I hate my life!"

Noah cranked up and bit his tongue. Now wasn't the time to castigate her for her poor life choices. She needed his sympathy and his help. "I'm taking you to the emergency room. We'll get you some help."

"How did I end up like this, Noah? I used to have it all together." He handed her a handkerchief and she blew her nose. "We used to have something special. What happened to us?"

Noah hit the steering wheel with the palm of his hand. "You threw what we had away, Harper. I begged you to step away from that shit! But no. You loved it more than you loved me. I regret, more than I can say, what happened to you, but you let yourself get in over your head. So far, you haven't learned your lesson, you just keep going back after more, time and time again."

Harper quit crying, and looked at him with narrowed eyes. "Maybe, I've made mistakes. I don't deny that. But this…" She gestured down her body. "This is your fault."

Noah slammed on the brakes, pulled off the street and stared at her. "How in the hell could this possibly be my fault?"

"Because, as Ajax hit me, over and over again, he said 'you have your boyfriend to thank for this, little girl. The McCoys will learn not to mess with me.'"

* * *

"I love your room, especially this shower." Avery was having the time of her life. Isaac had tenderly carried her to the shower and washed every bit of the oil and evidence of their loving from her body. Now, it was her turn. "But, I love your body the most. You are the sexiest man in the world. I can't believe I'm here with you like this. I am so, so lucky." She had soaped her hands and was washing him skin on skin.

"I'm the lucky one, Avery-mine." He cupped the back of her head as she went to her knees and soaped his muscular legs from knee to ankle. When they had first entered the shower, he had been flaccid. Now, next to her cheek was his HUGE manhood!

"Can I…?" She stole a kiss from the side of his swollen rod.

"Don't tempt me. But no, I have other plans for this erection. I want to be inside you. Now." He pulled her up and out of the shower, wrapping her in a big, fluffy towel.

"No shower sex?" Foot! She'd been counting on that.

"That's on the agenda, but I have other things in mind right now. Do you trust me?" he asked as he kissed droplets of water from off of the mounds of her breasts.

"Haven't I already proved that?"

Isaac swung her up in his arms and bit her cheek, playfully. "I could just eat you up. You're too damn cute. Yes, you proved it. But that was elementary sex, Baby. Now, we're moving up to the big leagues. Are you ready?"

"Heck, yeah!" Her enthusiasm was showing.

Isaac was thrilled by Avery's willingness and responsiveness. "Don't you think you should wait and find out what I'm talking about first?"

"So, show me!" She challenged him with a grin. Kicking her legs, she wiggled until he put her down. "I'm ready."

"Getting cocky, aren't we?"

With a mischievous giggle, she closed her hand over his manhood and squeezed, gently. "Me? I think cocky describes you a little better, big boy." She pumped it once, then twice, lovingly.

Never before had he played like this with his subs. Although that term might be a bit premature, she was redefining what made him happy in this room. "I know you played with toys while in Nevada, but I think I can teach you a trick or two."

"Is it permissible for me to make a suggestion?" She might be overstepping her bounds, but she was learning as she went.

Isaac stopped in his tracks. "Of course." He couldn't wait to hear what she had to say.

She sidled up to him. Was she flirting? Naked flirting? Avery Rose Sinclair was totally out of hand.

Placing her hands on his shoulders, she rose up on tiptoe to whisper in his ear. Her nipples tangled in his chest hair and she could feel his heart pounding in his chest. Leaning over, he wondered what she would say. He wouldn't put anything past her. She was constantly surprising him. And this time, she didn't disappoint. "I would really appreciate it, if you would spank me. Not hard, just a little bit. Please?" She dropped off her tiptoes and the bouncing of her breasts drew his eyes like a magnet.

Clearing his throat, he struggled to maintain a serious expression. What he wanted to do was grin from ear to ear. Frankly, he couldn't remember being this happy in a long time. "I think that could be arranged."

"Where do you want me?" She spun around and that curtain of hair had a hey-day bouncing around on the top of her butt cheeks.

"On the spanking bench."

Wheeling around she faced him with her mouth agape. "On the what?" She didn't wait for him to repeat himself. "Are you serious? They really call it that? Which one is it?"

"Guess."

She looked around and let her imagination run wild, and then she saw it. "That one?" she said with a point.

"You're learning quickly." He held out his hand to guide her. Avery loved how attentive he was. Dominant may be his goal, but making her feel important was what he was accomplishing. "They call it a punishing bench, but don't let that scare you. I like the way it's made, perfect for doggy style. See, there's a place for your knees and it'll make that perfect butt of yours stick up in just the right position. Here, hop on." He helped her up and showed her how to lean over. "I don't think it'll be necessary to lock you down, because this is your request, not a punishment."

She leaned over the waist bar and felt completely vulnerable. Now, she was ready to receive any and all things he would dish out. Her forearms and knees rested securely on the comfortable padding. "What are you going to spank me with?"

He began by palming her rump, rubbing the round, firm globes. Petting her would ensure that she knew this was an exercise in pleasure. Anytime pain was administered to heighten erotic play, it was paramount that love and affection be communicated above all. "I could use a small wooden paddle or a soft leather quirt. Both of those things make beautiful pink markings on pearly white skin. Or I could use my hand. Either way, I was wrong earlier. This time, I insist upon a safe word." As he rubbed, he teased the crease of her behind, dipping his finger into the crevice and playing a bit. Dipping down further, Isaac swirled his fingers around her clitoris, gathering cream and bringing it back to adorn her petite backdoor. "What'll it be? I need a word and the implement you'd prefer."

She huffed out a breath. "You expect me to think right now?" She let out a sigh when Isaac pushed the tip of his finger up inside of her. "Right now, when I'm so turned on I might self-combust?" He withdrew his finger and popped her once, lightly, drawing a giggle out of her. "I felt that in my good spot. So, the implement is settled." Her voice dropped to a husky level. "I want your hand and my safe word will be...Jezebel."

"Interesting choice. I like it. It's so you." He enjoyed joshing with her. Avery was fun. For just a second there was quiet. He stepped behind her, his manhood still stiff and distended. This state was almost a natural way to be around this woman. Soon, he promised it, soon. Her body was already wet for him. All he needed to do was introduce her to a new way of feeling good, that is, if she liked it. With both hands he framed and caressed her ass. "A perfect heart shape. Beautiful." Oh, this was going to be fun. Drawing back he delivered a spank. It wasn't really hard, for he had no intention of causing her any real pain.

She let out a little yelp. "Oww!"

"Not what you expected, Jezebel?" He waited.

"Do it again. Please," she added hastily.

Pop!

Pop!

He intersperse the love-taps with rubs. Her butt cheeks were turning the most delicious shade of pink. "Ummmmm..." She made a little noise that he strived to interpret.

Pop! Pop! Pop! Pause. Glancing down he saw a trail of excitement. Her body liked it. But did her mind and heart? That's what was important. Still, he hesitated until she pushed her bottom back and tilted it up. "More, Isaac, please." Thank, God. He resumed the erotic spanking, becoming more turned on with every blow. Soon, she was begging. "I need to finish, Isaac. I ache. I'm so empty."

"You're so hot. I've always known you were beautiful and sexy, but damn, love, there's no one like you." He grabbed his engorged rod and fitted it to her waiting heat. Soon, he would introduce her to the joys of having her sex spanked and how the taste of the quirt could be incredibly sweet. They would only do what made her happy, but so far she was taking to this like a fish to water. She groaned as he began to push his way inside of her. "Tight. My God, you are so tight." The walls of her vagina enveloped him and treasured him. Lord, he loved to be inside Avery bareback. "Oh, you are hungry, aren't you?" As soon as he'd tunneled in, she began to tighten on him with a steady rhythm. She wasn't climaxing. Avery was multiplying both of their pleasure.

She bowed her head and arched her back. Oh, this was so good. Being taken from the back was not a position she had ever fantasized about. She'd always thought it would be impersonal. Instead, it was primal. Isaac was powerful. His thrusts moved her whole body. She was being mounted, his hands at her waist controlling the depth of his penetration, and all she could think about was how incredible it felt. She was spiraling out of control. Nothing in her life had ever prepared her for the raw, raunchy reality of being dominated and taken by her soul mate. She reveled in his grunts and groans, animalistic in their cadence. They did nothing but make her want to beg for more. "More, Sir, please!"

A satisfied, conquering thrill shot through him. She had called him 'Sir', in the throes of passion where only truth won out. She had shown her true colors. Avery Rose fit him to a tee. Moving his body over hers, he pumped into her over and over again. This was what it should be like. Always. Sliding his palms underneath her chest, he cupped her breasts and squeezed them, pinching the nipples, adding just a dash of spice to push her over. There was no way he could keep this up. His orgasm was boiling up from his balls and he was ready to explode. Just last week, he had wondered if he could ever take joy in this room again. And now it would never be the same. Avery had changed everything.

"I can't take it, it's just too good," she cried. "God, Baby – Yessssss!"

Burying his face in her neck, he nipped the soft flesh. She was clamping down on him, squeezing. Her orgasm was all over his driving member. "You're mine, Avery." He jabbed into paradise, hard, taking the tender flesh of her neck into his mouth and sucking as he poured his seed deep within her. This was his way of marking her, leaving evidence of possession behind. Until he could get his ring on her finger, this would have to do.

* * *

After their loving, Isaac carried her back up the stairs to his apartment at Hardbodies. Now, all he had to do was convince her to marry him. Surely, it wouldn't be that difficult. Hadn't he proved how perfect they were together? He had to admit it seemed like a miracle to him. Never in a million years would he have guessed at the wildcat living within the body of this cuddly kitten. After tending to her needs, kissing her awake enough to brush her teeth, he carried her to the bed and wrapped himself around her. The next thing he knew, his cell phone was demanding attention.

"McCoy," he growled. "This had better be good."

"Oh, it's good," Jacob answered. "Jessie and I are getting married today. No fanfare. I'm just making her mine, but we're having a family dinner tonight. I know it's on the heels of the party, but this will just be us. You think you could get Levi to cover for you tonight? Oh, and Jessie said to make sure you talk Avery into coming. She likes her."

Curling a ringlet around his finger, he wanted to brag that she was with him right now. But this was too personal, too precious. "I'll see what I can do. And congratulations, but I'm sorry you're missing out on the festivities. I was there when Cady's grandmother told Jessie her feelings about the double wedding."

"Listen, like I told Jessie, I want to marry her more than anything. The how's, when's, and where's don't make a hill of a beans difference to me. So, we've decided to tie the knot before. There ain't a damned good reason to wait another second."

"Can I bring anything?"

"I would say some champagne, but with all the pregnant women we've got around us, that would just be cruel. So no, just you, Bud, and the little woman." Isaac could hear talking in the background. "Nathan said for you to bring that dog collar home to Lady that he saw in your truck. Do you know what he's talking about?"

Damn! That wasn't a dog collar. That was Levi's sub collar he was talking about. It must have fallen into the back seat. Levi didn't have a steady lady at the moment, but he did like to adorn the lady du jour. "Tell him I'll make sure Lady gets a collar." Now, he'd have to go by the pet store and hunt something as near to what Nathan had seen as he could. Jacob rang off and he cuddled back up to Avery for a few minutes. He'd never been one to collar a woman, but he knew what it meant. It was a visible, recognizable sign of possession, ownership and commitment. Among his kind, it was as meaningful and binding as an engagement ring, maybe more so. He didn't know how Avery would feel about being collared, but it would make him happy to give her both, a ring and a collar. And the one he had in mind would be a girl's dream, a platinum circle encrusted in diamonds, not your ordinary collar.

Nuzzling her neck, he stroked his hand down her body, just enjoying the touch of her skin. "Hey, Sexy. Do you have to work today?"

With a small yelp, Avery almost levitated off the bed. "Foot a duck! What time is it?"

"Calm down, Sweet. It's only eight o'clock. We've got plenty of time." She wiggled in his arms like a slippery eel. Finally, he let her go before she tangled herself any farther in the covers. "Where do you think you're going?"

Going to her knees in the bed, she plunked herself over on top of him, just climbed right on, laying full length on top of him. "I'm supposed to go help Tricia. I can't let her down." Taking his face in her hands, she kissed him long and deep, her tongue delving in and rubbing against his. "Mmmm, you are such a temptation." She snuggled down, fitting her head under his chin. "Am I taking too many liberties?"

Moving that wealth of hair to one side, he rubbed her back. "Impossible. Consider me your playground. Wanna ride the roller coaster?" He pumped his hips up and let her feel his bulge that was beginning to rise to the occasion.

"God! I wish." She licked his chest, kissing all around his nipple. "Maybe, we could get together later in the week or something. That is, if you want to."

What was it going to take? "Avery, my Avery." He took her chin between his thumb and first finger. "I'll take you to work and pick you up when work is over. Tonight, we're going to a family dinner, celebrating Jessie and Jacob's wedding. They're sneaking off to get married this afternoon. I want you moving in with me, today."

"Wonderful, I'm so happy for them," she beamed, then went very still. "About us, I would love to move in with you, but we're still making sure this all works. Right?"

He reiterated his last mental point. "What is it going to take? I thought we proved something here last night."

"We did," she agreed. "Still, I think I have a ways to go." She was purposefully vague. What she wanted was for him to tell her that he loved her. During their lovemaking, he had said that he loved her just the way she was, but people said things like that all the time. Avery dreamed of Isaac holding her face, looking in her eyes and telling her that he loved her more than life itself. When that happened, she would have everything she'd ever wanted. She'd have Isaac.

Isaac was feeling a bit frustrated. He had her in his arms, but he felt like she could fly away at any moment. It was like trying to hold on to a small wild creature that didn't know whether they could completely trust you or not. "If we still have a ways to go, Avery, you might ought to try giving me a map so I can find my way."

Not knowing how to answer, she chose to change the subject. Glancing at his watch on the bedside table, she sighed. "I've got to get ready to go and yes, I'll go to my house and pack a suitcase and go home with you tonight. Where we stay doesn't matter to me. Home is where you'll be." She could tell that admission pacified him, somewhat. "If you could pick me up at, say six? I need some time to talk to my agent."

She began scrambling off of him. To be so graceful on stage, she was adorably uncoordinated. Most likely, he would spend a lifetime catching her before she fell. Funny, that sounded perfect to him. Tearing his eyes off of her bobbing rump, he thought about her comment. Agent? What agent? "What are you talking about, agent?"

No time like the present. After all, they were sharing everything else. "I write romance novels. Most of them have been just contemporary, but I've started writing erotic novellas, and they're selling like hotcakes. I'm a smut writer!" she announced proudly.

"Holy Hell!"

Chapter Eight

As Isaac went about his day at the bar he attempted to digest the information that his pure and innocent little church girl had, in a matter of a few days, emerged from her cotton wool cocoon and revealed herself to be sexually adventurous, fun as hell, sweet as sugar and the weaver of erotic words. "That beats all I've ever heard," he talked to himself as he wiped down tables with a grin on his lips.

His morning had been full of the things that came with owning a bar. Doris had insisted they hire a cleaning crew, and she had been right. So he'd interviewed three different services this morning, and settled on one that ought to work out fine. Crowbar did all he could, but he needed help. The cleaners would start tomorrow. Plus, he'd placed his liquor order. All of the family fun had depleted his stock. They still had Aron and Libby's wedding on the 16th and then his birthday on the 31st. He couldn't believe his big brother would be tying the knot in less than a week and Jacob was getting hitched, right about now, he realized as he glanced over at the clock.

Isaac didn't worry about money, not really. Hardbodies wasn't making a killing, mainly because he used a lot of his inventory for private use. As far as he was concerned, that's what it was for. He wasn't accountable to anybody but himself and his employees. Tebow kept them all going and Noah deposited his share of the profits into his checking account monthly. That money was what he used to take care of his 'projects'. None of the family questioned one another about their profit sharing funds. Each brother did their own thing. Noah and Aron made sure that proper investments were made, the ranch was updated, expanded and ran like a well-oiled machine. Jacob was the mogul of the group. He had made some private investments and now had his own mineral company. Still, they were a family and families took care of one another.

"Boss!" Levi called from the back. Isaac laughed. In many ways Levi was such a cut-up. "The bull is here!"

Ah, the mechanical bull. "Excellent. I'll be right there." When he got to the back, the deliverymen had just unloaded the big box and were ready to take it in to bolt it to the floor. "Do we have all the electrical hook-ups ready to go?"

"Sure thing. We'll be bouncing around on this thing before the sun goes down."

Levi's off-hand comment just gave Isaac an idea. He wondered if Avery would want to ride him while he rode the bull. Hell yeah! Together, they worked with the installers until the simulator was in proper working order.

"How much are you guys gonna charge to let somebody ride this thing?" One of the deliverymen asked.

"Nothing," Isaac answered. "This is to draw customers in and keep them happy once they get here."

"Makes sense." The two shook hands with Isaac and Levi and took their leave.

As they picked up the scrap pieces of cardboard left over from the box to burn, Levi cut his eyes at Isaac. "Did you meet that new girl last week, Pawnee Baker?"

"Yea, I did. She seemed like a nice lady." Just a few days ago, his response would have been, 'she's a looker or nice rack', but that was pre-Avery.

"I heard something about her." Levi's tone, more than his words, told Isaac that whatever he was about to say was important to him.

"What's going on?" He walked over to the bar. "It's five o'clock somewhere. Right?" They didn't open till five, but ownership had to count for something. "Wanna beer?"

"Yea, I think I need one."

Taking two longnecks from the cooler, he opened them and walked over to join his friend. "So what did you hear about the lovely Miss Baker? I saw quite a few cowboys checking her out. If you're gonna throw your hat in the ring, you'd best do it in a hurry." Isaac poured half the bottle down his throat. "She into kink?"

"Hell, she gives kink a whole new meaning." Levi leaned back and took a long swig. Isaac thought he looked miserable. So, he waited for his bartender to continue…and he waited.

"Well, don't leave me hangin'!" Isaac complained.

"That's the whole problem. She's hangin'," Isaac mumbled.

"What are you talking about?"

"She's pretty, you know. I mean *real* pretty. And I was attracted to her, big time. It's not like I don't get women, but there was just something about this woman that seemed so soft and vulnerable. I guess you could say that she brought out the man in me."

"So, what's the problem?" Sometimes he had to be drawn a picture, but he just wasn't getting it.

"Man, I mentioned to Terence Lee that I intended to ask her out and he laughed at me."

"Why?"

"He said that it's rumored Pawnee has a....damn, a p..." He stumbled with his words. "A p..."

"A P?" Isaac held his hands out in supplication. "Spit it out, Levi."

"A penis."

Isaac almost swallowed his tongue. "Damn."

"Yes, a penis. A little one, but a penis, nonetheless. Supposedly everything else is there and all of it functions perfectly. It knocked me for a loop, I tell you." He slouched over with his forearms on his legs, the beer bottling dangling between his knees.

"That beautiful woman is a hermaphrodite? I thought they were, you know, rougher looking. She seems so...normal...beautiful, I mean." Isaac had seen a lot of things. He knew transsexuals, bisexuals, homosexuals, even some who claimed to be asexual, but never had he met someone with both male and female genitalia. "God, I bet she's lonely."

Levi looked up. "That's what hit me. A person like that, there'd be nowhere for them to go, you know? Can you imagine how cruel people would be?"

"Yeah, she seemed so fragile and feminine. I can't imagine anyone being mean to her." Isaac felt sympathy for her. He had an open mind about things, more so than lots of people. "Does it give you the willies?"

"I don't know, man." Levi looked down at the floor. "I just don't know."

"You still going to ask her out?"

"Hell, part of me wants to. And part of me is scared to death. So, I just don't know."

Isaac stood up and held out his hand for Levi's empty beer bottle. "Whatever you decide, you have my support."

"Thanks, Man."

Isaac left his friend sitting there with a big decision to make.

* * *

Noah had stayed with Harper until she had been looked at, cleaned up and admitted to the hospital. The doctor said she had broken ribs and deep lacerations. There was also a tear in her rectum from rough anal sex. That bastard Ajax had beat the hell out of her. Oh, she bore some of the blame. After all, Harper willingly put herself in these risky situations. But there was something strange about this and he seemed to be involved whether he wanted to be or not.

Against her will, he'd phoned her folks. They were good people, who had been friends with his own parents. Old Kerrville stock, they simply didn't know what to do with Harper. Her mom had asked Noah if they should try and get her some help, and he had been a strong advocate. Counseling was critical, as far as he could see.

For a few minutes, he considered calling Kane, but this seemed like it should be kept private. All day a creepy feeling had been crawling up and down his spine. Something told him that he needed to see to this personally. Harper didn't know for sure how to find Ajax, but she gave him several places to look for him, primarily dives and strip joints. He'd asked about sex clubs and BDSM clubs, but she said he didn't do those anymore. Apparently, he'd been banned. That struck Noah as funny. He didn't realize those kind of people had a conscience at all. With list in hand, Noah set out to find Ajax and see if he could get in a few licks of his own.

***

"So, you're moving in with him?" Tricia stood over Avery as she packed her signature pink suitcase.

"Yes, and don't just stand there. Help me! He'll be here any minute. We have a family dinner tonight."

Tricia gave Avery's suitcase a little tap with her foot. "So, WE have a family dinner tonight. With the McCoys"

"Stop that. Would you quit smirking and hand me the underwear out of that drawer."

Tricia stopped smiling long enough to dig out a dozen pair of white cotton underwear and some plain serviceable bras. "This stuff won't do. We need to get online to Victoria's Secret and do some serious shopping for you."

"Just grab anything, I ran out of time. Damn agent kept me on the phone too long. All of that writing I did last summer paid off." She looked up at her partner and smiled. "I got a three book deal!"

Tricia folded panties and arranged hose and slips in the side pockets of the soft-side luggage. "Three books?" she squealed. "Congratulations, I guess you're not going to have time for me." There was a hint of hurt in her voice.

"Nonsense, I gave you a good eight hours today and I intend to do that five days a week. Isaac doesn't have a problem with my working, and I enjoy what we do. You're not getting rid of me that easy."

Tricia perked up. "Good. When am I going to get to read something you wrote?"

Turning, Avery opened a drawer on her nightstand and handed her friend a book. "There you go. I hope you enjoy it. Remember, it's sort of risqué. Not as spicy as my current WIPs, but pretty racy, all the same."

"Sable Hunter, I like that name. Neat." She held the book close to her chest as a distinct rumble was heard in the living room.

"I thought I told you to lock these doors. Anybody can walk in here on you two," Isaac fussed as he found them in Avery's bedroom.

"I see that. Don't you believe in knocking?" She grouched at him, but she was all smiles. She let him gather her close for a kiss.

"Hi, Tricia, how are you?"

"Jealous." She sighed. "Are there instructions in this book of yours on how to find a man like the one you've cornered?"

Avery made a wry face at Tricia. "Very funny, like you need any help? You're gorgeous. Isn't she, Isaac?" Held close in Isaac's arms, she felt completely safe and...yes, loved. If he didn't feel the same way she did, he was doing a heck of an imitation.

"Hey, is that one of Avery's?" Keeping one hand on her arm, he reached for the book. "Let me see." He thumbed through it. "I want to read everything you've written."

"That's no problem. We have no secrets. Do we?"

"No, we don't," he assured her. And he was damn thankful he didn't have to lie to her. Avery knew all of his secrets and she loved him anyway. That knowledge was extremely freeing. "Are you about ready? The family will be gathering soon."

Snapping her suitcase shut, she looked around. "Yes, I have enough. I can get the rest of my things later." Avery was going to be positive. Everything was going to work out. Isaac would learn to love her, she hoped. He just had to.

* * *

Cady, official McCoy fiancé, had stepped up and prepared the wedding supper for Jessie and Jacob. Joseph had helped, playing zydeco on the music system. They had concocted gumbo, grilled shrimp, rice pilaf, and bourbon chocolate bread pudding. It was going to be a meal to remember. Cady's family had returned to south Louisiana, but their gift had been to fill their freezers full of enough shrimp, crawfish, and Andouille sausage to last till the next visit.

"Do you think Jessie will like the little bull we're all giving them as a wedding present?"

"There's no doubt in my mind that both of them will take to him right off, Little Bud. Jacob has been hankering after one of Machine Gun's offspring for years. Those little guys are worth their weight in gold." Joseph was sitting at the dining table, on his laptop, registering for his first dirt-bike race since the accident. He didn't type fast, but used the hunt and peck method. "Nathan has been in charge of getting our gift all spruced up and ready for presentation," he explained to Cady.

"I've made pralines, Nathan. Would you like one?" Cady held out a platter of the pecan caramel confections.

"Yes, please," he accepted one of the sugary treats. "Isaac just drove up with Avery. You know, if Noah brings home a girl, everyone will have one but me."

Cady was amused. "Does that mean you are ready for a girlfriend?"

"Heck, no!" Nathan was emphatic.

"This is a family dinner, but I think it would be okay if you asked a date, Nathan." Joseph took the opportunity to josh his brother. "Haley probably loves shrimp. Why don't you give her a call?"

"Nah," Nathan rejected his brother's idea. "I think I'd rather spend time with that bull calf and Lady."

"That will change." Joseph laughed.

"Sooner than you think," Cady added as she stirred the pot of gumbo. "Why don't you take the little bull some sugar cubes? And you can give the horses a treat while you're out there."

"Can Lady have a piece of that candy? I think she'd like that." At the mention of her name coupled with the word candy, Lady peeked her head around the door.

"Does Libby know you've been sneaking Lady in every chance you get?" Joseph tried to sound stern, but he liked to have animals in the house. His Mom had never stopped them from having pets, even in their rooms. But Sabrina, Aron's first wife had put a stop to the animals and they hadn't had any in the house since, until now.

"She don't care, but she said I had to clear it with Jessie and Cady, too." He gave Cady such a pitiful look that she walked over to the dog and offered a piece of the pecan confection. "You have my blessing, Miss Lady. You can sleep with me anytime." She ran her finger down the dog's head. "I bet she's smarter than we all realize. Aren't you, Girl?" The dog seemed to give her a knowing smile.

"Now, wait a minute. Your bed is occupied, by me." Joseph was teasing. Maybe. Nathan filled his pockets with treats and he and the black lab were about to scamper out the back door when Lady perked up her ears.

"Isaac's here!" Nathan announced as Lady dashed over to meet the man who had saved her life by rescuing her from the side of the road.

"Something sure smells good." Isaac and Avery came through the door. "Hey, Girl," he stooped to pet the dog and Nathan came over for his hug. "Man, I missed you today, Nate. Guess what I had delivered at the bar?"

"What? A new bike?" Nathan couldn't wait to have his own motorcycle, but Isaac was the one who had put his foot down. He wanted Nathan to wait until he was at least sixteen.

"No, a mechanical bull."

"Wow, can I ride it?" Nathan's level of enthusiasm spiked a thousand percent.

"Yes, you can."

"Man, O man." He pumped his fist in the air. "Can I come over tonight?"

"No." Isaac glanced at Avery. "I plan on letting Avery try it out first."

His wink told Avery that he was up to something. What it was, she didn't know.

"Where is everybody?" Isaac wanted to know. "Are the newlyweds back from the courthouse?"

"Yes, they're in their room," Cady whispered. "Jessie was tired, and she needed a nap."

"Is that what they're calling it now? A nap? And Jacob's napping with her, I presume?" Isaac held the refrigerator door open for Nathan as he filled a plastic bag with apples and carrots for the horses. No one answered his teasing questions about his brother and his bride's short honeymoon.

Seeing the pink Hello Kitty suitcase in Isaac's hand, Joseph asked, "Going on a trip?"

"Just up to my room, Wise-Ass. Avery's moving in."

"Sweet." Joseph grinned. "There's definitely something in the water around here, Nate my Man. You'd better start drinking Kool-Aid."

"Kool-Aid is made with water," Nathan explained patiently.

"Dang, Cady. So, that's how you caught me," Cady never blinked, she just whacked Joseph playfully with a wooden spoon.

"When's dinner?" Isaac asked. "I'm starving."

"Everything's ready. As soon as Libby, Aron and Noah get here, we'll call Jessie and Jacob and get started." Cady handed Nathan a jacket. "Put this on and hurry back. Don't make me have to send Joseph out to tear you away from the animals."

"Yes, Cady," he promised as he led Lady by the collar. "Come on, Girl, two down one to go."

Cady saw Avery's curious expression. "He still has to get the okay from Jessie about letting the dog in the house."

"I love dogs and cats. Once, I even had a white mouse in the house." She looked around wistfully at the big, comfortable kitchen. This was so obviously a home inhabited by people who loved each other. Would she ever feel at home here?

Joseph patted a chair. "Come sit by me, Avery, and tell me what you see in this badass brother of mine."

Isaac jumped over and pulled out her chair. "He's a gentleman," she offered as a start. "And I can get all the Shirley Temple's I want for free." Isaac roared with laughter.

"See, I have my uses." He wrapped an arm around Avery and pulled her close. "I'll show you my other 'assets' later." She kissed his forearm that rested just under her chin.

"I enjoyed your engagement party," Avery spoke to Cady. "The food was out of this world."

"I can't take credit for the buffet. The men prepared the meat and Jessie, Lilibet and Libby did the rest." She set the platter of pralines on the table. "It'll spoil our appetites, but these are wonderful warm."

"Oh, these are my absolute favorite candies in the whole world," Avery exclaimed as she laid claim to one of the treats.

"I'm glad. I made enough of these to fill the Mississippi. At the rehearsal dinner Friday night, guests get to take a little bag of these home with them. They're my contribution to the celebration."

"Oh, I want mine and yours, both," she told Isaac with serious eyes. "I love them."

"So, I gathered." Isaac took one for himself. "I wonder if they make praline flavored massage oil." Avery punched him. She knew exactly what he was getting at.

"Can I set the table for you?"

"Please do."

Cady seemed glad of the help and Avery wanted to be useful. Joseph put up his laptop and he and Isaac pitched in until they had everything ready.

"Have you received any word from Austin Boot Company on whether or not they'll help sponsor your rodeo?"

Joseph carried the heavy tureen of gumbo to the table as he answered Isaac's question. "As a matter of fact, Beau called me today and gave me good news. Austin Boot is in and so is Barrington Rifle."

"All right!" Isaac was so proud of his brother. "Avery, Joseph is putting together a benefit rodeo that will give handicapped children a chance to get up close and personal with some cowboys and all profits will go to help paralyzed kids."

"Wow that sounds great. I do some work for the Christopher Reeve Paralysis Foundation."

"Avery, you have got to meet Joseph's friend, Beau. He is one of the most colorful characters you could imagine. He lives on the banks of the Atchafalaya Swamp and has more alligator stories than you can count."

"I can't wait to meet him."

"You'll get the chance soon. He's coming to the wedding."

"Who's coming to the wedding?" Aron asked as he sauntered into the room carrying an armful of packages.

"Beau."

"Excellent, the more the merrier. I want everybody to witness me marrying the most beautiful girl in the world."

"Speaking of marrying..." Jacob escorted Jessie through the door. She was blushing and looked happier than anybody Avery had ever seen.

"Congratulations, you two." Libby hugged Jessie, then Jacob. After much backslapping and kissing of cheeks, the family began to settle around the table.

"Where's Noah?" Jessie asked.

Aron thought a minute. "I don't know. I haven't seen him since the party last night." He looked around the table. "Who talked to Noah last?"

"I didn't talk to him, but I did see him take a call and then he left. I thought he had a date." Joseph didn't look concerned.

"If it were any of the rest of you, I wouldn't worry. But this isn't like Noah." Aron got out his phone and rang his number. Everyone waited. Finally, he closed it. "He didn't answer."

* * *

Noah walked across the parking lot to where Ajax sat on the tailgate of a beat-up Ford pickup. "You Ajax Dirkson?"

"Who wants to know, Pretty Boy?"

"I'm the man who is going to whip your ass, you perverted bastard."

"Is that so?" Ajax sneered at him. Noah wasn't worried. Ajax was big, but not that much bigger and he looked bloated and out of shape. But his eyes worried Noah. They were cold and dead looking like snake eyes. He could just imagine this bastard wielding a whip on Harper's small body.

"You went too far with a friend of mine, and I've come to make sure you never have the balls to do it again." Noah didn't enjoy fighting, not like Isaac or even Joseph. But he could. He had brawled often enough with his brothers.

Grabbing his crotch, Ajax belched. "The skinny blonde wasn't the best bitch I'd ever had, but I did enjoy making her scream. That was one little whore who enjoyed the whip." Noah lunged at Ajax, but he raised his boot and kicked Noah in the stomach. Noah grunted and sidestepped.

"Sick bastard, I'm going to stomp your ugly face." Noah grabbed Ajax by the shoulders and pulled him off the truck. He was able to land one blow, but out of nowhere he was grabbed from behind by two men and pulled off the rank biker.

"What have we here?" A gruff voice with a thick Caribbean accent snarled in Noah's ear. "Do you know who this is, Ajax?"

Noah fought to get away, but he couldn't. Hell, he was in trouble.

"This golden-haired sissy-boy is a McCoy."

Ajax stepped closer. "A McCoy, huh? Not the McCoy I was hoping to draw out. Maybe, I didn't use the right bait. Still, I'm not one to look a gift horse in the mouth. Turn him loose, Troy. Let's at least pretend this is going to be fair." Ajax reached behind him and pulled out a bullwhip and Noah prayed that he hadn't made the worst mistake of his life.

* * *

Noah hadn't come home at all. They had waited dinner until everything was cold, and finally eaten just so Jacob and Jessie's evening wouldn't be a total washout. Isaac was concerned, but Noah was a grown man and could do what the hell he wanted to. He just hoped he was all right. At this particular moment, as he walked into his bar with Avery, he had other things on his mind. "You said you wanted to learn how to ride. Right?"

"Yeah, that's what I said." The words came out slow and hesitant. "Although, I was talking about either riding you or a meek steed like your horse Molly. Libby says she's as gentle as a lamb."

"Zeus can be gentle. I've got a pre-programmed setting all figured out. Besides, you aren't going to be riding by yourself." He turned her around, kissed her at the corner of her mouth and began undoing her clothes.

"You're going to ride with me?" She didn't protest his efforts to get her naked. Instead she began unbuttoning his shirt.

"Close, sugar. Actually, I'm gonna ride the bull and you're going to ride me."

To his delight, she growled. "Oh, yeah. I want a T-shirt that says 'save a bull, ride a cowboy'."

"I bet I could handle that." He was already getting hard. She was excited, he could tell. Her nipples were hard, her skin was flushed and yeah, he dipped his hand between her legs and it was sweetly damp. With a smooth move, she pulled his pants down, all the while running her tongue and lips over his chest. "I love the way you touch me." He couldn't help but let her know.

"How about this?" She slipped her hand down his tighty-whiteys, cupped his nuts and began massaging them.

"Damn, yeah, that's so good." His balls weren't the only things that got attention.

"Two hands are better." He pulled his shorts down to give her more room to work as she began pumping his erection. Running her thumb over the tip, she found the dewdrop.

"I want you so much, Isaac."

Damn! Avery was such a firebrand. He was a damn lucky son-of-a-gun. "Come on, or the rodeo will be over before we get on the back of the bull." They shed their last few pieces of clothing and he led her to the mechanical ride. There was a small remote control device that he picked up before climbing on the back and holding out his hand to help her get in place. He stood up in the stirrups and leaned as far back as he could and still stay on. "Come to me, Sugar. I'll make you feel really good."

She placed her hand in his and used the stirrup to get on, scrambling in place facing him. Once she was there, he fit himself down and hauled her up next to him. She gasped with satisfaction and surprise as he picked her up by the waist and draped her thighs over the top of his. "Isaac, I'm so excited, I may melt from just being close to you."

"Good. I want you to enjoy everything we do," Isaac spoke in a low, heated whisper as he nuzzled her neck, licking and nibbling, causing goose bumps to rise all over her skin. "Lean into me. I wanna feel your nipples rubbing me. Touch me, Avery."

She got as close as she could and still stay in her own skin. When her breasts rubbed up against him, she couldn't be still. Wrapping her arms around his shoulders, she caressed his neck, petted his hair and nipped him on the earlobe, just because she could.

"You ready to bump and grind a little?"

"Please," she murmured, her head already spinning from the electric sizzle of his nearness.

"Tighten your grip on me. I'm gonna get this boy going, real easy like." It was slow, but the front of the rodeo simulator lifted, causing Avery to fall into Isaac. It was like coming to rest against a stone pillar. He didn't budge. She could wrap herself around him during any storm and he'd be like an anchor of safety. "That's right, give me all your weight, put your trust in me." No problem. She was already there. His manhood was like a steel rod between them, and she was more than ready to feel him stretching her. They'd only made love a few times, but she was already addicted to how he could make her feel. "Can we put him in now?"

"Hell, yes." He picked her up a few inches. "Guide him in." As she fitted the head to the opening of her channel, he sucked and bit at her nipples, making her close her eyes in ecstasy. "Now, ease down. Oh, God, yeah, just like that." The feel of their union was exquisite for both of them. "Okay, here we go. And this is the first time I've ever done this by the way, just so you know." His words weren't plain. They were gritted out between his teeth.

The bull spun to the right and she laid her head on his shoulder. "No, raise your head. I need you up here." Avery obeyed, and she was glad she did, because he covered her mouth with his and kissed her with abandon. She kneaded his muscles, holding tightly and his hands weren't still. They were everywhere. She felt adored, and she wouldn't have traded that feeling for anything.

Their bodies moved with the pitch and sway of the bull. He did all the work and all she had to do was give herself over totally to him. Even in this, she was submitting and it felt heavenly. She wondered if he realized. "I love to be in your hands like this. To feel your control is so hot."

"You're hot, damn hot." These words were mouthed against her lips.

And she was listening, truly she was, except her clitoris was getting a thrill every time the bull dropped down. Gravity and delicious proximity pushed it against the ridge of his pelvis and the hard muscles of his abs. He was so big, so strong. She loved to massage his thick hardness by tightening the muscles of her sheathe. "Does it feel good when I do that?" She rocked on him.

"Damn, I'm close, Avery." He tilted her head back and licked her breasts. The rhythm of the bull and Isaac's natural ability to move his body made the whole experience seem like an erotic dance. "Squeeze me, harder. Bounce a little, Baby." He turned the bull's movements completely off and gave her free rein. He let his legs drop straight down, giving her the stirrups. She braced herself against his hard body, stood up in the stirrups and slid up and down on his rock hard staff, impaling herself over and over. He reached between them and began to feverishly rub her clitoris.

"Not fair. I'm gonna come." She didn't want it to be over so soon. Avery wanted this feeling to go on forever.

"That's the idea. I love to see you come apart."

As he stroked her, she could feel her world narrow down to that sweet place between her legs. "I need help. I need you to pound me." She wasn't sure if she was making it clear as to what she needed. It was hard to think and communicate when all she wanted to do was be ravished. Yeah, that was it. "I need you to ravish me."

"Lay back." He helped ease her down to give him room to work. "Ravishing is my specialty." She picked her legs up and wrapped them around his waist, then he stood up and began to thrust powerfully. It didn't take but half a dozen strokes till her whole body began to jerk, and when he felt the fluttering of her vagina, he exploded. Ramming in hard, he pumped her small canal to the brim with hot semen, his seed, his essence. She loved how it felt. Unable to stop, she kept working him, loving the connection and the pleasure the movements were giving her as she savored each sparkling aftershock.

"Kiss me, Isaac. Please?" Before she finished asking, his lips claimed hers in a series of kisses that ran the gamut between tender and voracious. This bull wasn't the most comfortable of surfaces to be having sex on, but she wouldn't have traded the experience for anything. Hugging him tight, she told him so. "Thank you, thank you. That was incredible. I'll never forget this night as long as I live."

Isaac appreciated the sentiment, but she made it all seem so temporary, that it worried the hell out of him. "We're going to make a lot of memories like this..." A banging on the door caused Avery to startle and jump, almost dislodging them both. "What the hell?" He hopped off, handed Avery her clothes and started climbing into his jeans. The banging was insistent and he could hear Aron's voice. God, something bad was going down.

"I'm coming!" Isaac yelled. Not bothering to fasten his belt he padded barefoot to the door. Throwing it open, he saw his brother standing there ashen white. "What's wrong?"

"A passing motorist found your brother on the side of the road about a half-mile from here. He's been horsewhipped. Why didn't you answer your damn phone?"

Damn! "My cell was on vibrate and you can't hear the office phone from the bar. And, hell, we weren't in the apartment."

"I don't give a crap what you were doing, just get the hell home. He won't go to the damn hospital. I may just whip him again. He's asking for you."

* * *

Noah laid in the bed in agony. Cady had cleaned his wounds and she and Libby were applying a stinky herb poultice to the bloody stripes. "There's going to be scarring, but we can lessen that over time." Cady looked at him with pity. "I can make the pain more tolerable, I promise." He knew she was an empath. Belief in faith healing or supernatural intervention was hard for Noah to swallow, but he had seen Cady do some miraculous things. He wondered if she could heal his spirit as well.

"Thanks, Cady, I appreciate it." He had thought nothing could be worse than losing his parents, but he had found an equal agony. Tonight, he'd learned his brother was involved in something he despised. Bitterness welled-up in him like a geyser. He was ready to blow.

Footsteps and familiar voices on the stairs heralded Isaac and Aron's arrival. "Get Joseph and Jacob for me, please." Noah looked to Cady for assistance. "They need to hear what I have to say to Isaac."

Cady looked at Libby. Something was wrong besides the obvious. A worried look passed between the women. "All right. I'm sure they're nearby."

Isaac burst into the room. "Are you all right? Who did this to you?" His brother looked intimidating as always. Tall, broad, a warrior, and Noah had always looked up to him. Isaac was fearless. Now, he knew his hero had feet of clay. Avery stood small and trusting, close to his side. How had she been taken in by Isaac's perversion?

"I had a run-in with a friend of yours."

Isaac stared at his brother. He was pale against the sheets. The girls had bandaged him up, but he could still see the lesser stripes, painful evidence of a beating. "A friend? I don't have a friend who would do this to you."

"Really?" Noah's tone was sarcastic, his face a mask of disdain. Joseph and Jacob moved into the room to stand at the foot of the bed. Everyone was here but Jessie and Nathan. "Keep Nathan out of here. He doesn't need to hear any of this."

"He's asleep and so is Jessie," Jacob offered. His expression showed how confused he was. They all were. "What's going on, Noah? You act like you're blaming Isaac for this."

"I am," Noah stated flatly. "Ajax whipped Harper. She's been in the hospital, too. That's where I was earlier. She called me to come get her. I found her half-naked in an alley covered in blood." Libby gasped with horror. "Of course, she was a willing victim, at first. Isn't that right, Isaac? There are people who get off on pain. You know all about that, don't you?"

Isaac blanched. The shit was about to hit the fan and they were all gonna come away stinking. Hell! He stepped away from Avery. No use dragging her through his filth. "Is Harper going to be okay?"

"What is he talking about, Isaac?" Aron demanded. "You two better speak plainer, cause I don't like the damn direction this conversation is heading. Tell me that I'm misunderstanding."

"Oh, this isn't hard to comprehend." Noah tried to sit up and grimaced in pain. "Haven't you ever wondered why Harper and I broke up?"

No one said anything. They just waited. An uneasy feeling permeated the room. Only Isaac knew, but it wasn't his story to tell. A sick feeling washed over him. He'd never wanted to hurt his family. What he did in his private life was private, but not anymore.

Noah continued, directing his razor sharp comments at Isaac. "You know why, don't you, brother? She's into S&M, a pain junkie. She gets off on being dominated and whipped. Harper likes to be tied up and slapped around. Avery, I can't believe you're into that. What would people say?"

"Noah," Aron warned his brother. "Be careful."

"You leave Avery out of this, Noah. If you have something to say, you say it to me," Isaac spoke low and evenly.

"Isaac's a Dom." The words were spit out. "Isn't that right, Isaac? Ajax is one, too. He said that you and he have been members of the same clubs. But you two got crossways, didn't you? And he lured Harper into his trap to get back at you."

"What's he talking about, Isaac?" Jacob asked.

Isaac looked at his brothers. There was condemnation and confusion on their faces. Hell, so this was how it was going to be. Fine. So be it. "Ajax is not my friend. I had him banned from some clubs because he abused women, just like he abused Harper and you.

Ajax is an abusive jerk who calls himself a Dom. A true Dom gives pleasure, not pain."

Silence.

Noah finally broke the quiet. "You've never used a whip on anyone, Isaac?" A sick smile on his face told Isaac that he knew the answer.

"Yes, a quirt, not a bullwhip. I give erotic pain. There's a difference."

"Sure, there is." Disbelief dripped from Noah's lips. "I couldn't abide this sickness in Harper, and I can't abide it in you. I don't know you, Isaac. And I don't know if I want to know you."

"Noah…" Libby looked aghast. She couldn't stand conflict.

"Joseph, take Cady and Libby and Avery to the kitchen and ya'll make a pot of coffee," Aron directed, evenly.

"I'm not going anywhere," Avery stated as she stepped up closer to Isaac.

"None of you have to go anywhere. I'll leave." Isaac moved one step toward the bed where Noah lay. "You don't understand me. I'm not going to defend myself. There's nothing I can say that would change your mind."

"You're right," Noah barked. "I'm laying here scarred for life because my brother is a pervert."

"That's not fair." Avery couldn't be silent.

"No." Isaac stopped her. "This has been coming for a long time. It really didn't matter what I did. I've always been the outsider. I'll never be good enough for this family. It's time for me to face that fact."

"Hold on." Aron put a hand on his arm. "We need to talk about this."

"What good will talking do?" Noah asked. "I don't really want to hear about that mess."

"You don't have to. I'm outta here." Isaac turned to go.

"I'm going with you." Avery started to follow him.

"No." Isaac stopped her. "You were right. Your dad asked too much of us. This isn't going to work. We're from different worlds. We could never be happy together. We're through, Avery." He walked away, the chains on his pants ringing in the silence.

Avery's world collapsed around her. She felt like she was going to die. Should she go after him? Maybe, but not till after she had her say.

"Damn," Joseph said what everybody was thinking.

"Damn is right. What Isaac is involved in is poison. It's sick and twisted and anybody that can be a part of it is twisted," Noah spat out the words.

"I can't believe it. I sure as hell didn't see this coming." Jacob looked to Aron as if for guidance.

"Wait, that's enough." Avery stepped forward. She looked around at Isaac's family. "I can't believe you people. Don't you know how much he loves you?"

"Sometimes love isn't enough." Noah was still adamant in his condemnation.

"Let me tell you a little bit about your brother. I've been in love with him for years. There's no one like him. No one."

"You can say that again," quipped Noah.

Aron held up his hand. "Let her speak." Noah hushed, quelled by his brother's will.

"As long as I've known him, he has given more of himself than you ever dreamed. Did you know he funds the soup kitchen? By himself? Did you know he has a fund set up to build homes for newly returned vets? Did you know he gives most of his income to charity? Check the records, Noah. I'm sure there's a way you can tell."

"I didn't know that." Joseph sighed. It was apparent that he wasn't as ready to lambast Isaac as Noah was.

"He's always ready to help. I've worked for these charities through the church and I always knew Isaac McCoy was one of our greatest benefactors. He didn't seek attention or even a thank-you. What Isaac does for others, he does because he wants to help."

"That's all well and good, Avery. But it doesn't excuse his involvement in the BDSM lifestyle. And you? Isn't it true that you spent time in a brothel? And I even heard a rumor that you write porn. Maybe, you're not the best judge of character."

"Enough," Aron barked at Noah. "I hate that you're hurt, but you're stepping over the line, little brother."

Libby stepped closer to Avery as if to protect her.

"I've done nothing wrong, and neither has your brother." Avery stood up straighter, determined to say her piece. "As far as his sex life is concerned, Isaac never did anything to me that I didn't want. He put me first. When you compare him to that nasty man, you do your brother a great disservice. What we share is beautiful and I wouldn't trade a moment of it for anything. I love your brother and he's the best man I have ever met." Avery moved toward the door.

Cady went to her. "Do you want some of us to come with you?"

"No, I'll be fine. I'm going to look for Isaac."

But, she didn't find him.

* * *

Ajax couldn't hide from Isaac. He knew the places to look and when he found him in a bar on the outskirts of town, he backed him out the door before he could rally his cronies. "How dare you touch a member of my family?" Isaac picked him up and slammed his body against the side of the building. "And what you did to Harper has nothing to do with being a Dom. You're a sick bastard. And you've abused your last woman, jerk." Ajax didn't have his whip, so he had to take Isaac on in a fair fight, which wasn't fair, to Ajax. And when Isaac got through with him, he walked away leaving Ajax spitting blood and hatred through his teeth.

Isaac didn't know where to go. His fists hurt almost as much as his heart and all he wanted to do was go home. But right now, he didn't know where home was.

* * *

The week passed in a swirl of upset and frustration. Isaac was nowhere to be found. Levi was running the bar and Doris swore that she hadn't heard from her boss. The McCoys were torn between hunting Isaac, tending to Noah, running their ranch and getting ready for a wedding. Feelings were worn on sleeves and tempers ran hot. Avery moved back home. There was nothing else she could do. Even when Isaac came back, she wasn't so sure he would want her. Self-doubt ate away at her. She'd been so sure he had begun to care about her. Every time they touched, she'd convinced herself she could feel his love. Perhaps, it had been wishful thinking on her part. Tricia hadn't asked too many questions, perceiving that Avery was beyond hurt. Space was what she needed and her partner gave her that.

The bouquets she created made her cry. The charity meetings made her cry. It was odd. She had expected to be ostracized by the city and the town's elite, but that wasn't the case. One woman even asked for her autograph, saying she had read some of her work. How she came by the pen name, Avery didn't ask. She was just grateful rocks weren't being thrown at her at the Post Office.

After three days without hearing from Isaac, Avery had backed her ears and called her father, telling him the wedding was off and she didn't want to hear any argument from him. He had started to preach at her, but she'd told him that she adored him and her mother, but the days of browbeating her to do his will were over. Shock was the only word she could label his quick agreement. In fact, their conversation had progressed by him telling her how proud he was of all her hard work and writing. When he'd said writing, she had almost bitten her tongue off. Without her asking, he volunteered that one of the deacons had come forward with this bit of 'damming' information on her, but the church had been much more horrified to learn the deacon had been visiting a hooker than the revelation she wrote racy romances. Before she hung up, she'd promised him she would visit for Thanksgiving and bring his favorite ooey-gooey pumpkin butter cake. But despite her work, her writing, and an unexpected peace with her father, Avery was desperately unhappy. Without Isaac, life had no meaning.

Chapter Nine

"We've got to do something. Hell, I don't know where else to look or who else to call. It's like he's dropped off the face of the earth. Kane did say there was talk he had been in a bar fight the night he left." Jacob poured a cup of stout coffee. He had so much to be thankful for; a beautiful wife, a sweet baby on the way, and his home was taking shape. But knowing his brother was somewhere alone and unhappy ate at his gut.

"I'm not surprised. His tearing up a bar is par for the course." Noah was healing. Cady had helped and stiffness and soreness were going to be the only ill effects which would stay with him any length of time.

With a steady hand, Jacob set the coffee cup down. It wasn't often he lost his temper, but he had all he could stomach. "Noah, I love you. You're my brother and I wouldn't trade you for anything, but I'm going to tear you a new one if you don't let up on Isaac. Not everybody is as tight-assed as you are. I'm not into heavy kink, but if I thought Jessie would enjoy a light spanking...hell, why not? More than once, I've tied her to the bed and it only makes the excitement rise, if you know what I mean. Your brother is a damn good man. He may march to the beat of a different drummer, but so do you. And I hate to tell you this, but I much prefer his cadence to yours."

Noah could tell his brother was displeased. And for a minute, he felt anger. But this was the brother who'd held him at night when he had been broken hearted over the loss of their mother. This was the brother who'd stayed up late with him to make sure he memorized all the state capitals, and it was Jacob who encouraged him to study business when Aron had been pushing for a Law degree or at least an Agriculture degree. Jacob had seen where Noah's strengths lay and knew the family would only benefit by letting him follow his heart.

"Jacob, I..."

"No, let me finish. I don't often speak my piece, and this has got to be said. I love you and I've forgiven you, but I can't completely forget that your reluctance to accept Jessie almost cost her life and me my world. You push too hard, Noah. You're too unyielding. You think you have all the answers and black and white are the only two colors in the rainbow. Even you have to admit, you were wrong about Jessie, as wrong as wrong can be. And you're wrong about Isaac and Avery. After Jessie was kidnapped, it was Isaac who stuck with me through thick and thin. He never left my side. I don't discount what you did. You fixed up the nursery for her and you were the first on the scene and were wounded so she could be saved. But, and this is a big but, it wouldn't have happened at all, not like it did, if you hadn't interfered. You said things that made her believe I didn't love her. Now, you've pushed Isaac away and he, in turn, has pushed Avery aside. What if they're supposed to be together and what if your unyielding spirit and narrow-minded bullshit tears Isaac from our lives and destroys their happiness? How would you feel then?"

Noah just stood there in deep conviction. His brother was right. He was wrong. "What can I do? Let's go find him. We can call Roscoe if we have to."

Jacob patted him on the back. "That's my boy."

* * *

Later that evening, the brothers sat with Kane and Zane at Hardbodies. Their hope had been that Isaac would show up or at least they could get a word of encouragement from Doris. Because, if he was going to call anybody, it would be her. She was like a second mother to him. But she was adamant. He hadn't called and she was as worried as they were. "He beat the hell out of Ajax. And the word is, Ajax deserved every blow. The owner of the dive didn't press charges. He considered that Isaac did him a favor. Still and all, as Mama would say, I don't trust that man. He's trouble. He and all his friends are trouble."

"Do we know who he hangs with?" Joseph asked.

"Some of them, but I intend to talk to Levi. He might know more than I do. He's a Dom too, you know?"

"No way!" Aron exclaimed. "You know, there are more people into that stuff than I ever figured. I caught Libby reading an erotic romance novel called, 'Master, May I?' and I read some of that stuff, and well, all I can say is that a good time was had by all." He got tickled at his own joke and laughed. Sobering, he looked at his friends and family one by one. "We've got to make this right. Until we find Isaac, we can't do much on that end, but we can see about Avery. I want to make sure she's at the wedding. Zane..." He turned to Kane's twin. "Would you mind checking on her and, if you don't already have a date to the wedding, maybe you'd consider asking her to accompany you?"

Zane leaned back in his chair and smiled. "I can see your reasoning. She'll probably refrain from whacking me with a broom...seeing, as I'm blind and all. The rest of you might not be as safe."

"Exactly."

***

"I need to talk to you, Noah."

He almost hadn't answered the phone. It was Harper again. She had called a dozen times since his run-in with Ajax. "I don't see as how we have much to say to each other." Lord, he was being a hard-ass again. Jacob's speech came back to haunt him. "What can I do for you? Do you need anything?"

"No, my parents have let me move back home. But, I heard Isaac is gone and I want to talk to you about him. I don't want to do it over the phone. Is it all right if I come over?"

It went against the grain, but if he was going to turn over a new leaf, this was a good place to start. "Sure, I'll be waiting."

He didn't have to wait long. The slight tap at the door alerted him that she had arrived. Apparently, she was parked at the end of the driveway while they talked on the phone. Since his ordeal, he hadn't ventured out of the house. Too many people would ask questions. He hated other folks knowing his business. Guess that was how Isaac felt. Hell! When he opened the door, he was shocked at how thin and pale Harper looked. There were still some red marks near her face where the whip had wrapped around her neck. He fought down the attraction. Hell, would it always be there? "Harper, come in."

She looked at the floor, clearly embarrassed. "Thank you, Noah. I appreciate you seeing me. I won't keep you. Don't be mad at him, but I ran into Joseph and he told me everything."

"He had no right," Noah began, but stopped. "Joseph is family." If he could only remember that truth, they wouldn't be in the mess they were in now.

"I should never have involved you in this. I'm trying to get my head on straight."

Noah felt his heart stir. But, what about Skye? Dammit, he was confused. "I'm glad you're feeling better, and I'm glad you called me. That's what friends are for."

"I wish we were more than friends," she whispered. Shaking her head, she got to her point. "Someone beat Ajax up and he's mouthing off, talking about getting revenge. And he says it was Isaac."

"Damn, he did it for me."

"Yes, when I heard you'd gone back to confront him, I nearly died. I never intended for you to be hurt, not any of you. Now, I hear Isaac is gone and I presume it's over what we have in common."

"It came as a shock." Understatement.

"Well, see, that's the thing. We're not alike at all. What I'm into is nothing like Isaac. He's a good Dom. He's into caring and pleasure and protecting. When I went to him and asked him to do a scene with me, he turned me down. He was nice and concerned, mainly for you. But he begged me to let go of my pain fetish and get into something that would be good for me. I didn't listen. I thought he was too tame for my tastes. Although, he is the powerful one in the community, Isaac McCoy is well respected and admired. He polices the clubs in his own way. That's why Ajax has it in for him. Isaac got him expelled and banned for doing things to others like he did to me."

The more Noah heard, the deeper the hole in the pit of his stomach felt. God, Jacob was right. He'd done it again. He had needlessly hurt someone he loved just because he thought he was so perfect. "Harper, I'm sorry...about a lot of things." He wasn't ready to start dating her again, but he didn't want to lose touch with her, either. "Can I call you?"

"Oh, yes. Please do." Her face brightened, completely changed and he realized she thought he meant for a date.

"Just friends for now, Harper. I want to take it slow this time." That still sounded more hopeful than he intended, but that was how it came out. It felt right.

"Friends is more than I ever expected. Thank you." She leaned in and kissed him on the cheek and it was déjà vu all over again. That old black magick was back at work.

***

"Someone get the damn phone," Aron yelled from the living room. "I'm trying to memorize my wedding vows!"

Libby rolled her eyes at Jessie. "My beloved bellows." She skipped over to the landline and picked up the receiver. "Tebow Ranch. May I help you please?"

"Yes, you can. I was hoping you'd answer."

"Isaac! Are you all right? Where are you? If you don't come to my wedding, I'll never let you live it down." All of that was said in a rushed, exasperated breath.

She was relieved to hear his familiar chuckle. "I'm fine. I'm in Houston and I wouldn't miss your wedding for the world."

"Thank God! Let me get Aron."

"No!" The word was said quickly and with no room for misunderstanding. "I don't want to talk to him."

"Oh, yes you do, Isaac. Everything is all right. Come home. Avery told us how the cow ate the cabbage. You should have seen her. She defended you, took on the whole lot of us."

"Is she there?"

Libby paused, hating to be the bearer of bad news. But, what had he expected? "No, she left and went home."

"Have you talked to her?"

"No, I've been pretty busy with the wedding plans."

"Of course you have."

"When are you coming home?"

"I don't know, Libby." She could hear the sorrow and uncertainty in his voice. "But, I'll be at the wedding. Okay?"

"Oh, Isaac, we've got to get past this. Family is too important. Please?"

"Give me time, Libby. Give me time."

* * *

"I don't know why I'm going. It's just going to hurt." Avery talked to Tricia as she dressed for Libby and Aron's wedding.

"That lawyer you're going with is sex on a stick. At least you can look at him." She held out the dark red, velvet dress that Avery had bought special. "I can't wait to see you in this. Put it on."

"Zane just asked me because Aron told him to. He admitted as much. He said he was protecting me till Isaac got home." She pulled the dress over her head and covered up the decadent underwear she had talked herself into wearing. It was part of her bordello wardrobe, as she called it. "I don't know why I'm dressing up. Poor Zane can't even see me."

Tricia grinned with a naughty thought. "Oh, Honey. I'd love to be his personal braille project. He could feel off me all he wanted to. By the time he got through, he'd have a pretty good idea of how I looked, and I'd be happy."

"Tricia!" Avery laughed. "Do you have a crush on Zane Saucier? I didn't know that!"

Flopping down on the bed, Tricia clasped both hands over her heart. "Crush? Maybe. Definitely lust-struck. Have you seen his shoulders?"

"No, I've been a bit busy lusting after Isaac to notice anyone else. Should I wear my hair up?" Avery picked it up and swirled it around. "Probably not. I look like I've got on a Hawaiian headdress."

"Your hair is your crowning glory. I bet Isaac loves it."

"I don't think Isaac loves anything about me." She started attacking her hair with a vengeance. No matter how hard she brushed it, it just bounced back into those useless ringlets. "You know what I really think? I think Isaac just felt sorry for me. Tricia, I can't tell you how I ran after him. Looking back on it, I was pitiful. No wonder he kept pushing me away."

"Nonsense." She sounded so sure of herself at first, and then her voice dropped. "I don't think guys have hot passionate affairs with women they feel sorry for. Isn't it impossible for them to, you know, get hard, if they're not into you?"

At her uncertain tone, Avery whirled around. Tricia had always seemed light years ahead of her in experience. "Are you a virgin?"

Tricia set straight up and shushed her. "My goodness, Girl! Why don't you take an ad out in the paper?"

"How is that possible? You're so self-assured and popular and...worldly?" Avery was stunned.

"I was a theatre major." She stated that fact as if it explained everything. The doorbell pealing caused them both to giggle. "The hot hunk has arrived."

At least their conversation had taken her mind off of her troubles. "This conversation is not over." She hugged her friend. "But thanks for coming over and keeping me company while I dressed. I'll let you know what happens, or do you want to hang out here and wait for me?"

"Nope." Tricia pulled herself up. "But, I will go and let Mr. Cutie in. Don't tell him I have the hots for him. Last week I delivered a balloon bouquet to his office, but I don't think he knows I exist."

'He will after tonight,' Avery silently promised her friend as she followed her to the door.

* * *

Crowbar picked the lock of the McCoy's hunting cabin. "I'll deliver her to you as soon as I can," he promised his cousin. "Do you think it's wise to be messin' with the McCoys like this? Have you seen them? They're huge!"

"Of course I've seen them, you moron. I beat the hell out of the younger one. He'll think twice before he comes after me again." They went in and Crowbar helped Ajax set up the portable tower that he would use once he got his hands on McCoy's woman. The right woman this time. That was where his dumb cousin had come in. Crowbar wasn't real smart, but he did what he was told. "Do you have the hood? We need McCoy's hood if this is going to work."

"Yes, I have it." He pulled it from the inside pocket of his jacket. "The last time I cleaned Isaac's playroom, I took it. It wasn't hard. He keeps it out in plain sight."

"I knew he would. It was custom made. If you'll look, their brand is in the forehead like the mark of the beast, damn T in a rocking Bow. I had seen him wear it too many times. I knew he would still have it."

"She's a nice girl, Ajax. I don't like this at all. Levi has been good to me, and I hate to disappoint him." Crowbar was tired of being Ajax's lackey.

After he readied the cuffs and the chains, Crowbar got up from his squat to find Ajax looming over him. "Go over there and watch for her. She'll go to the bathroom and when she does, approach her. You're about the same size as McCoy and in that hood and cape, she won't know the difference. She'll follow you anywhere. You know the score, Retard. Anytime, you don't want to follow my orders, I'll chain you to the back of my pickup and drag your ass all over the county. The only parts of you they'll find is what they can scrape off the highway." The maniacal gleam in Ajax's eye told Crowbar that he was cold enough to carry out his threat. It didn't matter that their mothers were sisters.

This man would kill him and never look back. "Do you understand me?"

"Yeah, I'll do it." He didn't have a choice.

* * *

"I can't believe that tomorrow will be Sweetest Day." Libby fitted herself as close to Aron as possible. "It seems like I've waited forever to marry you."

"The only reason it's the sweetest day is because you'll finally, legally, belong to me." He kissed her temple. "You don't know how I thank God every day that you're healthy, you're having my baby and I have the privilege of calling you mine." Libby smiled secretively. Tomorrow she would tell Aron that there was going to be two babies, not one. Two little boys. Two more McCoys, God help the world.

"Keep your eyes open for Isaac. He promised he would be here." She glanced around, spotting Avery sitting with Zane, Kane and Lilibet. "Avery's here. She sure does look sad."

"Hopefully, all of this will right itself as soon as Isaac comes home. Our job is to convince him that this is his home. We want him here and we don't care what he and Avery do in the privacy of their own bedroom, or in their playroom, or club, or wherever in hell they choose to make one another happy."

Libby went up on tiptoe and spoke so low only he could hear. "I've been reading up and I sure would like to try a little of that. I think you're already a Dom and I sure do enjoy you taking me hard. Could we play like that a little? Please, Sir?"

Aron felt his manhood turn to stone. "Little Girl, you sure can make me hard. You could make me beg without even trying. In other words, you tell me what you want and I'll turn the world upside down to make it happen."

She rubbed her body against his, discretely. No one knew what they were doing but the two of them. "I want what you want. I want to please you," she purred.

"Hot damn!" Aron growled. "How long do we have to stay at this damn party?"

Libby laughed. "Just a little while longer, but when it's over, I'll make you a very happy man."

Aron believed her.

* * *

"Aren't these the cutest things? Cady made them and they're filled with delicious homemade pralines." Avery held up the net and lace bags of praline confections that Cady had made for each guest. They were part of the place settings and Avery had claimed hers and had already torn a tiny hole in it and indulged.

"My favorite New Orleans delicacy. I can smell them. They remind me of home." Zane picked up one. "And I can feel the delicate handwork that she put into them. Cady went to a lot of trouble." He laid the bag down and patted her hand. "Do you want to dance? Kane and Lilibet will stay on the dance floor a while. Lilibet loves to dance. Look at her. Kane's a lucky man."

Avery looked over at the dance floor and then at Zane with admiration. "You know I forget you can't see. You know so many things that a blind person shouldn't. How do you do that?"

He threw his head back and laughed. "A man has to have some secrets."

"I hear so many wonderful things about you. I'm surprised. I didn't expect you to have so many good, faithful friends."

Zane laughed again. "Really? Because I'm a blind man?"

"No," she replied sweetly. "Because you're a lawyer."

"Oh, I like you," he observed honestly. "Isaac is a very lucky man."

Avery stopped smiling. She looked down and didn't reply.

"Avery, look at me." He paused. "Do it. I'm very perceptive. I'll know." She did as he asked, marveling that he wore no dark glasses, nor did his gaze appear blank or unfocused. To look at him sitting there, you'd never know he lived in a world of darkness. "Isaac will return, and when he does, he'll grab you up, hold you close and never let you go."

"I hope he does come home. His family needs him." Was all she said. "Zane, my partner Tricia is a very sweet and lovely girl. She's also a great admirer of yours."

"Oh, she is ...is she? Well, I'll just have to SEE about that," he teased.

"You do that," she countered. "I'll put in a good word for you."

* * *

Lady was hungry. Not just for meat...that was good, but there was always meat to be had. Her masters ate meat all the time. And her Nate always made sure that she got her share. Sneaking sandwiches to bed in the middle of the night was their favorite part. It was her job to make sure all the crumbs were cleaned up off the covers. Looking for a friendly face, she moseyed through the crowd. No one paid much attention to her. After all, she wasn't very big. Someday, she would be tall enough to reach up on the table, and then she had plans. The other day she'd jumped up in the chair and that made grabbing a snack so much easier, but Nate had pulled her down and told her they had to be good or she'd be sleeping in the barn. That was okay. Her boy gave her plenty of bites under the table.

Under the table was fun. Nate slipped her treats, but so did all the others. It took all the attention she could muster to keep up with the hands sneaking under the tablecloth. Sometimes, she just had to make herself eat another nibble because she didn't want to hurt anybody's feelings.

The people were hopping around and holding on to one another. Sometimes they seemed so silly. Lady watched the humans for a few minutes, but that wasn't what was on her mind.

Oh, yeah. She could smell it. Dessert.

Now, all she had to do was look cute and hope someone gave her a bite.

Ah, there was someone she knew. Another female, one she hadn't seen in a few days. Maybe, if she smiled she would get lucky. Sidling up to her side, Lady smiled. It always helped to smile, and holding up a paw could seal the deal.

"Lady! It's so good to see you." Avery patted her head.

Time for a whine. Licking the lips couldn't hurt either.

"Are you hungry? Do you want some candy? I'll share. It's not chocolate, so it won't hurt you." She held down the treat and Lady grabbed it.

Wow! That was one of the best things she'd ever had in her mouth. I want another one!

"You have a sweet tooth, don't you? Here's one more, but that's all. I don't want to make you sick." Avery gave her another tasty morsel.

"Are you feeding the dog, Avery?" Zane asked.

"Yes, this is Nate's dog."

"I almost brought my guide dog, but I opted for my trusty cane, instead."

"You seem so self-sufficient, it's like you have built in radar."

Lady opted to put a paw on her knee. Affection never hurt.

"You're a sweetie. Aren't you?

Yes, I'm a sweetie. And I want more candy. Maybe, if I sit up and look cute.

"Begging isn't going to help. I'll give you another after a bit. Zane, I'm going to the restroom."

"All right. I think I'll go speak to Joseph. Could you spot him for me and point me in the right direction."

It wasn't hard to find Joseph. All you had to look for was a crowd. He was such a celebrity, even in his hometown.

"He's behind your right shoulder about twenty feet away. I'll take my stuff and meet you over there. Okay?" She gathered her candy and her bag. "Lady, do you want to walk with me?"

Yeah, why not. I like you, Avery. You're nice.

Lady followed Avery through the crowd, hoping she'd drop one of those candies. That'd be nice.

* * *

Avery made her way to the bathhouse. The McCoy family had thought of everything. It wasn't a great distance back to the main houses, but having bathrooms and showers near to the pavilion was definitely handy. It reminded her of the rest stops on interstates, except this was much nicer. A steady stream of people made their way back and forth. It was dark, but security lighting was everywhere. Despite Zane's good company, she couldn't help but miss Isaac. Disappointment made her heart hurt. She really thought he would've shown up tonight. Noah had really hurt him. Avery was surprised that the family had wanted her here tonight. When she and Zane had arrived, Noah had made a point to come and apologize to her. He'd been very nice, and she had been gracious. But she wasn't the one he needed to apologize to. It was Isaac who had been wronged. If Avery could have turned back time, she would have. Maybe if she had told him what a good man she knew he was it could have made a difference.

"What in the world?" Avery stopped in her tracks. "Isaac!" There was no one else he could be. He wore his costume, the one he'd shown her and told her it was reserved for special occasions. The cape and hood made him look dangerous and mysterious and when he lifted his gloved hand and beckoned her to him, she almost broke into a run. He was back! And he wanted to see her!

* * *

Where are you going? Lady kept up. Don't go over there. We don't know that man. And he doesn't smell right. He has family smells on him, but he's not family. Stop! "Woof! Woof!"

"It's all right, Lady. It's Isaac." She ran up to him and when he held out his hand, she slipped hers into it. "I'm so glad you're back. I missed you."

"Is that Isaac in that get-up?" Jessie, who was coming out of the bathhouse walked up and gave him a quick hug. "I'm glad you're back. You remind me of Zorro. All you need is a hat." She didn't delay. "You two have fun. Don't do anything I wouldn't do. 'Course that leaves it wide open."

Isaac tugged on her arm and she followed. "Where are we going?"

Lady growled.

"You don't have to walk so fast. You know I'd follow you anywhere." He led her off the trail and into the darkness. "Ouch! A stick got me." Avery stumbled, trying to keep up. And when Isaac jerked her deeper into the thicker trees, she knew something was wrong. "You're not Isaac, are you?" Her voice rose. A scream trembled on her lips, but the man jerked her up against him and covered her mouth with his leather-clad hand.

"Shut up! If you'll cooperate, maybe we'll both get out of this mess alive."

Avery struggled, but the man was so much bigger and stronger. It was futile. She tried to claw her way loose and in the process she dropped her things. 'Oh, Isaac,' she thought. 'I need you, so. Please help me.'

Lady growled. She was confused. Were they playing a game? Something hit the ground. Candy! The lady had dropped the whole bag! Lady picked it up, but there was too much stuff covering it. She'd have to sit down and do some serious chewing to get at the good stuff. The woman made a funny noise. Lady pricked up her ears and followed them, the bag of candy in her mouth. She'd just tag along and see where they were going.

* * *

The sounds and smells drew Isaac like a magnet. Tebow. There was no place on earth like it. For the past week, he'd just been riding around. Houston had drawn him. It was so big you could get lost in the excitement and the congestion. But, it wasn't home. The question was, could he come home? Was he welcome? A greater draw than the ranch was Avery, but he didn't know if pulling her back in the morass of his life was wise. Living without her would be impossible, but hurting her was unthinkable. "Isaac!" Nathan spotted him and broke into a run, coming at him as hard as he could. Isaac grabbed him up and hugged him.

"I missed you, Little Bud."

"I've been so worried about you. Why did you stay away so long? Don't you know we love you? We can't be happy if all the McCoys aren't together."

"You're getting so big. It seems like you've grown six inches since I've been gone."

"Nah, I'm the same height. You're just getting senile." Nathan giggled when Isaac goosed him. "I'm looking for Lady. Have you seen her? I've called and called. I'm worried."

"She's here somewhere. I'm going to go say hello to Aron and Libby and tell them I'm here. I'll see you later."

Nathan stopped and looked at his brother seriously. "Are you home? To stay?"

Isaac didn't say anything for a moment. "We'll see." When his brother's face fell, he was quick to reassure him. "Don't you worry. I'll never be far from you, I promise. Is Avery here?" He couldn't help but ask. He didn't expect her to be, but miracles still could happen.

"Yeah, she is. I saw her sitting with Zane."

Zane? A tingle of jealousy ate at his heart. Zane was his friend. He wouldn't cut in on his territory. But what did he expect? When he'd walked away from Avery and his family, he told her they had been a mistake. Was he crazy? "I'll catch you later, Bud."

"All right. I'm gonna walk around and look for my dog."

Isaac made his way toward the pavilion. He knew that the wedding rehearsal had been earlier in the afternoon and he had missed it. Aron had asked him to stand up with him, along with Jacob and Joseph. Noah and Nathan were supposed to be ushers. Noah. Lord, he hated to face Noah. Seeing the look of disgust on his face had cut Isaac to his very soul.

"Isaac!" It was Libby and she shouted it just as the music stopped. "Isaac!" She didn't wait, but started toward him, and she wasn't the only one. From every direction, McCoys began to move…Aron, Jacob, Joseph, and yes, Noah started in his direction. He moved toward them and the crowd grew quiet. The band didn't begin the next song. It was as if time stood still. It could have been a football huddle, but it was more, because they enclosed him in a group hug that said far more than words ever could.

"God, I'm glad you're home."

"Don't you leave like that again."

"I missed you, Brother."

"I'm sorry, Isaac. I was wrong. I love you."

"Hell, there's no place like home." He hugged Noah the hardest. "I love you, too."

"Avery's with Zane. We made sure she was here for you." Jacob slapped him on the back. "You've got some fence mending to do."

"Damn, straight." He picked Zane out of the crowd. It wasn't hard. The lawyer was a damn big man. No Avery, though. He made his way across the dance floor, meandering through the tables, speaking to people. Would she be glad to see him? Would she take him back? Did he have a chance or had he blown it? "Zane, hey man, where's Avery?"

"Isaac, glad you're back!" No judgment here. "She went to the bathroom. It's been a while, though. She ought to have been back by now. Unless she ran into a girl-friend and they're having a gabfest."

"Maybe." Isaac began to scan the crowd. That didn't sound like his Avery, plus she wouldn't be so thoughtless as to leave her escort all alone, especially her blind escort. His baby was much too considerate and tenderhearted. His baby. That's right.

"Hey, didn't I just talk to you?" Jessie tugged on his shirt. "You sure did change clothes fast. And what did you do with Avery? I was so glad to see you together. It made my day."

"Wait. What?" Isaac stopped her, not understanding. "I haven't seen Avery."

"Of course you have. I saw you surprise her down by the bathrooms. You had on a hood and a cape. She recognized you right off. I walked up and..." As Jessie talked she realized by Isaac's face that something was terribly wrong. "That wasn't you, was it? Who was it then?"

Damn! Isaac had the worst feeling and the last words that Ajax has said to him were ringing in his ears. 'I'm gonna hurt what you love, McCoy. I'm going to destroy what you love, if it's the last thing I ever do.' "I've got to find her. Tell the others that Avery may be in trouble."

Isaac had never known what true terror felt like until that moment.

* * *

She was bound and gagged, so no chance to scream. Who were those men? And why were they doing her this way? Avery wasn't crying, but panic wasn't that far off. What had she ever done to deserve this?

Crowbar wasn't expecting her to fight. She wasn't very big, but she had grit. Not a step was taken that she didn't make him work for every inch. Using everything she had, she clawed, she kicked, and struggled. He didn't want to hit her, but he didn't really have a choice. Her life wasn't the only one at stake. "Look, you hooked up with the wrong person. That's why I had to take you. And if you don't be still, I'm gonna have to hit you. Will you cooperate?" Her answer was just to pull harder, making it almost impossible to keep her headed in the right direction. It would have been easier to knock her out, but Ajax wanted her to suffer, and for that she needed to be awake. Letting go of her upper arm, he boxed her upside the head and she would have fallen if he hadn't been holding her up. "Now walk, dammit!"

He was surprised when she didn't even give a yelp. In his mind, he kept thinking about the time he had talked to her in the bar. She was going to recognize him when he took off this get-up. All the while he had been waiting on her at the bathhouses, he had tried to think this thing through. There was no way this was going to end well. 'This isn't some S&M chick like the other one. This girl will press charges,' he thought to himself, adding to his fear. And she was connected, to a damn McCoy! Ajax either wasn't thinking, or he planned to kill them, all of them. And Crowbar wanted nothing to do with murder, nor was he ready to die. What in the hell was he going to do?

It wasn't far as the crow flies from the party place to the cabin. By car it would have been farther, because they would have had to go around by the road. When they got close enough, Crowbar could see the lit end of Ajax's cigarette. Show time.

There were two of them. Avery's heart sank. All hope died. Perhaps she could have escaped one man, but not two.

* * *

Nathan walked and walked. He kept his eye on the ground. Joseph had taught him how to track and Jacob had given him a little flashlight, so he was in business. The only problem was the amount of leaves on the ground. But he'd found candy and he knew how Lady loved candy and it made sense to him that she had filched some off the table and was headed out in the woods to enjoy her bounty. "Lady! Lady! Where are you, Girl?" Usually she came bounding to him, no matter what. And that was the fact that was worrying him. Something just didn't add up.

Lady could hear her little Master. And she wanted to go to him, but her protective instincts were kicking in. A couple of times she had laid down to chew on the sweet smelling package she carried. But muffled noises from the woman made her pick up her burden and follow. They were out of her sight, but not out of her hearing. A sharp cry filled her with alarm, so she dropped her goodie and ran, teeth bared and ready to attack.

* * *

"Bout damn time you got here. What'd you do, stop for coffee?" Ajax jerked her up on the porch. "Well, lookee here. You're a pocket Venus, aren't you? Big tits, narrow waist, and a round spankable ass!" He slapped her hard on the rump and Avery jumped. "And look at all this hair! You remind me of Little Bo Peep. I'm gonna have a good time taking the bullwhip to you. McCoy won't recognize your body when he finds it. I'm gonna stripe you like a candy cane."

The venom in his voice made Avery fight that much harder. She had to get away, she just had to. Not just for herself, either. Isaac would blame himself. If this man killed her, Isaac would never forgive himself. She couldn't let it happen. It would ruin his life. With every ounce of strength she flung herself to one side, trying to tear out of the demon's grasp. It didn't work and he jerked her up and swung hard. When his fist connected, it wasn't with her face, but her chest. His aim had been off, and the blow drove the air from her lungs. It was agonizing. Gasping for breath, she almost didn't recognize what was happening. With a snapping snarl, Lady launched herself from the ground and dove right into her attacker's chest. She was growling and biting and doing her best to make the man sorry he was hurting her.

"Get this damn dog off of me! Kill it!" He thrust Lady off and the other man kicked the dog. A pitiful yelp confirmed that damage had been done. "Kill that shittin' dog." Rough hands dragged Avery inside and when she saw what awaited her, Avery knew she was about to be tortured beyond anything she could have imagined.

Crowbar picked the wounded dog up. It whined, but still tried to bite him. He liked dogs, so he couldn't bring himself to deliver the final blow. It was gonna die anyway, but he didn't want to watch it. The last time he'd been out here working with the surveyor, he'd seen an old well. He'd chunk the dog in there. It wasn't giving it a proper burial, but at least the buzzards wouldn't eat it. Walking the hundred yards or so, he came to the barricade. "Sorry, Mutt." He didn't throw it, but just eased it down to a ledge just a few feet down. "There, maybe the coyotes and carrion birds won't find you." This way he could tell Ajax that the dog was gone, but he didn't have to kill it.

* * *

"Help! Isaac!" As soon as he pulled the gag off, she screamed as hard as she could.

"Thank you." The creep smiled at her like they were friends. "You've answered my next question. I wanted to make sure I had the right chick. Of course, I enjoy making any woman scream, but with you there's an extra benefit. The more I hurt you, the more I hurt McCoy and that makes peeling the skin from your body irresistible."

"You son-of-a-bitch!" Avery lashed out, hitting him in the face with her bound hands.

He retaliated immediately and harshly, backhanding her with enough force to take her to her knees. "Bitch! Nobody's whore slaps me! You'll pay for that shit-ass mistake." He hauled her across the room, almost wrenching her shoulder out of place. "There will be no mercy. I'm going to whip you 'til you don't look human anymore." Avery frantically looked around, but she saw nothing to grab, no one to beg, and the man who was dragging her across the room was insane. Attached to the open doorway between the kitchen and living room, a metal pole had been affixed with chains and cuffs. Avery pondered her fate. There was a possibility that this man was going to kill her. She'd never feared death, but she had assumed she would live to get married, have children and possibly pass away at an advanced age with some heart ailment or at least get the chance to choke on strawberries. Never in a million years did she expect to end up in the hands of a mad man.

"I know who and what you are," she spat the words at him. "You're Ajax, the man who hurt Noah and Harper. Mostly, you're a coward."

He took a knife out of his pocket and she thought it was over, but he wasn't going to let her off that easy. He slit the restraints that held her wrists together, and then pulled them straight up and over her head. In a few moments, she was standing on her tiptoes.

"We're very close to the McCoy house and party, Mr. Ajax. The sounds of my screams may carry on the wind. Are you willing to chance it?"

"Screaming makes me hard. If it didn't, the first blood I'd spill would be splitting your tongue." Grabbing the neck of her dress, he took the knife and cut it off. "Damn, your body was made for sex. I may just screw you before I carve you up. How would you like that?"

"No!" Being beaten was one thing, being raped was entirely different. "I would hate it! Just the idea of your filthy body touching mine makes me want to throw up!"

"Bitch! I'll make you sorry you were ever born." With a careless knife he cut her bra and panties off, leaving a thin trail of blood where the tip of the knife nicked her skin.

"I can't stop you from hurting me, but you can't steal my memories. Isaac was wonderful to me. I love him and you can never make me sorry I was born. Loving him was worth it all."

"Don't talk to me about that bastard." He stepped close to her and pinched her left nipple hard. Tears sprang to her eyes, but she wouldn't give him the satisfaction of crying out. Instead, she made him regret he hadn't chained her feet first, because she brought her knee up hard and tried to jam his balls up into his throat.

"Goddamn!" He bellowed and clasped her around the neck and began to violently choke the life out of her. "I've got a gun, you little shit, and I know how to use it."

As she felt her consciousness begin to slip away, Avery thought this might be over sooner than she'd figured.

* * *

Isaac went straight to the place where Jessie had seen them last. He wracked his brain trying to figure out how someone would have gotten ahold of his hood. Damn, he needed to talk to Levi. But hell, he didn't have time. Just the thought of what was happening to Avery right now made his blood run cold.

"Avery! Avery!" He knew there was little chance she could hear him or even answer, but he couldn't stand not to try. The only thing he'd taken time to do was run to his truck, get his portable spotlight and his Sig 40 caliber. Walking to the back of the bathhouse, he shone the powerful beam around until he saw a lot of footprints. They were biker boots, much like what he wore. Not a big foot, but the idea of Avery at the mercy of another man made him sick. If it was Ajax, God! He was going to hurt his precious doll. All he could think about was her soft skin, her sweet smile and her delicate spirit. When he got his hands on Ajax this time, he wouldn't be walking away.

* * *

Nathan had found three candies. He'd quit calling out. A niggling feeling of awareness was making the hair stand up on the back of his neck. Like he had told Cady, and Cady was the only one he'd told, but since his near drowning, he just knew stuff. And at this very second, something was telling him he was walking straight into trouble. But he also had this sense that he needed to go, that it was important. So, he stayed on Lady's Hansel and Gretel trail of pecan pralines. That she hadn't stopped to eat them made him think that the retriever was on the trail of bigger game than a full belly.

Looking around, he realized he was near the hunting cabin. Knowing it was just under a mile from the ranch house, he wondered who could possibly have wandered over here from the party. It was probably a smoochy couple. He had seen guys and girls sneak off to the barn and lots of other places. Only lately had he begun to think that this might not be totally gross. But a faint female scream made him stop and listen. Was that a happy scream or a scared one? He couldn't tell. Moving slower, he kept his mind focused on hearing anything that was out of place. From out of nowhere, a familiar whine caused him to turn abruptly to the right. "Lady? Lady? Girl, is that you?" Making a few sweeps with his flashlight, he realized the old well was only a few feet away. Was Lady in the well? Hurrying, he stepped to the edge and shone the beam of light. Peering through the darkness, he saw his dog lying on her side. She didn't even lift her head. "Lady, you're hurt! Just hold on, Girl, I'll go get help."

He turned to run, but he didn't get anywhere. "Hold it, kid. I'm sorry, but you can't leave, not until I think about this real hard." Crowbar had considered letting the boy go get help and stop Ajax from hurting the girl. But, what about him? How much trouble was he going to be in?

"You let me go! My dog's hurt bad and I've got to get her some help."

"That dog is nearly dead. Ajax made me hurt her. She attacked him when he grabbed—"

"Who?"

"Avery." He'd gone too far to hide, now. Maybe it wasn't too late to do the right thing. The boy showing up seemed like a sign. "You go get some help and you tell them that old Crowbar helped you and that he was forced to be bad. Okay?"

"Uh, yeah, sure." Nathan tore loose and started running. He had to hurry! Avery was in trouble and so was Lady. His legs were pumping like pistons, his adrenalin was running so high he could have made the track team. "Help! Help!" He began to yell, when he thought he was a safe distance away. Barreling through the woods, he ran head long into someone. For a moment, he struggled, thinking that one of the strange men had him.

"Nathan, it's Isaac. What's wrong?"

Talking in a rush, Nathan spilled his terror. "There's a man back there in the woods and he says they have Avery and Lady is hurt. She's in the old well. And the slow-acting man said that it wasn't his fault. He was forced to do bad things. I'm scared, Isaac. And I'm glad you're back."

"Me too, Buddy." Isaac hugged him quick. "Are they at the hunting cabin?" At Nathan's nod, he sought to reassure him. "Everything will be fine, I guarantee it." If only that were in his power. "I'm going to go help Avery and I won't forget Lady, either. You go tell the others where I'm headed and what's going on, and make sure Kane's informed. Then you take care of the women. Can you handle it?"

"You can count on me, Isaac. Please help Avery and Lady. They need you."

Wasting no time, he made his way to the hunting cabin. Whoever talked to Nathan was nowhere in sight, so he had to assume Ajax would have help. A popping sound reached his ears and his heart sank. He knew that noise…the bullwhip. "No!" He ran harder. Bounding up on the porch he could see through the front window and what he saw made his heart come up in his throat. She was chained to a tower pole, arms over her head. His beloved had been stripped and he could see evidence of abuse, blood and bruising. Hatred boiled up within Isaac. The man who did this would die. Every instinct told him to plunge through the window and step between Ajax and Avery, but the pistol in Ajax's hand gave him pause. He couldn't risk her life. For just a few seconds, he surveyed the room and saw what had to be the man Nathan was referring to. It was Crowbar. What the hell? The look on his face was one of distaste. Why was he going along with and even helping with this travesty? It didn't make sense. Nevertheless, Isaac prepared to go in. Edging around to the side door, he found it open. Good.

"You won't get away with this," Avery gasped. "Someone will come."

Ajax walked in a half moon path in front of her, studying his handiwork. "Dream on, Slut. They're partying over there and your man isn't even in this part of the country. He left you. Didn't he? Why was that? You weren't woman enough for him, were you?"

Isaac could hear, and he hated what he heard.

Avery met the eyes of the other man who had brought her here. She knew him from the bar. He had been nice to her that day. Clearly, he was uncomfortable with all of this. She silently pleaded for help. How could he stand and watch this pervert hurt her? "I may not be woman enough for him, that's true. But he's more of a man than you'll ever be. Isaac is a good man, while you're a sniveling eunuch. I bet you can't even get it up, can you? Is that why you do this? Is hurting women the only way you can get off?"

Isaac listened to her bait him. "Don't do it, Baby." He moved cautiously, positioning himself to take Ajax down.

"Why, you little whore!" He lashed out at her with the whip, leaving a stripe that went from her breastbone to the middle of her abdomen. She flinched. He continued his tirade. "Submit to me, Bitch! Bow your head and plead for your life. That's the only thing that will save you!"

Instead, she fought back. "I will never submit to the likes of you. I will only submit to Isaac, only to Isaac. I love him."

Another blow. But what he said stung worse. "I know what kind of woman Isaac McCoy craves. A real submissive, and that's not you. You're not worthy to be McCoy's woman."

All the tenseness, all the fight left Avery's body. "You're right." She submitted to the bonds that fettered her, and bowed her head.

"That's more like it, bitch." He struck again, just like a maddened serpent. "Hitting you is sweet. I promised McCoy that I would hurt him by hurting the ones he loves."

As if his words strengthened her, she lifted her head one more time, almost triumphant. "Well, you're out of luck, you bastard. Isaac doesn't love me. You've failed. You may hurt me, but you're not hurting Isaac. And for that I'm grateful."

"Then I better make this blow count, whore!" Ajax drew back the whip to strike a blinding blow, but his arm came up short.

He had him! Isaac couldn't wait another second. He wound the leather around his fist and jerked—hard. "It's my turn to do the hitting, jerk! You do not abuse what belongs to me." Isaac lunged at Ajax and literally plowed him down.

"Watch it, Isaac!" Avery screamed. "He's got a gun!" She directed her next plea to the other man. "Help him. I know you didn't want to do this. I'll defend you. Please?" That was all it took. The other man stepped forward.

Ajax wasn't going down easy, and he didn't intend to go down alone. Before Isaac could stop him, he pulled back the gun and shot Crowbar in the stomach. The other man stumbled back, holding his gut, which was blooming with a red stain. Disbelief colored Crowbar's face and Avery screamed.

Ajax was big and furious, which made him dangerous. They wrestled and Isaac managed to knock the gun out of his hand, but when that hand was free of the gun, it didn't remain empty long. Isaac didn't see the knife, but Avery did. "A knife, Isaac! Ajax has a knife!" She struggled, to no avail. He had no need of her assistance, however. Isaac was like a man possessed. She'd never seen his face look this way. He was hard, dominant, totally in control. Wresting the knife from Ajax's grasp, he threw it across the room and took up his bullwhip and began whipping him across his body. Seemingly, this was the first time Ajax had been on the receiving end and he screamed and squealed like a stuck pig. Holding his arms over his face to protect it, he begged for mercy.

It seemed like forever. Everything was in slow motion, but it was only seconds before the other McCoys burst into the room. Avery was mortified for them to see her naked. But, she shouldn't have worried. Noah grabbed an afghan off the couch and immediately wrapped her in it. "Damn, Avery girl. Let's get you covered up and out of here."

Jacob and Kane assisted Isaac and Joseph went to Crowbar, getting towels to staunch the flow of blood. "It's a damn gut wound. A helicopter is on its way, Fella."

"He tried to help me, Kane."

"We'll get your statement later, Avery," he promised. Pulling Ajax off the floor, the Sheriff cuffed him and read him his rights.

"I'll take her." Isaac edged Noah out of the way and picked her up. "Let's get you to the hospital." He started out with her to one of their trucks. "Call ahead and tell them we're coming. And somebody see to Nathan's dog. She's in the old well, and she's hurt pretty bad," he directed in a loud voice.

Avery placed her hand on his cheek. "I don't need to go to the hospital. There's no need. I'm not hurt that badly. All I need is to get cleaned up and put some antiseptic on the spots."

"Are you sure?" His voice was hoarse and Avery could feel a quaking in his body. Isaac was scared. For her.

"Perfectly. I kept him too mad and distracted for him to do too much damage." Actually, he had landed some hard blows, but nothing was broken and the doctors couldn't do anything about the bruising. "The helicopter will take the other man to the hospital?" She wanted to hug him, she wanted to kiss him, but she held back. Having confidence about her place in his life was a thing of the past.

Stepping quickly into one of the back bedrooms, he stood her down, whisked off the blanket and began examining the damage done to her body. Despite their history, she crossed her arms over her breasts. "That was pretty bad, wasn't it? I can't believe your whole family walked in on me while I was hanging up there exposed." She was grasping for something to say.

"Sit right there while I get some warm water and medicine." He sat her down gently and took a moment to cup her cheek, rubbing his thumb gently against a tear trail. "God, I'm so sorry, Precious. I'm sorry for everything. You got swept up in a storm that you didn't create."

As he walked off, she whispered, "Great, he feels sorry for me." This didn't bode well. Taking in the room, she noticed how comfortable it was. She had heard of the McCoy's hunting cabin and now she was here. Pity it wouldn't hold very happy memories. And she had no clothes! That fiend had ripped her stuff beyond repair.

"Let's get you cleaned up." Isaac knelt at her feet.

"Hey, is Avery going to be okay?" Noah spoke from the hall, a few feet from the semi-open door.

"Yes, I'm taking care of her."

"I'm fine, Noah, and thank you and all the rest for coming to my rescue. I'm sorry I disrupted the party."

"You aren't to blame," Isaac whispered. "This is all my fault."

Remorseful was the best word she could think to describe his attitude.

"Are ya'll coming up to the house?" Noah was nothing if not persistent.

Isaac smiled. The first she had seen. It made her feel better. "Not now. We want to be alone."

"Sure. Look, since you came on foot, I'm going to ride with Jacob and leave you my truck. The keys are in it."

"Thank you, Noah," Avery answered before Isaac could fuss at him. "Isaac will be home in a bit. Oh, Criminey." Avery winced. "That burns." She heard him hold his breath, but he didn't say anything. His face was stoic, and there was a tick by his lips. "You look miserable. I can do this." She started to take the sponge from him.

"Damn!" He threw it to the floor and gathered her, oh, so carefully, into his arms. "What are we going to do, my Avery? Where do we go from here?"

What was he saying? She, tentatively, hugged him back. "If you can get me a T-shirt and some of your lounge pants like before, I can go home. You have lots to sort out with your family. I'll be fine."

"If you think for one moment that I'm ever letting you out of my sight again, you've got another thing coming." He said this close to her neck, his face buried in her hair and he was petting the back of her head. Elation desperately tried to get a foothold in Avery's heart, but she tamped it down. Disappointment and disillusion were too fresh. She had to be sure. And then she felt it…dampness. Isaac was crying. Her big tough Dom was shedding tears, for her.

"Isaac, what are you saying? You do realize that I'm not what you need. I'll never be the perfect submissive. Ajax was right. I'm too mouthy and inexperienced."

He drew back and the look on his face took her breath away.

"I'll tell you what you are, you're perfect. You're perfect for me, Avery Rose. I enjoy being in control, but only as long as it brings you pleasure. I've changed. You make me happy. Whatever we do together makes me happy."

She stemmed his flow of words by closing the gap between them and kissing the dickens out of him. "Let me explain. I like everything we did, everything. And if you want me, if you think I can make you happy. Well, I want to try more stuff..." she whispered in his ear. "Anything your heart desires. I'm yours to command." When he chuckled, she sealed the deal. "When you go all alpha and macho, it makes me feel soft." She kissed his neck. "You make me glad I'm a woman." Now, she felt like she could be brave. "Your woman."

"God, I love you." He rejoined their lips and kissed her like she always dreamed of being kissed. "I have loved you from afar for so long."

Wasn't that her line? Avery wanted to laugh, but she didn't. He was just too sweet, and this was just too wonderful.

"I love your sweet spirit, Avery. I love your giving nature, your spunk. I adore your body. I love everything about you."

Dreams do come true. Whoever said they didn't, was wrong. "I love you, too. So much. I'll love you forever."

"You had damn well better." There was that McCoy bravado. "Will you marry me, Avery? Will you bind your life and heart and body to mine, forever?"

Hugging him tightly, she ignored the little pains and protests her body was making. This was more important. "Yes, I'll marry you."

"Thank the Lord."

Epilogue -Chapter Ten

October 16 – The Sweetest Day

Avery stood to the left, all the way on the end and Isaac stood to the right in the same position. Soon, they would meet in the middle and walk out together. And boy, did she have plans for the night. But right now, they had a wedding to celebrate.

Aron and Libby stood side by side, facing one another, ready to pledge their love. She was beaming with health and he was beaming with happiness and the rest of the family was so grateful this day had finally arrived. All was well.

Before the ceremony, Aron had presented Libby with a statue of him on his knees at her feet, and she had given him the sonogram showing that they were having twin boys. Both gifts had been perfect expressions of their love. The small church was full. Besides family, there was Bess, their former housekeeper. Nathan had been especially glad to see her. Kane, Lilibet and Zane were there. Joseph's friend Beau had arrived with a beautiful Hispanic woman and Levi had braved gossip and brought Pawnee, who looked very lovely and very feminine. Trace, Lance and Terence Lee had parked cars and now sat in the back row, and the biggest surprise had been Bowie Travis, not the baby, but Jacob's friend. He had slipped in the back just before the ceremony started and Jacob had sent a message back by Nathan that he'd better be planning on staying awhile. Today was a happy day, and there were many things to celebrate.

Aron began his vows. They were heartfelt. "I stand here, today, the luckiest man in the world. Libby, before you walked into my life, I was blessed. I can't deny that. I had my brothers, the ranch and my health. Many people would say that I was rich. But they would be wrong. I was blessed, but I wasn't rich." He ignored the preacher's tut-tutting gesture and framed Libby's face and kissed her, slow and deep. "Now, I'm rich. I'm rich in love. I'm rich in laughter, and hope, Libby. My life is full of happiness and hope, and really, great sex." He whispered the last three words, but everybody heard them and laughed out loud.

"That-a-boy, Aron," someone called from the back.

He doffed his hat at the comedian. He had insisted on wearing his hat, and Libby wouldn't have it any other way. Libby didn't wait to see if he was finished. She couldn't be quiet another second.

"Aron, when I came to Tebow, I didn't know if I was going to live or die. I wanted to experience all that life could offer. I wanted to live. I'm not ashamed to say that I had been infatuated with you for years. You were my dream. So when I thought I had a chance to spend some time on the ranch, I thought life couldn't be any sweeter. I was wrong. I didn't know what living or loving was like until the first time you kissed me. My life began the first time you took me in your arms. Never had I even dreamed life could be so wonderful. I will love our children to the end. Even now, I would die for them in a heartbeat. But as much as I will adore them, I will never love anyone or anything as much as I love you. You are my world."

Again, there wasn't a dry eye in the house. The preacher took up the ceremony, and just before he was about to pronounce them husband and wife, Aron motioned that he wanted to speak again.

"This is highly irregular, Mr. McCoy." The pastor smiled. "But, since when has that ever stopped you."

Everyone laughed. At least no one could say they didn't have a good time at this wedding.

"Do you remember the night I proposed? I promised you that you would have bridesmaids. I promised you that our love would be contagious and that the boys would find beautiful, sweet girls to stand up for you. Now look..." Libby glanced over her shoulder at Jessie, Cady and Avery. Standing behind Aron were Jacob, Joseph and Isaac. Noah and Nathan had taken their seats together in the front row. As the preacher had read the scripture, Skye had slipped into the chair by Noah and gave him a big smile. And when she covered his hand with hers, his eyes had gotten big and wide, but he hadn't moved his hand.

"Can I finish now?" the preacher asked.

"Please do." At least Aron was gracious.

"I now pronounce you man and wife. You may kiss the bride, again." Libby squealed with delight when he picked her up, kissed her soundly, then let her slide back down his body. By the time her feet touched the ground, her eyes were glazed over with passion.

"I can't wait for the honeymoon," she whispered.

"Ahemmm..." The pastor tried to regain control. "It is my privilege to be the first to introduce you to Mr. and Mrs. Aron McCoy." Loud shouts of jubilation filled the church and as the organ swelled with the happy notes, the McCoys filed down the aisle, all paired up with the women that God had created just for them.

Jacob took Jessie's hand. "I love you." He kissed her palm. "I'm sorry you didn't have a big shindig like this."

"What we had was perfect for us. It was private, and as soon as our baby arrives, we can renew our vows. Think how perfect that would be. You, me and Bowie Travis."

"It's a date," he promised. "And guess what? The elder Bowie Travis has arrived and I can't wait for you to meet him."

Joseph took Cady's hand. "Hello, Beautiful. Did you miss me?"

"Always."

"You're my angel. Did you know that?"

"Heaven knows, I wouldn't have it any other way." They shared a secret smile and a kiss.

Isaac and Avery stepped forward. "Before long, we're gonna let that preacher tie the knot for us." Isaac winked at her.

"I've got a better idea." She winked back at him. "Let's go home and I'll let you tie some knots of your own. You can tie me to the bed and have your wicked way with me."

"Hell, yeah!"

Get a glimpse into another Sable Hunter book:

Burning Love

Philadelphia, PA – LibertyOne Plaza – Socorro – Present Day

Harley took the long walk. That's how she always thought of it, no matter if it were a mile, two hundred yards or twenty feet. It was a long walk. She faced death with no one beside her, no partner, no team, no one to back her up or take her place. What she focused on was saving the situation, she knew if she failed there was more at stake than the loss of her life, there were the lives of others.

At least she had no hostages to fortune. If the worst happened, Harley left no one behind that would mourn her passing. The fact that she was solitary gave her strength to face the unthinkable. She could look her mortality in the face and know she was expendable. She had no husband, no children, no parents. No one who would wake up the next day after her death and be devastated to know she was gone, and that's the way she wanted it. She had no desire to bear the burden of someone else's happiness.

The very name of her company Socorro said it all. A Socorro was a type of mourning dove and the dove was a symbol of peace. Harley felt that the work she did, ridding the world of dangerous explosive devices, was her gift of peace. And since the Socorro dove was known as the solitary dove, it was never spotted in a flock. Always alone, it just fit her. The very word

Socorro meant to offer help, so she identified with it. She was Socorro.

The construction elevator was small and rattled like a two-bit radio. All sounds were muffled in the suit and the ice vest cooling unit made her feel as if she were sitting naked in a deep freeze. Her arms ached from carrying the portable x-ray machine and her bag of tools, in addition to having to move around in the heavy suit. That was the only drawback she had ever had. Her size. But what she lacked in size, she made up for in determination and grit. With a jerk and a loud creak, the temporary construction elevator ground to a halt. She stepped out on the deserted platform, about 108 feet off the ground. Harley disliked heights with a passion. She picked her way across the girders and tried not to look down.

The bomb came into view. Good Lord! They had to be dealing with a seriously psychotic individual. Somebody wanted to do this city, and her friend's family, some major damage. On the way today, she had been informed who owned this building. It was quite a coincidence that she was close to the Gaines Family. Not that she would work any harder to disarm this bomb than any other that crossed her path. She put the same amount of effort into each one, everything she had.

The device had to have been brought up in sections. As she drew nearer, she determined that the explosives themselves were housed in three grocer boxes. From the report she received, the boxes were full of semtex, a deadly plastic explosive. There was enough power here to do untold damage. The blast wave alone would shatter glass for several city blocks.

Falling to her knees next to the bomb, she set up her x-ray equipment to analyze where the fuses were and how she could neutralize the threat with the least amount of invasive scrutiny. Looking through the LED screen, she saw a tangle of wires between the layers of semtex. This made no sense. Bomb makers today used remote controls and microchips that could be dealt with through trepanation, a boring of a hole in the side of the bomb where the triggers could be liquefied with an acid bath. No, this would have to be done the old-fashioned way. She would have to snip wires and pray she picked the right ones.

With delicate moves, she began lifting out bricks of semtex to get to inner workings. How tempting it was to just try and empty the boxes of the plastic explosive, but she knew time was of the essence. There was no countdown display, and that made her need to be methodical, maddening. Now, there were probably only seconds left. She would have to act, and act fast.

Quickly, she removed the last layer, exposing the colored plastic wires. For a moment, she was stunned. This looked familiar, she knew this pattern. Impossible. He was dead, she had seen him die. Was this some kind of cruel trick? Closing her eyes for just a moment, she used her secret weapon. Rubbing her fingers over the cluster of wires, she used a combination of knowledge and insight, took her wire cutters and held her breath. Snip. Breathe. Moving the blue wire out of the way, she snipped the green one. Breathe. She wore no gloves; they would just get in the way. Using one fingernail, she lifted the yellow wire. Yellow or black, yellow or black. It could be either. Making her mind a blank, she waited for the answer. Yellow. Snip. Breathe. No explosion. Every muscle in her body relaxed. She would live another day.

* * *

Deep in the South - Atchafalaya Basin – Louisiana

Beau LeBlanc steered his pickup down the levee road toward the Guidry homestead. He would have liked to be out in his airboat plowing through the water lilies, fishing for catfish. Instead, he and Indiana had been called to wrangle a big bull gator who had been plaguing the fisherman trying to make a living along Bayou Chene. These Cajuns had known too many problems, recently. The BP oil spill, the Mississippi River flooding and now a rogue alligator who was getting too aggressive around their homes. The locals had named him Godzilla; he had begun his reign of terror by tearing up their traps and snapping their trotlines and continued it by crawling up in their yards and eating their dogs and cats. Most of them were afraid to let their children out to play. So Beau had been summoned to move the old monster to a safe place before he became a man-eater and would have to be destroyed.

As luck would have it, Godzilla had got himself into a predicament before traps could be set for him. He had been in the process of crawling between irrigation ditches at the Guidry place, when old man Guidry had walked upon him. The old gator had tried to get away from the human and instead of heading for one of the manmade waterways; he slid underneath the connecting pipe right into an enclosed deep water well. The watery trap was likely to become his grave unless Beau could get him out. It was a wonder the homeowner hadn't shot the old reptile. But he hadn't, and for that Beau was grateful. He had a soft heart for things no one else cared about. Beau ran SAFEPLACE, a Sanctuary for endangered and threatened animals. Godzilla wouldn't end up there; he was still able to make it on his own. They would relocate him somewhere deeper in the swamp, away from man.

"That's the Guidry house." Indiana pointed over at the dog-trot style, Louisiana swamp house. A tall thin man stood out front waiting, two hound dogs flanked him on either side. Beau pulled in and climbed out, breathing in the atmosphere like life giving oxygen. The swamp was a spiritual place for Cajuns. He could close his eyes and smell his home, the bayou was where he belonged. The familiar aroma was so many things melded together into a gumbo of sights, sounds and experiences. The hot sun, dark green water, crawfish, mud, cypress trees, and humidity all carried on a thick damp breeze.

The cellphone on his hip buzzed. Glancing at the number, he turned to Indy. "It's the store. I wonder what's up? We left them working on converting those stock Uzi's to competition grade." Punching the talk button, he answered. "LeBlanc, here."

"How much longer are you gonna be, boss?" As Beau listened to his employee, he poked Indiana, pointing out at the water. Out in the bayou, they could see the tell-tale eyes and a little bit of a snout showing above the water. An alligator.

"Not too much longer, we've gotta pull Godzilla out of a hole and then Indy will move him deeper into the Atchafalaya. I'll come on back as soon as he heads out. What's going on?"

Rick Gentry was excited. When he got excited, he stuttered a little bit like now. "You, you, you will never believe what's coming into our shop this afternoon. A woman called and she, she, she has a Ma Deuce she wants us to look at."

That got Beau's attention. "A Ma Deuce? Damn! I'll be there. If she arrives before I do, don't let her leave, or at least hold on to the gun."

***

Mon Dieu! Beau stood frozen at the entrance to the lobby, stunned at exactly what had fallen into his lap. If Indiana only knew! This sweetheart was much better than a gun, no matter what the caliber.

There was no way in the world he could take his eyes off of her. She was absolutely delectable. The Ma Deuce was forgotten, he'd check it out later, much later. He'd much rather talk to this hot little honey. Lord Have Mercy! She had her back to him, but what he could see caused his cock to swell. Tight little blue jeans cupped a behind so round and sweet, he wanted to go to his knees and genuflect. Her hair, swear to God, hung to the top of that little rump and all he could think about was lying beneath her, letting that curtain of dark silk enclose them in their own private paradise. Damn! And he hadn't even seen her face yet.

She was making a point and he was entranced at the way she moved her hand and cocked her hip. It really didn't matter why she had come, he would give her anything she wanted. Hell! What if she was married? Surely God wouldn't be that cruel.

"There you are." Dandi motioned him over and when she did, sweet-doll turned around and Beau audibly growled. Okay, he surrendered. It was over. This was the future Mrs. Beau LeBlanc. His eyes almost crossed, he couldn't decide whether to stare at her perfectly adorable face or the two handfuls of tit-heaven that seemed to be begging for his touch. "What's wrong with you?" Dandi asked. Thank God, his cousin couldn't recognize that he was completely lust-struck. "Come meet Harley Montoya. She has a couple of questions for you."

Her heart almost stopped beating. It was impossible – absolutely impossible. Harley couldn't believe it. Every psychic nerve in her body tingled – even before she made a move to turn around. Never, ever had she expected to see Beau again. All breath fled her body. It was Beau, and he was drop-dead gorgeous. Taking one-step toward him, she prepared herself to greet the person who meant the most to her in this world. Did he recognize her? Her mouth had gone dry. Meeting his gaze, Harley searched his beautiful blue-black eyes for any hint he knew who she was.

He didn't.

He was smiling, but there didn't seem to be any surprise in his expression. He grinned and there it was, that little half dimple she had dreamed about so often. Her Beau. God! She wanted to sink to her knees and thank heaven. He was alive and within touching distance. She had to drive her fingernails into her palms to keep from reaching for him. Harley didn't know what to do; she was so tempted to just launch herself into his arms. But, she resisted. Not only would it shock him but her ingrained fear of intimacy made her skittish. There was no need to embarrass both of them. The only thing she allowed herself to do was extend one trembling hand in greeting.

"Hello, cher," Instead of shaking it, Beau surprised her when he brought it to his lips and kissed it. "What a pleasure it is to meet you. I'm Beau LeBlanc."

No, he didn't know her. At all. Harley didn't know whether to be relieved or disappointed. "I'm Harley. It's nice to - uh - see you, Beau." The name slipped off her tongue like a prayer. She had known the owner of Firepower Munitions was named Beau, but Beaureguarde and its derivative were common in South Louisiana. Plus, she had never known her Beau's last name, and he certainly had not known hers. Details like that hadn't been important. They had been more concerned with just staying alive. Still, she drank in his face with her eyes, her whole body shaking from the shock. "I've heard wonderful things about your weapons business."

"Thank you, I'm proud of it," he was staring at her face so hard, she just knew any moment he would realize who she was. But he didn't. "Do you live near here?"

"Yes, I just moved from Southeast Texas, before that I lived near San Diego." Why was she being so specific? There was no need for her to share so much, unless she intended to remind him of days gone by. Would he want to know? Harley wondered if Beau would even remember the thirteen year old scrap of humanity named 'nothing' that had clung to him like he was a life preserver.

"Well, welcome to the Atchafalaya Basin. I'm sure you'll love it here. As a home-grown boy, I sure would be glad to show you around. Would you like that?"

He looked so expectant she had to smile. His voice had the same sexy Cajun cadence she remembered from their youth. Sixteen years might have gone by, but she would have recognized him anywhere. His hair was the same. Longish, slightly curly and black as sin. High cheekbones, a chiseled face and a smile that would make any woman in the world sigh with longing. It was all just as she remembered, except mature and perfect. The last time she had seen him, he had been climbing out the window to safety. She had stayed behind to provide a distraction for Pell while he escaped. Harley had never seen Beau again, until this moment. She had often wondered how he had fared. Hopefully, better than she had. Pell had beaten her six ways to Sunday for aiding in the loss of his star pickpocket. And that wasn't all he had done. But, she pushed the painful thought from her mind. No use dwelling on that nightmare. Beau had gotten away, and she had escaped. Pell's final attack on her had given Harley enough courage to take the risk and get out of that hellish place. After all, with Beau gone, there had been no reason to stay.

Wait! What had he said? He was asking her out? Harley was so distracted by the wonder of finding him again that it was difficult to process simple English. She was about to try and answer him, but Dandi cleared her throat, reminding them both she was there. "Harley wants to talk to you about a conversion job." It was obvious she was growing bored with their by-play.

Beau's mind was fogged by arousal. Conversion job? He wasn't familiar with that term; all he could think of was blow jobs, hand jobs. You know, critical jobs. "Did you bring your weapon with you?" He didn't need for her to answer that; he could tell she was fully armed and dangerous. And he was cocked and primed and on a short fuse. Hell, he was beyond aroused!

"Yes, I did." Harley tore her eyes from his and unzipped the gun case, removing the Remington rifle for his inspection. "I'd like to see about getting a reaper conversion and having it accurized, if that's possible."

Beau held his breath while he asked the next question. "Is this a surprise gift for your boyfriend?" There was no way this baby-doll could handle a sniper rifle. Everything within him hoped her answer was no.

Boyfriend? Harley paused before answering. "No, there's no boyfriend. This is a birthday gift. Do you think you can do it?" She didn't explain that the gun was a gift to herself.

Boyfriend? That was almost funny. If he only knew her crazy history. To start off with, for three years she had lived as a boy after leaving Brownwood. After escaping, Harley had run off into the night, hiding underneath one of the bridge overpasses near the river. A homeless man had loaned her a knife and she had sawed off all of her long, dark hair. After what had happened with Pell, if she could have stripped herself of her femininity, she would have. She handed the .308 to Beau, anxious to get the focus back on the gun and off of her.

No boyfriend. He couldn't help but smirk. Okay, so the coast was clear. She sure as hell fascinated him. All he could think about was what her kiss was going to taste like and how it would feel to run his hands all over her incredible body. Taking the gun from her, Beau admitted that Harley handled the firearm pretty well, for a girl. Beau was intrigued. He had seen women shoot big guns before, but the thought of this woman handling a rifle was turning him on to no end. God, he'd love to feel her hands on his weapon. "Well, sweetheart, it would be my pleasure to do this for you."

"Okay, good." Harley felt so torn. What should she do? But, he deserved the truth, didn't he? "Beau, there's something that I need to..."

"Here's the brochures," Dandi breezed back in and gave them to Harley. "Have you brought in the Ma Deuce, yet?"

That got his attention. "You're the owner of the .50 caliber?" Damn! He hadn't even thought about the machine gun. She was just so beautiful everything else had slipped his mind.

"It's in my vehicle."

"She drives a Hummer." Dandi shared the information like she was whispering the most delicious gossip.

"Dehelyousaye?" There was more to this woman than met the eye, and he couldn't wait to peel back every layer…of clothing. Feeling his cock jerk in his jeans, Beau found himself smiling again. "Shall we bring it in? And what do you want to do with it?" Fighting to regain a little decorum, Beau couldn't believe he was acting like a sex-starved teenager and liking it.

"Sure," Harley felt like she had gotten a reprieve. It would give her a few more minutes to get her thoughts together for her confession. "I inherited the machine gun. I hope you can help me find a buyer for it."

"Damn! I'd sure love to have it." Beau ran a hand through his thick hair, ruffling it.

Harley was entranced by his hands. They were strong, wide and capable. The veins stood out prominently on the top and she found herself wanting to trace them with her tongue. Land sakes! What was wrong with her? Beau was talking; she tried to focus on what he was saying.

"Depending on the condition, those things are going for fifty to fifty-five thousand dollars."

'This was perfect,' Harley thought. "It's in mint condition. Of course, I encourage you to check it out." She could get rid of the gun and do something nice for Beau. "If it passes your inspection – how does ten thousand sound?"

"Ten thousand?" Beau was flabbergasted. "Why? If it's all you say it is, I could find you a buyer in a couple of days who would be glad to pay you full price." Was she that hard up for money? He had no desire to cheat her.

"No, I'm not interested in making a big profit. I just want to get rid of it. So, if you're interested, it's yours."

"Hell yeah, I'm interested." This was turning out to be his lucky day, in more ways than one. "I'm interested in the gun, but I'm more interested in you." Beau grinned. He was happy. There was no two ways about it. And he wasn't shy, so he just decided to lay all of his cards on the table. "You are the most incredible looking woman I've ever laid eyes on." Behind him, Dandi choked. Crap! He had forgotten about his cousin being in the room. And his little bombshell, Harley? She blushed! Good Lord in Heaven, the little darling blushed!

Digging the keys out of her jeans pocket, Harley held them out to him. "You've just bought yourself a .50 caliber machine gun. It's in the back of my truck. Let's go get it." She decided not to comment on Beau's admission that he found her attractive. It would be better if she just ignored it. Her body seemed to have other ideas, however. Harley felt her nipples puffing up and her pussy began to swell and an unfamiliar ache started deep within her sex. God, she was turned on! A myriad of emotions flooded through her. This type of reaction to a man was unheard of for her. But this was no ordinary man, this was Beau. "Come on."

**Warning: Contains explicit details including sexual content. Intended for 18+ Audience
myBook.to/BurningLove

BADASS

About the Author:

Sable Hunter is a New York Times, USA Today bestselling author of nearly 50 books in 7 series. She writes sexy contemporary stories full of emotion and suspense. Her focus is mainly cowboy and novels set in Louisiana with a hint of the supernatural. Sable writes what she likes to read and enjoys putting her fantasies on paper. Her books are emotional tales where the heroine is faced with challenges. Her aim is to write a story that will make you laugh, cry and swoon. If she can wring those emotions from a reader, she has done her job. Sable resides in Austin, Texas with her two dogs. Passionate about all animals, she has been known to charm creatures from a one ton bull to a family of raccoons. For fun, Sable haunts cemeteries and battlefields armed with night-vision cameras and digital recorders hunting proof that love survives beyond the grave. Welcome to her world of magic, alpha heroes, sexy cowboys and hot, steamy to-die-for sex. Step into the shoes of her heroines and escape to places where right prevails, love conquers all and holding out for a hero is not an impossible dream

Visit Sable:

Website

http://www.sablehunter.com

Facebook

www.facebook.com/authorsablehunter

Amazon:

http://www.amazon.com/author/sablehunter

Pinterest

https://www.pinterest.com/AuthorSableH/

Twitter

https://twitter.com/huntersable

Bookbub:

https://www.bookbub.com/authors/sable-hunter

Goodreads:

https://www.goodreads.com/author/show/4419823.Sable_Hunter

Sign up for Sable Hunter's newsletter

http://eepurl.com/qRvyn

SABLE'S BOOKS
Get hot and bothered!!!

Hell Yeah!

Cowboy Heat
(Hell Yeah! Book 1)

Hot on Her Trail
(Hell Yeah! Book 2)

Her Magic Touch
(Hell Yeah! Book 3)

Brown Eyed Handsome Man
(Hell Yeah! Book 4)

Badass
(Hell Yeah! Book 5)

Burning Love
(Hell Yeah! Book 6)

Forget Me Never
With Ryan O'Leary
(Hell Yeah! Book 7)

I'll See You In My Dreams
With Ryan O'Leary
(Hell Yeah! Book 8)

Finding Dandi

(Hell Yeah! Book 9)

Skye Blue
(Hell Yeah! Book 10)

I'll Remember You
(Hell Yeah! Book 11)

True Love's Fire
(Hell Yeah! Book 12)

Thunderbird
With Ryan O'Leary
(Hell Yeah! Book 13)

Welcome To My World
(Hell Yeah! Book 14)

How to Rope a McCoy
(Hell Yeah!)

One Man's Treasure
With Ryan O'Leary
(Hell Yeah! - Equalizers)

You Are Always on My Mind
(Hell Yeah! Cajun Style)

If I Can Dream
(Hell Yeah!)

Head over Spurs
(Hell Yeah!)

Hell Yeah! Sweeter Versions

Cowboy Heat - Sweeter Version
(Hell Yeah! Sweeter Version Book 1)

Hot on Her Trail - Sweeter Version
(Hell Yeah! Sweeter Version Book2)

Her Magic Touch - Sweeter Version
(Hell Yeah! Sweeter Version Book 3)

Brown Eyed Handsome Man - Sweeter Version
(Hell Yeah! Sweeter Version Book 4)

Badass - Sweeter Version
(Hell Yeah! Sweeter Version Book 5)

Burning Love - Sweeter Version
(Hell Yeah! Sweeter Version Book 6)

Finding Dandi - Sweeter Version
(Hell Yeah! Cajun Style)

Forget Me Never - Sweeter Version
(Hell Yeah! Book 7)

I'll See You In My Dreams –
Sweeter Version (Hell Yeah! Book 8*)*

Moon Magic Series
A Wishing Moon (Moon Magic Book 1)
Sweet Evangeline (Moon Magic Book 2)

Hill Country Heart Series
Unchained Melody (Hill Country Heart Book 1)
Scarlet Fever (Hill Country Heart Book 2)
Bobby Does Dallas (Hill Country Heart 3)

Dixie Dreaming
Come With Me (Dixie Dreaming Book 1)
Pretty Face: A Red Hot Cajun Nights Story

Texas Heat Series
T-R-O-U-B-L-E (Texas Heat Book 1)
My Aliyah (Texas Heat Book 2)

El Camino Real Series
A Breath of Heaven (El Camino Real Book1)
Loving Justice (El Camino Real Book 2)

Texas Heroes Series
Texas Wildfire
Texas CHAOS
Texas Standoff

Other Titles from Sable Hunter:

For A Hero
Green With Envy (It's Just Sex Book 1)
with Ryan O'Leary
Hell Yeah! Box Set With Bonus Cookbook
Love's Magic Spell: A Red Hot Treats Story
Wolf Call
Cowboy 12 Pack: Twelve-Novel Boxed Set
Rogue (The Sons of Dusty Walker)
Be My Love Song
A Hot and Spicy Valentine

Audio
Cowboy Heat - Sweeter Version: Hell Yeah! Sweeter Version

Hot on Her Trail - Sweeter Version: Hell Yeah! Sweeter Version, Book 2

<u>Spanish Edition</u>
Vaquero Ardiente (Cowboy Heat)

Su Rastro Caliente (Hot On Her Trail)

BADASS